Versions of the following stories have previously been published: "The Universe in Miniature in Miniature" in *American Short Fiction*; "No Sun" in *New South*; "Vaara in the Woods" in *Time Out Chicago*; "Easy Love" in *Storyglossia* and *Ghost Town*; "The Peach" in *The Madison Review*; "Hair University" in *Barrelhouse*; "Confused Aliens," "People Like Me," and "The Wildlife Biologist" in *Five Chapters*; "Pangea" in *ACM*. Thanks to the editors.

Published by
featherproof books
Chicago, Illinois
www.featherproof.com

First edition
10 9 8 7 6 5 4 3 2 1

Library of Congress Control Number 2009944043
ISBN 13: 978-0-9825808-1-3

Design and Illustrations by Zach Dodson at Bleached Whale Design
Except Figure VB7009 and the faces of The Abacus by Rob Funderburk; Figure 24.7k8 by Mark Rader; Helmet, p. 259 by Alex Kostiw

Printed in the United States of America
Set in Dante

The Universe in Miniature in Miniature

★ by ★
PATRICK SOMERVILLE

featherproof BOOKS

Table of Elements

for slartibartfast

Discussing emotions is always tricky for people. But ultimately
the society we need to create to sustain the planet depends on our
ability to speak emotionally with some sort of comfort or fluency.

– *JOSH BERNSTEIN*

But perhaps we shouldn't chase our technology…after all, journalists…
compress life into tiny representations, which remain compressed and
unreal, unless we take the time to mentally expand them back into a
reality wide enough for every life to be genuinely fathomed and felt.
And this, I think, is true compassion.

– *ERIC DANIEL METZGER*

Tell them, that, to ease them of their griefs,
Their fear of hostile strokes, their aches, losses,
Their pangs of love, with other incident throes
That nature's fragile vessel doth sustain
In life's uncertain voyage,
I will some kindness do them.

– *WILLIAM SHAKESPEARE*

The Universe in Miniature in Miniature

Lucy says we aren't watching to see if he will die. "That would miss the whole point," she says. "And besides," she says, "that would be, like, cruel."

It's the third time I've asked her in the last month. Now she's frowning and staring at her monitor. She's pretending she hasn't noticed that I've asked her three times.

We are in our van. Dylan stole it. I think he stole it. He won't tell us, one way or the other. If he did steal it, he stole it from a pedophile, that is certain. It's night-black and gladiatorial. It has bubble windows in the back. Sometimes when we drive up Lake Shore I look out the windows and see the waves and imagine we are all onboard a submarine, and out there in the water that is air there are fish and bubbles and everything like that. Inside, it's nice—there's a long bench in the back where I usually sit. Most of Lucy's gear is up on hooks. I have my own cushions.

We're not moving now. We're on stakeout, parked at the end of Yellow Oak Lane. We're way out in the 'burbs. The black felt is in the windows.

"So you don't think it's cruel, anyway?" I ask. I think I might already be so far down the path of hating Lucy that it will be impossible to come back. This happens with best friends, doesn't it? If things don't go smoothly forever, you have to hate them eventually. Sometimes you come back and sometimes you don't.

"Do you guys think Sprite or 7UP is more evil?" Dylan asks from the front.

He's got his feet crossed on the dashboard—I can see that his right sneaker is untied.

"What do you mean by evil?" Lucy asks, not turning away from her monitor. She's got on a blue knit cap and her bangs are peeking out over her forehead. Her bangs are dyed dark red and I hate them.

"I don't know," Dylan says. "Which gives you a worse feeling?"

"That's your idea of evil?" Lucy asks. "Whatever makes me feel bad?"

"I don't know," Dylan says. "It's a gauge."

"Questionable," Lucy says.

"Okay," Dylan says. "Which makes you feel worse, then? That's all I'm asking. Sprite or 7UP?"

"When I drink it? When I look at it? What are we talking about?"

"When you imagine it."

"Totally Sprite," Lucy says. I see her eyes flick to me over the top of her monitor. "What about you, Rosie?" she asks me.

"I don't know," I say. "Not either of them, really. It's soda."

"You've gotta dig for it," Dylan says. He's leaning his head back over his shoulder. I still can't see his face. I can see one beautiful cheekbone. "These are feelings that hide themselves. Marketing and what have you. It's really hidden in your mind. But it's in you. Embedded, like how the military embeds journalists."

"I have soda-hatred buried in me?" I ask.

"We all do."

"Why?"

"Because," he says, and I can see that he's staring at the black felt. When he gets frustrated he doesn't raise his voice or make angry expressions, he just stares in a different direction. "Because it's soda. We all hate it, right? Just because we all had to...you don't really like it. No one really likes it. I mean soda—do you really think it was like a market-driven thing originally, like someone out there was wishing for a bubbly...I mean it had to be invented before we even wanted it, so—soda is an embarrassing item. It's colored? It's as though we're in a zoo, isn't it? I mean we didn't choose for it to be here with us. You know? It's just here." Dylan is frustrated.

"What?" I say.

Lucy giggles, then says, "Dylan's about to admit to us that he got sexually abused by a can of soda when he was little."

Dylan, I see, smiles at this, closes his eyes. They're a strange couple. I can't understand them and I want to. Dylan is soft and ephemeral—I think of him as a fairy. Lucy is sharp, jagged metal inside. They are in love. I'm in love with Dylan. I think we all know that.

"Sprite," I say, turning back to my model. "I guess I do have an opinion."

"Sprite," Dylan says, making a mark in his notebook. He gives me a long smile, then smiles once more at the felt. "Thank you, Rose. I was going for Sprite, anyway."

I met these two a year ago, when all three of us started at the SSTD—the School of Surreal Thought and Design. There are nine people in our class, even though there isn't really a class, and even though I don't really know the other six. We don't meet in a room to talk things over. We don't have any professors. There is no paperwork. All we have to do, to graduate, is complete our projects. Our projects are whatever we want them to be. We have total freedom and I'm not sure anybody even looks at our projects when we're done.

You are asking questions now. Do we pay for this? What manner of degree do we earn? Are we employable in the future? Is there a framed certificate?

None of that matters.

We are in this van, on this court, doing surveillance on this house, because of Lucy. This is her project. There on her monitor? It's a boy. His name is Ryan Conrad, he's twenty-seven, he's in a bed, and he has brain damage. Lucy's project is large and many-tiered. She says she is breaking down the walls that went up after Milgram was deemed offensive. She says it's up to the artists now, if we want to understand people. Her project is to observe the wholesale collapse of a family following major trauma. Her chosen family is the Conrad family; three years ago Ryan Conrad went from a good-looking and somewhat free-spirited law student with an IQ of 132 to an invalid incapable of dressing himself with an IQ of 50. He slipped on the ice and hit his head on the concrete. He was in a coma for a week, then woke up not the same. I will tell you about his mother and father later. I will also later explain the further love complexities. Lucy and I are both in love with Ryan Conrad, too, but neither of us has admitted that yet.

She has placed eighteen spycams in the Conrad house. There are six in Ryan's bedroom. We watch him every night.

My project is about little models.

Dylan's writing a novel about scientists who accidentally destroy the planet Earth while trying to devise the perfect carbonated beverage.

It's that melancholy springtime. It's gray and cold and there have been no amazing days. It's the same in the morning, and I spend hours in my pajamas, sipping coffee in the chilly sunroom, wishing for the sun. After I make coffee in the French press I clean it out and then pour boiling water into it alone. I press the plunger up and down and watch the bubbles. I think I'm depressed. I think we're all depressed.

Later, I decide not to sit with Lucy and Dylan in the van, and instead I go to a rock show at a club down the street from my apartment. The band is called SAUSAGIZER and they sing half their songs in French. I do a little dance near the bar, sipping at my drink. Almost the whole dance has to do with my toe.

A few hours later, the bar has cleared out a little. SAUSAGIZER's bass player sits down next to me and asks me my name.

"It's Rose," I say. "Are you guys French-Canadian?"

"Bill is," he says. "The frontman." He points at Bill, who's in a booth with three really, really hot girls who look like maybe they live in a magazine somewhere. The drummer is also there. He is ugly.

"You're not?" I ask him.

"No," he says. "I'm just Carlo. Carlo Rodriguez."

"Is that actually your name?"

"No," he says. "My name is Kevin Johnson."

Kevin Johnson asks me what I do. I tell him I make accurate models even though they are technically not to scale.

"Models of what?'

"Do you know," I say, "how sometimes little boys, for science fairs, decide they want to make a model of the solar system?"

"Sort of."

"So they find maybe a basketball and cut it in half for the sun? And then they use, like, a marble for the Earth? And so on? And their dads probably help and it turns into this huge project with cardboard and rope and everything? And how maybe sometimes the dad even says to the little boy, 'You know, Timmy, if we really wanted to be accurate about this model we'd have to drive five whole miles away to properly include Uranus,' and the kid is totally into it? Like his mind is blown by the scale?"

"Yeah," says Kevin. "I know about that."

"I make models of that."

"Cool," he says. "Wait. Of what, now?"

"I make models of little boys and sometimes their father making models of the solar system."

"You're saying this is your job?"

"Kinda," I say. "It a long term project. It's art."

He nods, tilts his head, like maybe he's starting to see it. "So you make the universe in miniature in miniature, then," he says.

"No," I say. "I make the solar system in miniature in miniature. But that's close." "Let's do some shots," he says. "I like Jack."

I agree to do some shots. I tell him Jack's a friend of mine, too.

A week goes by and I don't call Lucy or Dylan. I want to drift away from them—more than anything, I want to drift away. I sometimes imagine myself totally alone and I enjoy the feeling. And I mean something by alone, something more than the word holds. I mean something blank and pure and vacant, plus me. And also moral. This blank and pure vacancy that includes me that is also moral is so empty, it is so one, that my presence in it makes me not exist, although I am still there, and that's what lifts all the weight.

I have tried to explain my religion to both Dylan and Lucy. Neither of them get it. Dylan sometimes says it sounds romantic, the way that it's confusing and lonesome, and he says that he wishes he had a machine that could let him be me for one minute so he could feel what it feels like to live with this idea of mine. He said he would call the machine The Machine of Understanding Other People. I told him I thought *that* was romantic.

But I'm not that kind in the end. I'm a faker when it comes to suffering. I don't want it at all.

Dylan shows up one afternoon. When I open the door he's standing there, wearing his headphones, hair wet, distracted by the cracks in the hallway's drywall. I'm not used to seeing Dylan standing. He's usually behind the wheel of the parked van with his feet up, notebook in lap. He's about nine hundred feet tall.

"Hey," I say.

"Hey," he says. He's lurking.

Dylan once told me that he was an octoroon. I said to him, "You don't look totally white, it's true," and he said, "That's because I'm not white." "What are you?" I asked. "I'm an octoroon," he said, "but also other things." "Like what?" "Polish."

"What's up?" I say. "Do you wanna come in?"

"I felt like maybe walking for about a half a mile and then having some tea," he says. "So, no."

"Okay," I say. "That's specific."

"Yeah," he says, nodding, looking over my head. "I'm just into that kind of thing lately. Just, like, totally knowing."

"I think this is a time I should wear my Ducks, then," I say.

"Okay. Do that."

I bought my Ducks on eBay for fifty dollars. They are those old shoes from the eighties that are rubber and shiny and resemble ducks, but just in the way that the constellation Orion looks like a guy.

"Lucy thinks my Ducks are twee," I say to Dylan as we walk. "I think she thinks my models are twee, too."

"Maybe," Dylan says. "I don't know. Lucy thinks a lot of weird shit."

"I think my models are twee, though," I say. "I condemn my own art as I make it. It's part of it. Is that okay?"

"Where have you been?" Dylan asks. "Why don't you come in the van anymore?"

"I don't know," I say. "Ryan. I feel bad for Ryan and his parents. I really do. I think we might all be evil for doing what we're doing to them."

"It's just Lucy."

"We're there," I say. "We helped put the cameras in. You wore the cat burglar outfit."

Sometimes Ryan Conrad cries, and Lucy records it all. He can't talk but he moans, and his mother sits with him and talks to him about the news. Her name is Katherine Conrad, Kathy for short. She's a small woman, tenacious, tough—I have admired her strength, watching her lift and pull at Ryan's body to help him bathe. She's maybe five foot three and a hundred pounds and sometimes she cries, too, and I can feel everything, and I cry, too. Lucy never cries. Once she told me she wishes she cried along with them. Another time she recorded me crying as I watched them and asked me to talk about why it was sad. First I said it was lost potential, because Ryan had once been strong and powerful and now he wasn't, and that is basically the saddest story there is. Then I closed my eyes and listened harder to the feeling and I realized it was sad for his mother in a different way, but I didn't understand it.

"Lucy's up in Ann Arbor," Dylan says, "interviewing people who used to know him in college."

"I don't think I'm an artist. Are you one?"

"No. I don't know. Yes."

"Is she evil, though?" I ask. "Are we evil for helping? Should we stop her?"

"It's not evil. We're just watching."

"But it's more, isn't it?" I ask. "Aren't we taking by watching?"

"No. Definitely not. And besides. It's her project."

We have tea in Lincoln Square and then Dylan walks me home and asks me, at the door, if I think that the two of us having sex would change the dynamic back and make me want to start sitting with them again at night. He says he misses me in the van and he says he and Lucy are having problems. He says he thinks he loves me more and he asks me if I love him.

I say no but somehow we still end up having sex.

Lucy says her project is about pain. There are many complicated factors, she says. I am listening again because I'm interested again, and tonight, she's riffing.

Lucy used to know Ryan Conrad, you see. She knew him in high school, and even loved him. They dated for two months. Lucy was one of those in-between popular kids, I think, and was allowed to date anyone she wanted. Sometimes art kids and sometimes Ryan Conrads. So for a couple of months their senior year they went out. They never tried to merge their friends and even ignored one another at parties. Lucy, though, told me the central story about their love. She told me that the only thing the two of them used to do together was meet up at Ryan's uncle's apartment—this uncle was away in Sweden for a year—in formal dress and eat catered dinners at the table and dance and pretend they were somewhere around forty-five years old. She said that they never once broke out of the game and they hardly even planned it.

Tonight, nothing's happening. Ryan's already asleep, and his mom and dad are watching TV in the den. We are watching them lazily on Lucy's monitor. This afternoon, Ryan fell out of his wheelchair at his day-clinic, and the main topic of conversation tonight, between husband and wife, has been a discussion of how mindful the employees are where he goes. Dad says not mindful enough, Mom says usually mindful, this was an anomaly. "He hardly has a bruise," she says to him, near the end of the conversation.

I have my smallest model yet in my lap. It's so small Mercury is just implied.

Lucy says, "I think I'm close to being done."

"Really?"

"Yeah," she says, cocking her head, still looking down at her monitor. She clicks her mouse and we switch to the night-vision camera in Ryan's room. "I'm getting these feelings of understanding them," she says. She looks at me. "I knew she was going to say that about the bruise. I heard it in my head before she said it. I thought it."

I am quiet. We look at Ryan. He's at peace when he sleeps. Lucy's never put her project quite in these terms—in terms of understanding— before. Up front Dylan has music playing pretty loudly in his headphones and he's writing away in his notebook. I tell Lucy about the Machine of Understanding Other People, and about what Dylan told me.

"Did he say that?" she asks, and smiles a little.

"Yes."

"That was my idea," she says. "He's using my stuff on you." She laughs, but it sounds like she's actually surprised, maybe a little hurt. If you're an artist you're supposed to get credit for the things you make up.

"Yeah," I say. "He is."

"I guess that's what I'm doing," she says, turning back to the monitor. She pans right and zooms. Ryan's foot is twitching and she's getting good video of it. "That's my project."

Then, after a few seconds, she says, "It's not because I hate him."

"I didn't think it was."

"I don't hate them," she says. "For being normal people. And a normal family. I mean Ryan was going to be an insurance lawyer or something. So maybe you might think I'm doing this all because it's okay that he's gone. Because the world doesn't need another insurance lawyer. Or because an insurance lawyer is not going to be the one who saves the world in the end."

"I don't think that at all," I say. "I've never once thought that."

"No, good," she says, "because that's not true."

"What are we—"

"Dylan said that you said you thought I might be evil. Because of this project."

I let it sit for a few seconds. Then I say, "Why are we doing projects at all?"

"To get our degrees."

"No," I say. "I mean, like, why."

"I don't know," she says, shrugging. Of course she doesn't like questions like this—they get broken on the metal inside of her. "Because we're fucked-up weirdos who can't work in offices? Or we'd die?"

"We wouldn't die."

"Maybe you wouldn't." She looks over at the model in my lap. I look at it, too. I think it's another way of saying that I'm twee. Things have gone sour. Again I can't understand.

On Sunday I go to church. I don't know what kind it is. I dress extremely well and look better than I have in two years. I wear my green dress. I pay close attention to my cleavage as I stand in front of the mirror. I try eight different bras until I get it right.

Suddenly there I am, sitting in a pew. Everyone stands up and sings from the book and I stand up with the book and move my mouth and pretend. I can feel the waxy lipstick smeared on my lips. So many sounds come out of us. We try to use our magic and tear open a portal that leads up to the center of the universe. We are attempting to speak to its core. We try for a few minutes, then sit down.

After, I smoke cigarettes in my nice green dress, standing in the parking lot. I hold one leg at an angle, arched, and stare off in the distance. I am trying to make the people filing out of church believe I am a hooker, or was once a hooker but I decided that church could help reform me, so I came back. A few men watch me, I think, but I won't turn to look at them. A few ladies, too. I keep smoking.

Once they're all are gone and I'm alone on the street, I drop my cigarette and I go back in and find the guy. I don't know what he's called—otherwise I'd use the word. He's the guy with the white collar who led us.

"Hi," I say. "Can I confess?"

"We don't actually do that," he says.

"You don't?"

"No," he says. "But we do talk."

Maybe it's better to not tell him my made-up story about my old hooker-life.

He asks me my name and I tell him that it's Rose. He says it's a nice name. I think it's only fair to tell him that I believe nothing he believes.

"That's okay," he says. "I don't mind that." He has a nice smile. He's young, too. I try to imagine the path that leads here.

"Did you grow up going to church, then?" he asks. We're sitting next to one another in a pew. Just a half-hour ago he was standing up at the front, telling a story about salt. Now he's turned into a person.

"I just have a question, I think. We don't have to talk about my history."

"Okay," he says. "Shoot."

"Can you describe to me, very accurately, what it feels like to be lost?"

He purses his lips and looks at the hymnbook in front of us. "Spiritually lost?" he says. One eyebrow goes up.

"I guess."

"No," he says. "I've never been spiritually lost."

"Oh," I say. "Okay."

"I'm supposed to have been," he says. "I think. I don't know, though. I just haven't."

"I'm sure it's okay that you haven't," I say. "It's probably better. It probably makes you more confident. You have to be because you're a leader."

"I'm not so sure."

"I think this one could really go either way."

He nods, then squints across the room. "Not all those who wander are lost," he says. He's still squinting. I wonder if he's practiced this squint—a squint-stare off into the metaphysical distance. I'm realizing he's kind of handsome. But then again, it might just be that he cares about something.

"What is that?" I ask. "Did Jesus Christ say that?"

"No," he says. "Bilbo Baggins said that."

For example, Ryan Conrad's dad, David Allen Conrad II, or the other question of Ryan Conrad, the question of why I love him, or how I love him, and how it's not the same as Lucy. Then there is evil. Then there is Dylan, who I sometimes now smoke cigarettes with. Lucy doesn't like that we have to break cover to go smoke but she won't let us smoke in the van, so every two hours we're allowed to slip out stealthily and go to the neighborhood park. We are there together the Monday after church and I ask Dylan if he told her about us.

"No," he says. "But maybe she knows. I think she wants it, anyway." We're on the swings.

"Really?" I ask. "You two have always been you two."

"Rose, come on," he says. He rocks himself a little by pressing his feet down. "She loves him," he says. "That's what this whole thing is. That's her project."

I don't want to talk more about this and so I ask him about his novel. He says it's going well. He says he didn't plan it, but it's turning into a tale of redemption. The scientists who lost control of their carbonated beverage experiment have agreed to return to the Earth and try to save it.

"So they accidentally turned all of the oceans into grape soda, and then the land itself is kinda this gummy worm stuff," he says. "So far the people who are left—the people on the Moon, who live in a city on the Moon—they've had the scientists up in a kind of exhibit prison thing as a warning about hubris and technology and all that. But the problem is that these guys are the only ones who might know how to reverse it. And one of them in the prison has this idea, and so all the scientists get excited because they think if they can return they might be able to save nature and bring all the animals back."

"Is it because they want to be heroes?" I ask.

"No," he says. "They really do feel like they did a terrible thing. They want to get back to even."

"Is it going to work?"

"I don't know yet."

"If it works I think that might make you a Republican," I say, and he laughs.

"What's the name of the city on the moon?"

"Moonopolis," he says.

We're quiet for another minute.

"All politicians are nihilists," he says.

We smoke another cigarette and then go back to the van.

I get a letter from the SSTD—my first one ever—asking me to come to the underground campus in East Chicago to meet with my advisor. It says her name is Eleanor Wright. I didn't know I had an advisor. I call Dylan and Lucy and they both say they got the same letter, but they have different advisors and have meetings on different days. It's nice outside. I make the ridiculous choice to ride my bike. It's 27 miles. Lake Michigan, though, is an ocean to my left, and the greens are all coming. Dylan's scientists haven't managed to do all their evil yet.

To get into the SSTD you have to enter through a bakery called Marvin's. You have to say a secret word to Marvin. My letter says that today's word is ANOREXIA and so inside the bakery, totally sweaty, I look at the man who must be Marvin and say, "Anorexia."

He says, "Well, you've come to the right place."

"That's not what I mean," I say. "I mean that as the code word. I'm not suffering from it."

"I know that," he says. "I was about to pull the lever that makes that wall of biscuits open." He points at the wall of biscuits.

"Sorry," I say. "You know what you're doing. I got confused."

"I do know what I'm doing," he says. He pulls the lever and opens the wall of biscuits.

I go down the secret elevator and down some secret hallways and get to the secret administrative offices.

"Do you have an appointment?" the secretary asks. She looks like my aunt.

I show her the letter. She smiles broadly. "Rose," she says warmly. "It's you. I've wondered what you look like in person."

"Yes," I say. "It's me."

"It is you," she says. "Okay. Now. Let me see. You need Eleanor, and Eleanor said that you could meet her—" she checks a post-it note—"in the Glass Palace of Mystery."

"What's that?" I ask.

"I'll get you a map of the tunnels."

It takes me ten minutes of wandering down tunnels—tunnels that are actually just very clean, well-lit hallways—before I come to the doors that say GLASS PALACE OF MYSTERY. They're not made out of glass. I try to push them open but they're locked, so instead I knock. I see a button and I push it.

Above me, a trapdoor opens, and confetti pours down onto my head.

After a minute a woman opens the door. She's a middle-aged woman with brown, frizzy hair. She's wearing a yellow cardigan and a pair of glasses hangs around her neck, held in place by a stringy, silver cord. "Hello," she says. "Rose?"

"Eleanor?"

"Yes," she says. She looks at her watch. It's half-melted. She nods, then looks at me. "You're right on time. I appreciate that."

"It's amazing that I am. I rode my bike. It took way longer than I thought."

"I wouldn't call that amazing."

"It's not amazing," I say. "No. Sorry."

Eleanor nods again and opens the door wider. Behind her, I see the Glass Palace of Mystery. It's one room, as large as an amphitheatre. The walls are all made of glass, or at least they're all transparent. We're 100 feet below the surface of Lake Michigan. Eleanor leads me further into the room and presses some buttons on a remote in her hand. Some lights go on, both inside the Glass Palace and outside, in the lake. A few strong white beams blaze out into the murk and gloom. They light up a pile of sludge and a pile of old tires.

"It's some of our best pollution to date," Eleanor says. "By that I mean most toxic. We've been petitioning the power company to increase their superheated water output in order to encourage more extravagant changes in wildlife behavior. "

"I didn't know I had an advisor," I say to Eleanor.

"And how is your project coming?" she asks.

"I suck."

"The models?" Eleanor says. "Oh, I don't know. I have to admit, part of me just loves the idea. We've had others here who have not been impressed. But I see what you mean by those. I really do see it."

"How do you know about them?" I haven't come to campus once since my interview.

"We watch," Eleanor says, watching the sludge. "We watch all of you."

"So you're like Santa Claus," I say.

Eleanor purses her lips, then puts both hands behind her back and strolls toward one of the glass walls. Her heels click against the glass floor. "You could drop out," she says, "if you'd like. If you do really find your work...sucking."

"I don't want to," I say. "But I'm lost."

"That's good!" she cries, turning, smiling. I doubt I look convinced, because she nods and says, "Really. For people like you that's a very good sign."

"People like me?"

"You know."

I don't know what people like me are. I say nothing.

"Boring people," she says. "You're boring, Rose."

"Oh."

"And you also don't have very much talent."

"Oh."

She says, "I wouldn't mind for you to expand some of your technical skills. In order to...deepen your work. All's not lost. I've never cared much for talent. Think about scope. Scale."

"That's interesting," I say, "because my whole project is about scope and scale."

"I don't think you understand your project."

"I think I have to quit," I say.

"Lucy," says Eleanor, watching the tires now. There are a few fish down there, I see. They probably think that it's coral. "Do you like what Lucy's doing?"

"Not really. Sometimes. I like Lucy better than what she's doing."

"The Machine of Knowledge of Other People," Eleanor says. "Such a fabulous title." Eleanor nods to herself at the other end of the chamber, turns back to me and, walking toward me, says, "I feel good about what I've seen here today. You pass. Carry on."

"What about quitting?" I say. "Also, I'm lost."

"Oh, it doesn't matter," she says. "At this point."

★ ✪ ★

The next night I ask Lucy to come over to my apartment instead of sitting in the van with Dylan. I don't think she'll want to, but on the phone she says, "Okay. Dylan's being really weird, anyway."

I have started working on a new model. It's a model of the three of us sitting in the van.

When Lucy comes in I show it to her and she says, "Less twee, I guess. You could be doing so much more."

"Like what?" I say.

"You need to break through," she says, "all your sentimentality and wonderment."

"Why?"

"It's just better."

"Why?"

"It's just better."

"Why?"

"It's just better."

"Why?"

"It's just better."

"I think if I did that there wouldn't be anything inside of me to talk about."

"Well," she says, flopping down onto my green cat-shredded recliner, "there you go."

My biggest model of a father and a son constructing the solar system takes up most of the kitchen, so to make tea I'm constantly stepping over Jupiter and having to hug the father as I go around him. "You suck sometimes," I say to her. My kitchen has an opening for the breakfast countertop. She doesn't react at all. "Do you realize you're mean?" Again, nothing.

When I give her her tea she says, "I'm sorry. I barely know what twee means."

"I hardly even know."

"You know the thing with Dylan?" she says.

"What?"

"He has this whole spacey art genius vibe and I'm pretty sure he's totally full of shit."

"Yeah," I say.

"He told me he didn't love me anymore. He said he was starting to think that love was invented, anyway." She sips at her tea and looks down at it. "What sucks is I think I said the same thing to him like two years ago. Now he thinks he's the one who thought of it. Again. And that he's, like, the first person who ever thought of it."

"Do you actually think that's true?" I ask.

"About love?"

I nod.

"It doesn't matter," she says, and smiles. "It doesn't matter at all, who invented what. It's there either way, right?"

Once, Ryan Conrad's dad almost found spycam 8. It's the one in Ryan's bathroom, where Lucy gets her footage of Ryan's mom bathing him. Ryan's dad was in the room, in a suit, chatting to them both during a bath. (He has a way of chatting with Ryan that must be how he used to chat with Ryan— no difference.) But as he spoke he kept staring right at the camera, which we'd mounted inside the heating vent when the Conrads were on vacation. We thought he was about to stop talking completely, open the vent, and find it. In the end we had Dylan go into the backyard and light their compost on fire to distract them.

Still, it has to stop. There's something wrong. Maybe, I think, it's my project. To stop Lucy's.

First I go looking for Dylan to tell him he might be the worst of all of us.

He's not at his apartment. I find him at the coffee shop, drinking a mug of hot water.

"It's something new I'm trying," he says. "Just water. Ever since I turned the oceans to soda in the novel I've been having these weird feelings about water."

"I want to talk for real," I say. "Just let me get a triple cappuccino."

When I'm waiting in line I plan out what I want to say. It's something along these lines: we think we're different and we think we're special, the three of us, but we're not. We really have no idea. We're all like Ryan Conrad. Everyone is like Ryan Conrad.

When I sit down, Dylan says, "So I finished the book and sold it for $750,000."

I stare at him.

"It also got optioned for a movie. So I'm rich."

"Dylan."

"What?"

"The scientists," I say. "What happens to the scientists?"

"What?" he asks. "In the book? They go back to Earth with their idea."

"Does it work? Do they reverse it?"

"I'm not telling," Dylan says. "I actually can't. I don't own the story anymore. They own it."

"I don't think that was the point of the project," I say, "when you were doing the project."

"I'm moving to New York. Next week."

I leave the coffee shop and take my triple cappuccino and my saucer with me.

That night I dream I am Lucy. I dream I am at my high school homecoming dance. Across the gym I see Ryan Conrad with his date. Her name is Jenna Fitzcarmichaelsimmonson, she is blond, and Ryan smiles at her as he hands her a plastic cup of fruit punch. As Lucy, I am hurt to see this because we are not allowed to talk about our strange dates dressed as adults or the dances we tried to do in his uncle's living room. It's not because our love would be taboo or impossible—no one cares about us. We could do it. It's because somehow we decided on this game and we never realized we didn't have to stay in the game. I become a wise older Lucy inside of the gym inside of my brain while I sleep. I look at him, thirty feet away, and realize that all along, one of the only true and good things in the world was right here, alive and well, right beneath the basketball hoop. It was just simple love and a good, clear connection between the minds of two people. And I couldn't tell because I was too young.

★ ✪ ★

I don't know if Lucy knows when I go to Yellow Oak Lane. The van is there and the felt is in the windows. It's very conspicuous. Nobody has said a thing.

I am standing on the sidewalk at the end of the block, staking out the stake-out van, when I see Lucy climb out of the side door. She sneaks across the street and climbs through a window on the first floor of the Conrad's house.

I stand still for a second, unsure what to do. Then I go to the van.

Lucy's laptop is on the utility bench, and I don't have to do anything to find her—as I'm sitting down she's slipping into Ryan's bedroom. The night-vision is on, and so when I see her she is green. Her hoodie is up and tightened, so her skin is a pale yellow-green circle, and the colors make me think that I'm not looking at a bedroom through a night-vision camera, but I'm looking at the Underworld, and that Lucy has snuck down through the caves, looking for him, and she has finally entered the cavern where he is staying. She has turned into a corpse to find him, but it was worth it. Her eyes are white. She stands in front of the door.

Slowly, she closes it behind her, so softly that the bars don't even jump on the audio.

Ryan is asleep. Or, if this is the cavern in the Underworld, he is gone.

Lucy goes across the room and kneels beside him.

For a long time she is still, just watching his face. I have imagined before that this, here—Ryan asleep—is as close as he gets to being what he was before. Lucy and I have seen both parents watching him and I've suspected they were thinking the same thing. We've seen both parents crying. And what does Ryan Conrad dream about? What can be inside of him? This, Lucy can't know. I can't know either, but I have guessed, and I think she's guessed, too, even though she would pretend she hasn't.

My guess is this: inside of Ryan Conrad Ryan Conrad looks up at the world and all it used to be from the bottom of a well. There's only a small circle of light. Faces pass over it and he sees them and his heart changes. The color of the water he is sitting in changes, too. He reaches out for the faces and he can't reach them.

There is a tremor of movement in the low-res green light. Lucy's arm is moving.

She touches Ryan Conrad's hair. She strokes it once, tilts her head, leans forward, and kisses his lips.

I get a postcard from Dylan a few weeks later—he says that he found a place to live and he tells me I should move out and live with him for a few months. He says he has a cat, and he says he lives in a place called Carroll Gardens, and when I read the words I imagine that all the characters from Alice in Wonderland live on his block.

He says in a P.S. that he found out he was allowed to tell me that his scientists do manage to save the world after all. It is a happy ending. One of them lost an arm. But beyond that, it worked.

I write Dylan back on a piece of toilet paper and tell him that he's missed only a little, but that we haven't missed him. I tell him I'm glad his scientists found redemption and saved the Earth and reversed the effects of their former selfish acts and I tell him that I don't think he is Republican just because he wrote a story with a happy ending. I paint the toilet paper in liquid plastic and attach one of my little AA-powered lights to the top and set it out to dry on some newspaper.

That night, I was waiting in the van when Lucy came back. I was crying and she said, "Please don't," to me, but maybe she was, too, or had been. Then she went to the laptop and loaded eighteen files and showed me all the times she had snuck in to kiss Ryan Conrad. We watched them in silence. When we were finished I said, "I think your project has to be done."

She was quiet.

"Lucy."

"Do you know what I thought?" she asked.

"What?"

"I thought that if the right person kissed him, he might wake up."

"He never did."

"No," she said. "Of course he never did."

★ ✪ ★

We each have a new project. Lucy's is already done. For her project we removed every single spycam and microphone from the Conrad house and we left no trace. We did it on Memorial Day, when the Conrads were away in Oak Park. We erased all her files. We threw away the gear. We left the van in an alley. We had never been there.

My project is more complicated. At first I just said little things to Lucy and didn't follow them up, but I have now decided it's time for the hard sell and I tell her directly, while we're eating pasta, that she has to go see him at his day-clinic.

She doesn't ask me why I think she should. She just finishes her sandwich and wipes her face with her napkin and says, "Will you come?"

And everything else is as you'd expect it might be. His mother is there but his dad is not. When we get there lunch has just ended, and other head trauma patients are spread out across the room. Some of them are with their mothers, too. Lucy is dressed in nicer clothes but she's not in formal wear. I stand back as she goes to talk to Ryan's mom—I am holding a reasonably-sized model of a boy and his father making the solar system for a gift because I think there's a good chance that Ryan and his dad maybe really did do it a long time ago. So I will give it to them. When Lucy talks to Ryan's mom I imagine she is saying simple, clear, true things, like, "I used to know Ryan," or, "We were friends ten years ago. I've been meaning to come see him but I didn't know what was the right thing to do." Whatever she says, Ryan's mom seems warm and happy and they sit down in front of Ryan. Ryan's mom talks and gestures; Ryan's eyes are empty, his head is tilted. His hair is cut well but his face isn't right. Maybe there is nothing inside of him at all anymore. It's too hard to imagine what there is inside of him.

Instead I imagine Lucy, what she thinks. She thinks that in another universe, one of the many that has split off from ours, Ryan's foot slid and he reached out and grabbed her shoulder and they laughed heartily together. They laughed about how close he'd come to falling. Then they went on with their lives.

Here is Ryan, gone from the world, he won't be waking up, and nothing, I really mean nothing, is irreversible.

No Sun

On the morning of the third day I walked through the dark streets of our home town, Grayson—the government had already turned off the grid—to my uncle's offices, which were on the second floor of a corner building on Jackson and Naismith, right above the hardware store. I knew that Uncle Drake, when he first moved to Grayson, had intentionally chosen the spot to make a statement: beneath the theoretical, even with buildings, there must always be the practical to enforce it. The hardware store below was action. He, the man above, was mind.

There was no one else around as I made this small journey. There were no clouds, many stars, no cars, an eerie calm. It hadn't gotten cold yet. I could hear that Fallon's still had drinking customers and a few houses had candlelight in the windows, but despite the disembodied voices and other small signs of activity, it was difficult to imagine people inside structures, still living. Not because a wave of destructive force had rocked through the community and killed us all—this hadn't happened yet, clearly—but because, since that first morning, a feeling of incredible doom had overwhelmed me, and I was having trouble believing in the existence of life.

Sara was still alive. It was the first time I'd been away from her in 72 hours. And it had become obvious that she was essential, that she would be essential, if there was going to be any kind of future for us.

This morning I had left her more for her sake than out of any compulsion to get away from her. Of the two of us, she was the one who liked to be alone, and I had begun to see the same fidgeting and irritability that meant she needed two hours to gather herself amidst her introverted rituals, developed over a lifetime of quiet moments within her own mind, without me wandering around the house, making noises, planning, asking her questions about her allergies.

She was faced with the prospect of never being apart from me again. We had been dating for five weeks. She was scared.

Finally she'd said, "Can you please go find...something?" Understandable. So I left.

I had been worried about looters since the darkness started; it now made me anxious that she was in my house alone, but the town, amazingly, was still quiet. Probably because we had no television, and could not see images of the other side of the planet, which we'd heard was on fire.

"Good morning, Joe," said Uncle Drake, after he'd pulled open the door. "Although there is no longer such a thing." He was actually smiling.

"My watch is still running," I said, and held up my wrist to show him. "So it's morning, Doc."

"Eh," he said, shrugging, and he moved out of the way.

I entered his offices and he closed the door behind me. I let him take my coat. He was running a generator; I could hear it grinding away in some other room. How fruitless it seemed. Still, his consumption of electricity was modest, only a lamp at his desk and a small tape recorder, the old flat kind, playing some soft classical music that I thought might be either Erik Satie or the soundtrack to *Star Wars: The Phantom Menace*.

"Curious tattoo on your wrist," he said. "What is it?"

I looked at it. "It's the sun," I said. I watched him nod appreciatively. Considering the circumstances.

"It's a coincidence," I said. "Don't start pontificating."

"Come again?"

"I thought it was cool at the time," I said, even though this was not true. "It's not like I knew this was coming."

"The sun is not cool."

"Not what I meant."

"Would you like some tea?" he asked, and I was glad we were dropping the subject.

I nodded yes, and he went into the kitchen. I sat down on his sofa.

This, exactly, is what I wanted. A conversation before Sara and I left. Some advice, maybe. He was the smartest person I knew, and as I am not a smart person—book-smart person—I'd always found it a good idea to talk to such people in times of crisis. He had been a physicist at the U. of C. for 25 years before moving up from Chicago; he'd arrived quietly, relocating the hundred miles to Grayson, and now it seemed that he'd come just for this, to be our personal interpreter for the end of the universe. He had no family but me and did nothing but sit in his offices, reading, working out old paradoxes to keep himself busy. Sometimes he strolled.

I'd last seen him late into the first day, during what should have been dusk. He had been in the library, speaking at a lectern in front of an impromptu crowd of maybe 150 people. He had been trying to explain—no, not explain, just describe, since explanations, as such, were no longer possible—the physics of what had happened, but in the end I think his lecture upset people, which was impressive, because people were already so upset. There were some screams. I saw a lady push her husband and storm out. All they had wanted to know was when normalcy was going to start again, and he hadn't been able to say a thing on that topic. Deep down I could tell my uncle didn't think it would ever return. Oh, and this: the deceleration was still going on, and Uncle Drake had been pressed forward into his lectern as he spoke, as though the whole library had been built on a slope. At one point his glasses had fallen forward, horizontally, from his face.

"I've been thinking about time," he said now, coming across the apartment with a silver tray. "Your watch reminds me." He wasn't European—actually, he was from Michigan, like my dad—but he behaved like he was. Or tried to. He had a small white beard on the tip of his chin and a mustache that curved around his lips to greet it. It had been intense back when I was little; now it was extraordinary. His hair was white, too. For some time I had been convinced that it was dyed, and that he was intentionally cultivating the image of a batshit crazy theoretical physicist in order to impress the whole town. Now, given the situation, I wondered to myself whether it was possible that being a physicist actually made your hair turn white and gave you a hint of a German accent.

I looked at my tattoo.

"What about time?" I said.

"It's all gravity," he said, flipping his left hand casually—time, how annoying—as he dipped the tea with his right. "Our whole feeling for it." He looked up. "Of course we ourselves participate as well. But now, I don't know what will happen with it."

"I don't really—"

"I woke up with an image in my head," he said, "of every person in town frozen. Not by ice but in time."

I nodded, then leaned forward and took my own small cup of tea. "Sure," I said, stirring in my sugar. "Wait, what?"

"If this happened, Joseph," he went on, "would we know?" He stared over my head. "If our movements were slower, and our metabolisms and synapses slowed down as well, does it seem possible to you that no one would know the difference? That the course of human civilization would continue on at this new rate? Perhaps our understanding of nature would change, but we would call that a phenomenon of nature, not of us."

I felt afraid imagining this, and I moved my neck a little to verify the speed of everyday life. I started to wish I hadn't come to see him at all. "I guess it would take someone who wasn't slowing down," I said, "to be able to see it."

"This is not relevant to our current situation. Gravity is still more or less intact," he noted gravely, moving on. "Something that behaves like gravity, at least."

So I had happened into a larger conversation he was having with himself. I thought then he might demonstrate his comment about gravity by dropping something, but he didn't need to, since we weren't floating in the middle of the room. So he didn't.

"Listen, Uncle D," I said. "Have you figured out anything new?"

He talked then for some time about his guesses as to who would go first, the hot side of the planet or us, the cold side. Each side had its merits. He guessed that Africa was dying the fastest, that the temperatures could possibly be 130 or 140 degrees by now, the continent baking as it was beneath permanent sunlight. Europe and Asia were probably not doing much better.

"But then again we've lost photosynthesis," he said. "And energy. The scales of the geological systems are out of balance. The weather will be coming soon. That will probably kill us all before any of the more interesting questions are answered."

"Sara and I are going to go up to my dad's old cabin."

"Oh? I vaguely remember something about that. Where is it?"

"It's in the Porkies. It's way up in the U.P."

"Suit yourself," he said again, and shrugged, just like he had when I came in. "I will not be joining you. Fools rush out."

"I know," I said, and sipped at my tea. I would have invited him, actually. It would have been okay to have him.

We sipped a little more.

"I'm going to kill myself," he said.

I could have had a strong reaction to this, but it had already started to happen around town, and he was by no means the first with the idea. The entire Funderburk family had eaten rat poison, and no one had seen the mayor since he left to "look into things" in Milwaukee. I didn't doubt Drake's will to do it. But I had one question, and it was at the core of what energy I had left, at the core of going north with Sara.

"What if we start to spin again?" I said. "What if we go back to normal?"

"Yes," he said immediately, nodding. "We have no reason to assume the planet won't correct itself, just as—well—just as we had no reason to assume that it would never stop." He was quiet then. I wasn't proud of my thought, I didn't think that I had outsmarted him, and knew something other people didn't know. I didn't understand what he'd just said. But I knew that my idea was a simple and clear idea, and it seemed to be the best one to hold on to. Why not go all-in for hope? Every time? What other arguments made sense? It had taken apocalypse for me to see it.

Uncle Drake finally came up with an answer, one that I am still thinking about during these long, long days.

"It may start again," he said. "But it won't make a difference. Not now."

"There's too much damage?"

"No," he said, shaking his head. "The earth can always heal itself, given time. It's us. We're the ones who've been destroyed. I mean that now, and forever, we won't know what to believe. Our knowledge has fallen apart."

He smiled again. "Causality. Simple and horrible."

★ ✪ ★

All around I was reacting well to apocalypse, frankly. And more than just the deeper thoughts. Something inside of me—maybe this came from my time living on the West Coast— just understood doom, and had understood since the beginning of the long night, when we woke to the bed sliding across the floor, and then our backs were pinned against the wall like we were two insects, hands and feet squirming a little but the majority of our bodies stuck in place. Uncle Drake told us later that it was the Earth slowing down that had pushed us all in one direction. When he said it I found an eerie beauty there. It made me think of surfing—we were all surfing through outer-space, but on a cresting wave. He told us that Tycho Brahe would have been proud to be alive to see it. I didn't know what that meant.

I was not a doomsday prophet and had never thought much about these kinds of things. I remember a man named Clive who used to scream at the streetlights on my corner when I lived in Portland. I'd see him when I went to get cigarettes. He thought that unnatural light was tied up in with the many sins mankind had committed against nature, and that the punishment, when it came, would involve the melting off of our skin by aliens with horns and metal mouths. It was never very convincing back then, but then again, nothing had been. Portland. Portland was a dark time. I'd almost killed myself with drugs, and not at all on purpose.

These days, though, these days of my new life, I was a practical person. I usually looked for ways to solve problems, not understand them. It hadn't taken me long to start acting. And besides whatever intuition I'd had, you could feel the significance very quickly, even as we were just beginning to be able to move around again, and were realizing that it had been first twenty, then thirty, then forty hours since daylight. I'd hit the grocery store and the hardware store early, before people were panicked, before the lines snaked out the doors, before the best supplies were snatched up. I was ready.

"He said he thought it was a good idea," I told Sara about an hour after I left Drake's, after I'd again checked over what I'd packed into the Cherokee. There was enough for maybe a year. I didn't think that water would be a problem, and so I'd concentrated on food, guns, ammunition, and clothing. Also condoms.

"What kind of good idea?" she asked. She was standing in the kitchen with a cup of tea, wearing her bathrobe. It was tied loosely, and I could see her bra and panties hidden underneath. There were candles all around. This was not sexual, however; this was depression minus electricity.

"What does that mean?"

"Like oh, good idea, the same as any other idea you can have? Or oh, good idea, like it makes sense and could be good for many reasons?"

"I think the second," I said. "I wasn't sure. He was distracted."

"By what?"

"Thinking."

Of the many bad things happening and the indescribable feelings of this strange time, the worst was maybe the most selfish. Here we were in the endtimes and I couldn't stop thinking about my own inner world. And the day before it started. It was the best day Sara and I had ever had together, and because of that, very possibly the best day of my life. It wasn't anything incredible. We'd had lunch together at Denny's, and had then driven out to Kettle Moraine. We first went and looked at the kettles from a wooden observation deck, then went down to the grass in the park and sat on a blanket, watching some kids play on the park's jungle gym. Later, we drove back to town and ate Chinese food at her apartment, then made love for the first time. I have the image of her still—she's lying beneath me on the cheap white couch, small breasts bare, shoulders back, odd smile on her face. Eyes closed. There couldn't be eye contact.

We'd met in N.A. I was still going as much as I could, although the details of my former addictions were confusing to me, and so sometimes I avoided meetings because I didn't want to have to articulate what had happened. I wasn't a normal addict. In fact I don't think I was ever an addict. I just did everything, all the time, and when I felt like not doing it anymore I stopped. But I had fucked up my emotions. I could tell. Whenever I smiled I heard a voice in my head saying, "You are smiling."

She hadn't been clean for quite as long as I had, but she was doing well. Now she was a librarian. I knew that she had had problems with depression, and was on meds now, but she had a wry way to her that fascinated me. She could let cynical barbs go, softly, from a place of psychological resignation that she had arrived at years before. There was power to that. I loved her darkness.

"Are they saying anything on the radio?" I asked her. This to avoid saying, "Are you coming or not? Because I'm leaving now, baby, into the forest, bravely."

"I haven't been listening," she said. "I'm scared to use up the batteries."

"I've got some in the car." By "some" I meant 256 Cs and 256 Ds.

"Have you seen your brother?"

"You've only been gone for like two hours," she said, turning away from me and going back toward the kitchen. "No."

I knew she was thinking about her brother and his family, but she hadn't said it out loud yet. I honestly didn't know what to think. That was another four people, including two children. The food that would last us a year might last us three months.

"I think we should discuss it."

"Why?"

"Because we have to go. Today. Now."

"I haven't decided that I want to go."

"I can tell you don't want to go without him. We should discuss that."

"Why do we have to go again?"

"Because there are too many people here."

"So this whole thing about going up to the mountains is just about getting away from the population? The world is ending and you want to get away from other conscious life? You realize that many people would have the opposite reaction."

"Don't act like you don't know what people are like."

"What are they like?"

"No one will hesitate to take everything we have and kill us if they think it means it will help them."

"Did you see that in a movie?"

"Don't."

"What?"

"You're acting like I'm being crazier than you actually think I'm being."

"What are you? A holocaust survivor? You don't know about this kind of thing."

We had done this more than once. But I knew that she believed me, and that she would in fact leave with me. It was a feeling, again. All of this was just her building it up in her own mind, so when she looked back and wondered about her brother and her nieces and nephews, and wondered whether or not they survived, and wondered whether or not she should have left, whether she was an immoral person, she could recall all of the soul-searching she did, recall that I had pushed her, and not think of herself as greedy or a bad person. She hated her sister-in-law and always tried to get out of babysitting, anyway. She didn't want to stay. I was just making it easier for her by being tough about it.

You just want to live, I told her. We both do, and I want to live with you. And we could start spinning again, and we could come back, and we could have a new life. Don't discount the possibility of having a new life.

It's funny that we think of the sun as something that comes up, still. Even after they realized that it was us turning around, not the sun. That it never came up, just that we came around.

I imagined it as we drove. I never had, not the real one. Who thinks hard about the sun? I had seen the dramatic shots of it, flaming and alive, regal in its sun-way, with dark spots all over it, as though piles of black fire floated around on a sea of liquid fire on its surface, and so that's what my mind gave me, and it was as though something inside of me was asking for it, and I tried to remember that it was there, still, either way, and that we just couldn't see it anymore. I tried to take away the feeling that what I was seeing was a photograph, or an artist's rendering, and just imagine what it must be like out there, in space, floating in front of it. On its own. It's not there for a reason—that's the heart of it. It's not there for a reason, but there it is.

I'd gotten the sun tattoo while unconscious. I suppose that means I can't say that I was the one to get it. Someone got it for me. First I was sitting in a bar and then I was in an alley. Then nothing. I never found out exactly how it had gotten there, who had taken me down to the parlor. I can only remember waking up, sitting perfectly upright, and seeing that I was sitting at a coffee shop. There was a bagel in front of me. There was a bandage on my arm. I was sitting with a girl named Ruth, and she watched as I peeled the bandage away and we both looked down at the new black tattoo. Ruth was into heroin. I think I was in a gasoline phase.

"Would you look at that," I said.

"That," Ruth said, "is the motherfucking sun."

★ ✪ ★

We passed the occasional car, lone headlights first only a blip on the road. Once, Sara said, "I wonder who's in there."

"People with the opposite idea we have."

"You mean people going to bigger towns. People gathering down in Chicago. People not going to hide in the mountains because they can't think of anything better to do."

"I guess," I said. "I don't know. I can't see."

"Wouldn't you ever think," she said, "that rather than all of us, like, turning into animals and ripping out each others' flesh and becoming the absolute worst we could be, that maybe the best in people will come out? Maybe we'll help each other? Maybe it'll be easy?"

"I guess," I said. "But maybe not. How can you know?"

We had a game that we sometimes played when we drove, a game about movie stars and movies. You would say a star's name and then the other person would say a movie they were in, then you'd say a different star in that movie, and the other person would say a new movie.

"Don Cheadle," I said.

"*Boogie Nights*," she said.

"Marky Mark," I said.

"*The Departed*," she said.

"Jack Nicholson," I said.

"*Five Easy Pieces*," she said.

I thought for a minute. "I don't know anyone else from that."

I looked over and saw that she was staring out the window, her head resting against the glass.

"Look," I said. "I'm sorry. I honestly think—"

"What else did your uncle tell you?"

"What?" I said. "About the sun?"

"Yes."

"He mentioned something about weather."

"What?"

"That bad weather was probably going to start coming. Because the atmosphere. And everything."

"Oh," she said.

"What am I going to do when my Wellbutrin runs out?" she asked.

"You'll be okay," I said. "Things are different. You'll adapt."

"There's no sun, though," she said. "I mean what's it going to be? An ice age? Like a whole ice planet? Isn't the sun supposed to be the thing that makes you happy?"

"It'll come back," I said. "You'll see. We'll just stay warm and safe for a while, then it'll come back."

"You keep saying that," she said. "It's not like we can sit there and play the movie game the whole time."

"We'll adapt," I said. "We're people."

★ ✪ ★

I could not resist stopping at the fully-lit gas station that was about a mile after we'd passed 64. I knew we were not going to see people again. And here it was, lit up and apparently open for business. I thought that we might be able to find a few more things to eat, maybe fill the tank one last time. There were five or six cars parked in the small lot beside the building. I thought it might be a gathering place. This made me nervous, it's true, but still I couldn't resist. What if they had gas?

"See if you can get the pump to work," I said to Sara. She had come out of her haze a little, and was looking curiously at the lit station. We could see at least one man through the window, leaning on a countertop.

It looked like his mouth was moving, that he had an audience, but I couldn't quite see. Just then he turned and looked right at us.

"This is weird," she said. "Let's just go."

"I thought you liked communities." I had the Smith and Wesson .45 under my seat and pulled it free while she was watching them. I ticked the safety and tucked it into the back of my pants.

"Just weird that they're open. How are we going to pay? Do you think they actually want money?"

"I'll go see."

The temperature had dropped. I felt it when I opened the door. I didn't bother to get my coat, but I could see my breath now. Someone else came out of the station's door before I got to it. His body was round and portly, and he wasn't especially tall. He had a toothpick in his mouth and wore glasses. He had a friendly face—he looked like he might have been a preacher. I can't tell you what preachers look like, that's not really what I mean. It was just a feeling. His hands were in his pockets.

"Welcome," he said. "I see you're partaking in our gasoline bartering collective." He nodded with a little smile. "Go ahead and fill her up. What would you like to trade?"

The way he said it had a certainty to it that I didn't like. As though already a new economy was in place, one that had been agreed upon without my vote.

"We've got some things," I said. "How about batteries?"

"We've got those."

"Food?"

"What kind of food you got?"

"Not too much," I said. I wondered about value now. What was a can of beans worth, at this point? Gasoline was like gold. I looked over my shoulder. Sara was still filling up. To fill the whole tank she'd probably use fifteen gallons. I thought of calling out to her to stop filling as we negotiated, but he knew and I knew both that we needed the gas, and were going to pay whatever we had to pay to get it.

When I looked back there was another man standing beside the preacher. Also a boy, ten or twelve.

"I said what kind of food?"

"Mostly canned," I said. "Beans, soup. Some of those Campbell's Chunky Soups."

"How many of them you got?"

"How about I give you fifty cans?"

Finally the other man spoke; he was taller, and had long gray sideburns. He was wearing a baseball cap. Something like GO AMERICA! And Suck a Cock If You Don't Like It!

"Sounds like you got lots," he said. "We were thinking more like 300."

"I can't do that," I said. "We don't even have that much."

"Why don't we just go and take a look at what you've got back there," said the preacher.

"I'll give you fifty cans of the Campbell's Chunky and fifty cans of chili beans," I said. "I've also got a couple extra flashlights I can give you." I was worried most about the axes. If they took the axes we were done.

"Why don't we just go and take a look at what you've got back there," said the preacher again, in the exact way he'd said it the first time, very amiable, and now the three of them were already moving.

Sara looked to be finishing up with the gas, and as they approached the car, I heard the Lambchop man say, "Hello, dear," to her in a too-nice voice, and she nodded back at him. When she looked at me I nodded at the car and she understood and she got back inside. I could see her locking her door.

The preacher leaned toward the back door of the truck and pulled on the handle. It popped, and he leaned back as it slowly opened. "I have to be honest with you," he said to me, after taking a long look at everything I had back there. "This isn't really a negotiation. It's more like a requisition." He turned back to look at what was there. "It ain't like it matters much one way or the other."

"No?" I said.

"You see what people—"

I shot Lambchop first, in the back of the head, only because he looked to me like a biker, and I was sure that he was the one, out of the three, carrying a weapon. It did, then, feel like time was slowing down a little, but only for them, not for me. I moved fast for me. I'm usually slow as it is. I thought that maybe somewhere Uncle Drake was smiling, noting how well I was paying attention—I wondered too about whether he'd been on to something about the time. We wouldn't know, would we?

Lambchop's big body crumpled to the ground in front of me after the bullet went through his head and the preacher turned, stupid words caught in his mouth, one hand still on some of my batteries, and I shot him in the face, and his brains sprayed out over my supplies.

I pulled him off and dropped him down next to Lambchop. The kid was just standing there.

"Run," I said.

He was staring at the ground, at one of the two men.

"Run, moron."

He shook his head no, his eyes wide. He opened his mouth while his head was still shaking, and for some reason I thought that I couldn't bear to hear him speak, I didn't want to hear anything about his interpretation of what had just happened, because it would not be properly grown up and subtle. I didn't want to hear a sound from him. I didn't want anything about him to be there, as he had seen what I'd done, and what I'd felt nothing about.

Inside the station I found some empty gas cans and brought them out and filled them up. There was just enough room to fit them into the back, but I had to arrange a few things. Then I went back in again, just to see what else there was that we could fit. I thought for a second about having Sara drive one of their trucks and filling the whole thing up. But that would take too long. It would also make us like them.

We had to leave. There was no one else here, but there probably would be, soon. The lights attracted us, like we were moths. It was obvious now what had happened to all the owners of the other cars I'd seen parked in the side lot, and I had no interest in happening upon their graves.

It was just as I was going out the door that I saw the meth on the countertop, beside the cash register.

There were six or seven miniature baggies, all lined up in a row, and inside each of them a good, solid diamond-chunk.

I recognized it from the one time I had done it in Grayson, when I'd first come back to the Midwest. I'd met an old friend and we'd gone to the playground at the same elementary school we'd attended twenty years before. He had gotten into ATV sales or something. I'd spent a lot of time having fourth-grade memories come into my head, not really knowing whether they were real or whether I was making them up—they'd been too pleasant, in a way, and didn't fit into my haunted, dark-enchanted-forest sense of childhood. The kind where the trees eat little boys. He'd asked me why I came back, and I said, "It was so lonely out there," which had felt basically true, and then we'd smoked the meth.

I stuffed all of the baggies into my pockets. It was just something else that we probably needed.

"Please tell me something," Sara said in a tiny, meek, almost inaudible voice after I'd started up the car again and we were on our way. "Tell me that boy—I mean I know what those men probably tried to do, I understand that—but Joe? But that boy? Please tell me that he ran away from you, but straight back, directly away from the truck. That's why I didn't see him. Right?"

"Right," I said. "I told him to run and he ran."

"Who did you shoot twice, then?" she asked.

"The fat one," I said.

It took us another two hours to get up into the mountains. For a half-hour I played with the radio, and high on the AM band I found somebody broadcasting, just a lone tinny voice talking about everything that he'd heard. He apologized for not having any music to play, but he figured that information was more important. He was in Indiana, he said. He said that as far as he knew, everyone in the southern half of Africa was dead. He said that in Indiana, there were tornadoes, larger than he'd ever seen, except that it was snowing, too, so ice crystals were flying through the air like shrapnel, moving so fast they were breaking through the walls of houses. Then he started talking about why he thought it was happening. Basically: God decided to be done with us. He had all these explanations.

"Turn it off, please," Sara said. "I don't want to hear his theories."

I thought of bringing up my optimistic thoughts about it starting again. Instead I reached for the radio and clicked it off. I think we both understood that it was probably now going to be a long winter, perhaps a forever winter, and that it would be dark, and that there was no reason to think that it would ever get light again. What had the preacher said? That it didn't matter. "It ain't like it matters much, one way or the other."

To me, either way, it still felt like it mattered.

Three weeks later I was outside chopping wood in the middle of a blizzard. Around me the landscape was starlight white and icy; I had worked hard every day to keep a hole open outside of the door, so I could crawl out through the tunnel and find wood. Then Sara insisted that we do the same for the windows of the cabin, and we spent a week digging our way through. "For the air," she told me. "The circulation." Then I spent two weeks wondering what would happen if the forest itself ended up underneath the snow, and so I chopped wood intently, piling it in the basement, filling the upstairs bedroom and loft, burning it often to keep us warm and lit, and to keep the snow from our walls. Of course I thought of the boy and what I had done. It was a shame, because it probably mattered.

There is more, and I could explain it. Once, I thought I saw a bear and ran toward it, through the snow, instead of away from it, like I should have done had it been a bear. But it was a stump. Another time, Sara and I played cards for three hours, and I argued with her about the rules of gin rummy. I was mad and she said, "The world ended," and I said, "That's not the point." To cool down I went for a walk and I hiked the road, to the highway, just to see what I could see, and to get away. I was worried we were both going crazy—the real kind. It was barren, too, and my flashlight showed me only a long whitish strip of ice both ways. I still had the meth in my pocket. I hadn't smoked any. After a long time of breathing the ice air I threw it all away, into the ditch, and went back home.

Here we are.

The only other story worth telling is when I crawled through the front tunnel after a few hours of shoveling and chopping and opened the door and found Sara upstairs in the corner of the loft with the broom, sweeping up broken glass. She had brought the lantern up with her.

"What happened?" I asked her. I saw then that there was a hole in the window. I could feel the wind.

"No," she said, seeing my stare. "It's okay. I thought we could just fill it with insulation."

"Did you do it?" I asked.

She shook her head no.

"What?"

She set the broom down and went to the corner. She knelt and picked up a shoebox that was there. She came back to me and set it in my hands, and as I held it, she lifted off the top.

"It just came in like a missile," she said. "I put it in the box. Like a bed."

There was a bird inside. It was a bright red cardinal. She lifted it out and held it cradled in her two palms. It was curled up and almost spherical, its beak tucked far down into its chest. It looked like a heart.

"Is it dead?" I asked, and just as I did, it opened one yellow eye and flapped its wing.

Vaara in the Woods

It's night. Alexis and I are in the bedroom, putting the new bed together.

She's wearing a white T-shirt that makes the pregnant curve of her belly obvious.

"It seems substantial," she says, looking at the bed.

"We'll definitely be supported," I say. "This will be…very comfortable." Eyebrows up.

I can think of the monster while lying in the dark, as both of us are drifting off, and I can dream it, too, and see the white pines and the groups of men huddled around a fire. How many years can such things last? That's an important question. And why does it feel so important to imagine apocalypse?

My family tells me this happened in Forest County, Wisconsin, far from Chicago, and I would like to say that it isn't or wasn't true, because I am a modern person who uses computers, not a lumberjack. This was eighteen-something or nineteen-something, somewhere close to there, and the most important thing to know is that people who spent time in lumber camps suffered tremendously. The lumberjacks and the bosses lived in their killing zones for months at a time, used oxen to drag logs through the woods after they'd been felled, and often these oxen died of exhaustion, just crumpled first to their knees and onto their sides with a wail or a moan, and to hear that dying moan was like you had died as well. Sometimes they were just beaten to death by whips or shot for being not strong enough. When the jacks burned the dead oxen at night, it was said among the camps that the smoke collected up in the trees and came together, and later, not far away, it coalesced and drifted down to the earth, and it became the monster.

The pain. That's what drove the magic. It came alive again in the shape of something that looked like an ox but an ox made in a cave of hell, standing low to the ground with razor teeth, the horns on its head twisted around one another, its eyes burning red, a fire-liquid dripping from its rotten lips. The night after it was created, the monster would return and pull men from the camps.

My grandfather's grandfather, a man named James Somerville, worked those camps, and he worked them so long and so hard, so mercilessly, that he became a boss as a young man. He drove the jacks in the camps harder than anyone, and they hated him even more because he wouldn't eat with them at night; instead he ate in his shanty with his pregnant wife and his baby boy. It was uncommon for there to be any women in a camp, but James had demanded she come along through the summer. There had been what he once called "indiscretions" having to do with the pregnancy, and he wanted her by his side where he could watch her. She came. Her name was Martha. And when the story plays in my mind, for some reason I am one of the young loggers in that camp watching this happen, I am seventeen and outside of it and I see her through the open doorway some evenings as we come back to the camp, sitting in a chair with that baby in her lap, rocking it, her black hair loose around her shoulders, and I sometimes hear her singing to the child, and I realize why other men would be so quick to love her: She doesn't fit here.

Then it's that terrible June day and James, out in the woods, has been watching a Finn named Vaara. Sometime around lunch, sitting on my log, slapping at the black flies on my sweating neck, I see James walk by and spit at Vaara's feet. Either Vaara has been with her or James believes he has, and it doesn't make a difference which version is true.

Vaara takes a long look at the wad of spit by his feet and considers it and James keeps walking past him, to the oxen, and among them he finds one of the healthiest we have and he pulls it into the middle of our lunch gathering and he begins to beat it with his short whip.

It takes him fifteen minutes to kill it. No man says a word. The ox cries out at every strike. I shut my eyes.

Once it has gone to its knees, a bloody mess, James takes the pistol from his holster and shoots the ox through the head.

He looks at Vaara for a long time, breathing hard, and says, "Help me drag it back to camp."

Vaara, pale now, looks at the dead ox and says, "Would be impossible," in his thick Finn accent.

James says, "Come with me, then. I'd like to speak to you."

Vaara puts his sandwich down. Together the two men walk out into the woods. Not long after that we hear the shot.

James tromps back and says, "Far more to do before the day is done, boys."

I am part of the group left behind to burn the beast in a pyre, and we shrug and think two birds with one and don't think about the pain and we go find Vaara in the woods and put him in the pyre as well.

We burn them both up and go back to camp, but as I eat I think back to the smoke I saw coming up from the pyre and think of how it seemed different and think of the stories of the monsters but let that go from my mind quickly, as I'm not the type to believe it. Near dusk, as I'm washing up, I see James come out of his shanty and go out into the woods. Twenty minutes later he's back and he walks straight to me and says, "Where is Vaara?" "We burned him," I say, and he says, "Where?" And I say, "With the ox you killed." James's eyes go wide and he stares at me for the longest time. "The same fire?" he says, and I say, "Yes." "You goddamned fool," he says, and his neck snaps around and he looks out into the woods.

It's night. It's right then we hear it, this low moan but with a force behind it, like it's coming from far away but loud enough to get to us. James begins to run toward his shanty and that's when the monster comes into camp. It's not even like the stories say it should be; it is shaped like a man, but terrible, awful I tell you, enormous, burning and moaning its way into our clearing, its long, blackmuscled arms nearly dragging on the earth, and eyes red and its teeth gleaming. Vaara and that ox have fused together. James is already in the shanty to protect his wife and the monster throws one of those long arms out into the side wall, wood explodes, and that's when I feel myself running toward them, which is opposite, because every other man in the camp is screaming and running away.

The shanty is burning by the time I get to the door and when I pull it open I can see that James is already in the arms of Vaara, amid a fire, that the monster's torn through the wall, and that the woman, Martha, is crouched near the bed, and she sees me and my eyes are wide and she holds the baby out toward me, and I scream, "Run outta there!" and see in the corner of my eye James smashed up into the ceiling of his shanty by the monster, and he is on fire, he is a rag doll, his neck's already broken, but she only thrusts the baby into my arms and backs farther into the smoke and chaos of that place coming apart, and a piece of the porch collapses beneath me with this baby in my arms and then I am only running, not looking back and not hearing the sounds of her screams as I plunge into the woods.

In Chicago, in the night, I look out the window at the bare trees in the wind and the yellow lamp lighting my street corner, and of course the *I* is not the right *I*, that baby was my great-grandfather, directly above me, or so the story goes. I am not lying to you when I imagine the real ending to be Vaara trundling down Winchester Avenue in Ravenswood. Up into our building. He finds us in our new bed, Alexis and me, and takes us with him as well.

I cross the room and go down the hall to the bedroom door, and through the crack I can see her asleep in the bed.

I go back out to the window.

Once the baby comes, it will pass. I believe. We're safe.

Even so I hear myself whisper, then, still watching the clicking trees. I tell the night, "Vaara, I'm sorry, I'm sorry but it wasn't me."

Easy Love

Seven or eight years ago I saw Alex, the Iraqi man who used to own my corner store, chase a neighborhood boy out onto the sidewalk and throw a can of Diet Dr. Pepper at his head. I had just two days before I sent off my applications for medical school, and I remember feeling lighter as I walked, relieved I was through (for the time being, anyway) with the paperwork, the staplers, the lost files on my computer, the carefully-crafted emails to old professors, pleading with them to send my letters of recommendation. Relieved that I could get on to more important things, like reading the veins of leaves and rescuing farm animals from barn fires.

Almost everything was changing; my mother had died of MS over the summer and I had gotten engaged to a girl I'd met only a month before. Her name was Corinne Jones, and we'd met at a bar called Saxony. By December Corinne was married to someone else, but at this moment it was all roses, not a bad feeling in the mix. When Alex threw the Dr. Pepper she was away in France for six more days, there for some kind of international conference, presenting a paper regarding something maybe having to do with recycled paper. I knew little about her. I couldn't tell you details of what she was doing there, or if she was passionate, or even what kind of work she liked to do, but I hadn't slept, thinking of her return, and her hair piled up neatly beside me on her pillow in the night. I loved that girl.

By then I had known Alex for two years. I was intrigued by his corner store—Windy City Liquors, it was called, with a square blue sign bordered by bright, globular light bulbs, not unlike what you might see on Broadway, New York City. The floors were sticky. It was understocked, served homeless alcoholics as much as anyone else, and often contained, instead of customers, three or four members of Alex's family sitting behind the counter, watching a small Zenith television, smoking cigarettes and drinking exotic-looking shots of charcoal-black coffee. Transactions there had a ceremonial air to them involving greetings, nods, and thank yous from both sides, from many different people, consecutively. To buy a box of saltine crackers could make you feel like you were ratifying a constitution.

I knew the family was Iraqi because Alex had once told me proudly that the picture on the wall beside the condoms, the one of the clean-shaven young American soldier who stared straight into the camera, was his son. I asked Alex what country the family had come from.

"Originally, I mean," I said.

"Iraq," he said, staring at the picture. "Joseph is there fighting Saddam now."

This day Alex was the only one at the store. Maybe he was nervous, and when he saw that a kid was stealing from him, he didn't have his family there to hold him back. I could see, from where I was on the sidewalk, the candy bars spilling out of the kid's pocket as he ran out of the door. He had made it to his bike and had stood up on his pedals to begin his escape just before the barrel-chested Alex emerged, wound up, and released, and the Diet Dr. P hit him square in the temple, and he sort of accelerated and veered into a metal garbage can at the same time. The front tire hit it with a metal crump, and the bike stopped moving, and he kept going—through the air above his handlebars, then went down onto the pavement, where he remained, facedown, not moving, for quite some time.

"You don't do that!" Alex yelled at the boy's body.

After no response, Alex yelled, "This is a business!"

Still no response, and Alex looked over at me. I could see he was surprised by the violence.

"Is he dead?" I asked.

"Oh, no," Alex said then, laughing very nervously. He shook his head, then went and knelt down beside the kid. "I am sorry, boy. Hello?"

He shook the kid's shoulder, then looked back at me. He smiled, and his mustache curved up below his nose.

To fill this embarrassing time of someone else's unconsciousness, Alex picked up the kid's bike and leaned away from it, as though inspecting the purity of the frame.

Satisfied with the angles he saw, he carefully leaned the bike against the side of the building and went back to the kid.

"He's fine. Look." He pointed. "He breathes."

A minute later, the kid was sitting against the brick wall that was the side of Alex's store, sipping at the very Diet Dr. Pepper Alex had thrown at him, waiting for Alex to re-emerge with ice for his head. Alex had not requisitioned the candy bars on his way back in, I noticed. Guilt.

The kid stared coolly at me.

I was beginning to feel a little too caught up in the incident. I had just been on my way to buy an apple. I was innocent.

"Don't fall asleep," I told him. "You might have a concussion."

"Fuck you, dude," said the kid, shaking his head and pursing his lips at me. "That shit was assault."

"I don't think it counts if you're a robber."

"Fuck you, dude," he said again. "It's still assault."

★ ✪ ★

The farm animal comment requires explanation. I do want, though, a discussion of love, ultimately, because **that's the focus of this story**, and I'm not sure it's important for you to know this part about the fire. But who am I to omit? I've decided that one can't tell about these things, and that the feeling matters more than what happened. This Dr. Pepper incident, and my subsequent date with Alex's daughter, came on a Thursday. The previous Tuesday was the day, as I said, I had sent away my medical school applications. It had been a nightmare of paperwork, more than I ever knew it would be when I first began filling out forms, and honestly, had I understood the amount of work just to get in, I probably would have found a different career. God forbid my future self being able to contact—via new time travel technologies—that version of me and describe what it would be like after the school, in residency, or after that. My hospital at this very moment is being eaten by an HMO that I think about in terms of Pac-Man, and the insurance costs alone have cut so far into our cash flow that yard work is looking like a good alternative business. Being an ER doctor is like being an astronaut; it sounds cool until you accidentally fly the ship into the sun, or you forget to turn on the oxygen before you go to sleep, or your partner forgets to recharge your jetpack before a spacewalk, and you float off, at three miles per hour, infinitely. It's then—a key moment in all lives—when the optimism of your dreams becomes stupid.

I couldn't quit at that point. I had just spent two years back in college hanging out with nineteen year-olds who called me Dad because I was 30, getting through the prerequisites, and now there was nowhere else to go but forward. In a sense I already was that astronaut. I dropped the envelopes into the blue mailbox on the corner, and to reward myself on that Tuesday, I decided to drive out of the city and to get into the countryside. I didn't know where to go, not really, and so I just got onto the expressway and headed south, deciding I would pull off whenever things looked rural enough, find some field somewhere, and start walking and getting in touch with my deepest and most complex emotions, which you have greater access to when you are near trees.

When I parked at a gas station I was probably forty miles south of Beverly, and there was nothing around but farms, their fields, and a few patches of woods here and there.

For no reason I bought a bottle of Gatorade at the gas station, then asked the guy behind the counter whether there were any big parks around.

"What do you mean?" he asked.

He was disappointingly American in all ways, and I wished I was back home, in my neighborhood. There are all different degrees and qualities of transactions with anonymous vendors; you can be blocked from the start or you can immediately be pulled in to someone else's kindness, someone else's world, by a look. Not unlike love. A comment about the weather can be a bridge. If I want anything in my life, I want bridges.

"I don't know," I said. "Something with trails. Or like a bridge going over a creek?"

"There's some ATV trails back that way."

"That's not what I mean," I said. "Just for walking."

He started laughing at that. I left the gas station, trying to hold my head up, gripping my Gatorade as though it were a source of dignity, which is in fact the opposite of what a bottle of Gatorade is.

Standing beside my car in the parking lot, I looked out at the nearby wall of trees and thought to myself that this was as good a place as any. I went in. There didn't seem to be any sort of path, but that didn't matter; three feet in and I had forgotten the man behind the counter and felt the feeling I had been looking for: the dampening of the noises around you, the calm, the noble trees themselves, each a singular history, a life form and system in and of itself, and then you, silly as you are with your human-being accoutrements, a couple floppy arms and legs and a pail full of wet organs in the middle (how could we not need love?). Trees, I thought. Trees are the things with dignity. I thought of Corinne, and how her body was leaner, and had a tougher edge to it than mine. That if she were an elegant white birch then I was at best a blue spruce suffering from canker. My softness was embarrassing.

She was, I'd suspected since we met, a better person than me. She hadn't figured it out yet, but I'd known it all along. What was going to happen to us? Could you meet somebody like I had met her, fall in love, and a few months later be together at the front end of a lifetime's marriage? I had taken to thinking about the relationship in terms of months. If it was going to work, it was going to be 480 months. 480. I considered the length of a month, the amount of events that could occur inside of just one, the way a given August could stretch out and feel endless. I tried to multiply that feeling by 480 and could not get a sense of it. I thought about how strange it was that we are given a whole life and not enough brainpower to appreciate even its outline. Then I looked up and realized I was standing in front of a burning barn.

It was an old barn, and red, just like you would imagine a barn if I asked you to imagine a barn, which is what I'm asking you to do now, I suppose.

The roof was entirely engulfed, and inside I imagined piles of hay going up faster than tanks of gasoline. There was no one around; no Mennonite women running through the fields, their shawls and dresses billowing behind them, no farm families huddled beside a well, the father dumping pails of water over the children's heads to protect them, no stampede of horses, no telling, overturned lantern beside a guilty-looking cow. I could see a house a half-mile away, in a haze, but no cars, no trucks, no people anywhere. There were no sirens, no neighbors rushing forward to take charge. Just a barn and flames, and me, small person on a nature hike, watching.

And hearing some bleating.

Let's be clear: I don't want to be thought of as a hero for this. And I have no explanation for why a barn full of hay would contain one small goat. But I will say this: I surprised myself with my ability to not only enter a dangerous situation and to put myself at risk but to do so for no reason other than the sound of a bleat, the guess at a life. Perhaps I was a little suicidal, okay. Again, I think of the mysteries of personhood and connection. I have already mentioned the bridges.

The goat was crouched low in the corner of the building, and I made my way as quickly as I could, one arm raised up in front of my face to shield me from the waves of cracklingly hot air that whipped through the barn's interior, thinking, as I hoisted it up onto my shoulder and then did my best to run, to actually run from the barn with this thing, its little hooves digging into my back, through the cotton of my T-shirt, that who this was for, really, was Corinne, the girl I didn't know very well, but whom I loved. Maybe there was something here, when I told her the story—I imagined it happening in the car, just after I'd picked her up from the airport, myself cast as hero, her falling in deeper—that we could both inject into those 480 months, and *voilà*, there's a life.

Alex had a daughter named Matilda. Unlike him, she spoke with an American accent, and by all accounts had grown up in the States. She wore sweatsuits, and had a lazy beauty to her; she usually looked like she was either about to go to bed or was just getting out of bed. Her face could sometimes be caked with foundation. You would see her because she sometimes worked the counter in the afternoons. Once when I went in I got my milk from the cooler and then pointed at her T-shirt.

"I went to Wisconsin, too," I said. "I didn't know you went there. Don't you miss it?" I had seen her enough times to speak to her like we were friends.

She said, "God, I'm so glad I'm not you."

"Oh."

"Bougie frat-boy college sentimentality," she said, rolling her eyes. "I so know you."

"So you're saying you didn't like it?"

"I studied yeast cultures for four years straight and didn't talk to anyone at that school. That milk is $4.27."

The day of the Dr. Pepper, Matilda pulled up out front in her Toyota Camry a few minutes after Alex had sent the kid away. Alex and I were inside the store, watching Bob Ross painting on the tiny television.

"I love this guy," Alex was saying, shaking his head as Bob Ross worked on the sky. He looked at me.

"He is amazing, no?" He patted me on the shoulder, as though I had sculpted Bob Ross out of magical clay and then brought him to life.

"He is," I said. "Was. Yes."

Alex looked at me, eyes wide. "Was?" he asked. "He is dead now?"

I nodded.

"Only in America," Alex said, turning back to the television.

Just then Matilda came in, looked at me and at her father, and said, "What's on fire?"

I had been having some trouble getting the smell out. It had to have been in my hair, but no amount of shampooing had helped.

"I was involved in a barn fire on Tuesday," I offered. I didn't mention that currently, the small goat was back in my apartment, and was engaged, I would find later, in eating my couch.

(I had a habit of trying to make pets, to rescue things. There were other examples, but you understand the basics. I also have other personality traits. But this one matters most—that is why I'm telling this story. I liked the feeling of reaching out for other minds, human being or otherwise, and drawing them near to me and my own. I liked to think that other people could perhaps even become you and you could become them if you pulled them close enough. Love is just as much about the relief of no longer being yourself than it is about other people.)

"You two," Alex said. "Why don't you two go down to the hot dog stand together?" He winked at me. Alex had been wanting me to take Matilda out for months. Never mind she had an engagement ring on her finger. It was, I think, an extension of his obsession with assimilation. Yes, he could wear his Cubs sweatshirts and watch his Bob Ross, but the ultimate coup, I think, would have been to marry his daughter off to a product of the American suburbs. The neighborhood white kid—weirdo or not. Coup against whom or what I wasn't sure—Alex's wife and mother both wore robes and headscarves inside of the liquor store, but no burqas or veils. Considering they spent their days owning and operating a liquor store, their connection to Islam seemed to be, at best, tenuous.

I didn't understand the situation, in the end, the situation of Alex's family in America—who had made whom move where, who wanted to be here, who did not. Whose life had been destroyed to come. Whose love was fading because of it.

I looked at Matilda, expecting her to be rolling her eyes at me, but instead I saw that she had an amiable look on her face, and said, "Sure. I'm starving."

Alex, beaming, opened the register and gave us four dollars in quarters.

"You kids have fun," he said.

We walked down Damen on our way to the hot dog stand. On the way, I told her about what had happened with the Diet Dr. Pepper. She laughed at that.

"He hates stealing so much," she said. "He gets insane. But he loves all the kids in this neighborhood, too. He has a temper."

"I wonder if there's a physiology to temper," I said. "I wonder if we can quantify it."

"Nice questions," she said. "Nice investigation of the world."

"I can't tell if you're being sarcastic," I said. "The other person has to be able to tell if you really want it to be sarcasm."

"I could sneer more."

"Try that."

We walked the rest of the way with her practicing different sneers. I would say something I guessed she'd find stupid and she would respond with different sneers and tones of voice and then I would rate the quality of her sarcasm.

"I really like the sit-com *Wings*," I said.

"Oh, so do *I*," she said. When she said the word "I" she bared her teeth and opened her eyes wide and raised her nose up so high she seemed like a pig.

"That was good," I said. "Here's another one. They say that for one of the first times in America, the younger generation will not be able to make as much money as their parents' generation."

"That's so interesting," she said, but she said "interesting" without moving her lips at all, which was amazing in its own right.

"That was good too."

"The ending of *Cocoon*," I said, "is underappreciated by serious film critics."

"ObVioUSLy!!!!"

Matilda ordered a dog with everything and I felt compelled to order the same. That's the kind of person she was, I was realizing, the kind of person you wanted to emulate but the kind of person you knew would be able to see clearly your ambition to emulate. But I couldn't help myself. She could see and I could see her seeing.

"So who are you marrying?" I asked her, after we'd started in on the dogs.

"A guy," she said. "His name's Faruk."

"What does he do?"

"Computer," she shrugged, and despite only one non-plural word I understood what she meant. Squinting, tapping at a keyboard, and a lot of money.

"Is he American?"

"No," she said. "That's why my dad wants me to marry you."

"He doesn't really want that, though."

"Yes," she said, "he does."

It couldn't actually be true.

"Does your dad know my name?"

She looked at me. "I'm not sure I know your name," she admitted.

"Well," I said. "That makes two of you."

I finished eating in silence, wondering what it would be like to marry Matilda. It seemed, actually, possible. Sort of. I let it be possible, let's say. I had eaten many jalapeño peppers, and I was sweating—I was in a heightened state, and I wasn't thinking straight. But this is my problem, this has always been my problem—I fall in love all the time. Too easily, obviously, and with everyone and everything. Think of me as a Love Monster.

"Faruk is a hard person to know," she said. "My dad doesn't like him. He reminds him too much of back home."

"So the war," I said, thinking of the most sober, unromantic topic I could come up with. "What do you think of it?"

"I mean I don't want my brother to get killed. But I'm for Saddam being killed."

"That's—"

"What?" she asked. "Too hawkish for you? Coming from a young woman? Of color?"

"No," I said. "I don't know."

"Of course you'd be against it," she said. "Of course you're the young liberal white guy who's against it. How could you not be? But have you really thought about it? It's so simple. Do you want more or less tyrants in power in the world? Tyrants who kill people for no reason?"

"Less," I said, "but that's not—"

"You're again predictable."

"Listen, Christopher Hitchens," I said. "Hold on. First of all, you're allowed to have this opinion because you're Iraqi."

"Allowed. And why are you not allowed?"

"Because I would be an asshole if I had that opinion."

"Why?"

"Because I'm the young white American."

"I'm American too," she said.

"You know what I mean."

"This country," she said, shaking her head, "is so fucked."

My married life with Matilda had puppies in it, I don't know why. Later, when I would close my eyes and imagine it, imagine her naked, near-perfect body above me as we moved together in our dim, very bourgeoisie master bedroom, her face finally makeup-free, our central air cooling the whole place, even after Corinne was back, and then later, after she'd left me, I'd see Matilda look down at me through half-closed slits of eyes as sweat glistened on her forehead near the end of making love, black hair hanging just above her breasts, lulled into my own dreams, this unbearably beautiful insouciant Iraqi woman, wrists bent, hands pressing down onto my shoulders, happy. I saw us owning a home, something safe, and in the backyard there would live 800 or 900 puppies.

The hot dog date ended in a way that was surprisingly reminiscent of the way things had ended between me and the burglar kid, out on the street—Matilda simply looking at me with a kind of frown after our debate about the war, not talking on the way back. No more games about sarcasm. No bridges whatsoever. We'd had, literally, a twenty-second window of what to me had felt like love. That is easy love. It comes and goes, but has no staying power.

I don't think of love in terms of relationships. It happens in terms of seconds, but goes away like that, too. I pass a nurse, I love her, it ends when

I go around the corner; at a restaurant I see a forlorn man at the table next to me, and I love him, and the conversation pulls me back, and it's ended. A patient comes in, and she is sick, and I love her, and then she dies, and I never see her again. This is what I live for. Don't think that it's sad.

I just had a kid who died.

He was in his twenties—he'd been stabbed by an insane man.

I did what I could but there was no chance—none. He was just on the edge of the wet pail of mush already. He stayed conscious.

He was screaming for a long time, and do you know what? Doctors stay very professional in these situations.

But I could feel that he was dying—you get a sense about that, you feel the energy in the air.

We put him under and I tried. He didn't make it.

Stabbed by a crazy man.

Corinne was justifiably confused at finding a goat living at my house, and when she noted this out loud, I remember saying, "I'm also confused by it," and I immediately then drove the goat back south, to where I'd found it, and left it walking around the burned husk of the farm house. We broke up. A few months later I moved to Louisville and started school. When I was done with it all, I came back to Chicago.

Before that, I had more pleasant stops at Alex's shop, leaning against his counter, watching television with him. Sometimes Matilda would come in and not talk to me, which was fine, because I no longer loved her. Joseph even returned on leave before I left town. He was working at the store, and rung me up when I bought paper towels. Who knows if he later died?

Even Windy City Liquors was impermanent. The last time I saw Alex was in February, during a week-long below-zero snap. It was noon and it was dark already, and I trudged through the snow, down the street, for soup. Out front, I noticed three black Jaguars lined up in a row, all with their hazards on. And inside, I found their owners. Five men, all of them tall, all of them in long dark overcoats, all of them standing in front of the counter, talking to Alex in what I think was Russian, and there was Alex, looking amazingly small, hands on his countertop, listening, nodding his head, complacent and meek, and I thought to myself: this is what the mafia looks like. When it's mad at you. He didn't acknowledge me when I rang up my can of Campbell's, but I thought of it as him doing something good for me, not letting me be involved at all. All the men stepped aside for me, and I paid, and then I was outside again, jogging back to my building. The next afternoon, there was an Eastern European man I'd never seen before working behind the counter, and a few days later he was there again, and finally I introduced myself and he nodded and said that he'd bought the store from Alex.

"He wanted to spend more time with his family," he said. "He was overworked."

I have wondered what one does to transplant an entire family from one country to another—from a country where a war is going on to the other country fighting the war—and what one then does to get a business, and what one does to make ends meet in the process. It can't be easy.

"Do you see him?" I asked the man.

"What do you mean?"

"Do you know him? Do you know Alex?"

"Me?" he said. "No. No, I don't know."

"Well if you do ever see him," I said. "Tell him I say hello. All right?"

"Of course, my friend."

I was back at home before I realized this man didn't know who I was.

The Mother

Here was a day. Here was a day I went down and tried to find my son and tried to bring him home. Here is what I find out earlier that morning. I find out Jeremy did not almost quit school last week like he told me, but that he quit three months back, from before I even started seeing Michael and before the semester began. Can you believe that? I find this out because I call into the UIC bursar and they tell me. So first thing I wonder back aloud to the lady is where is all the tuition, but she don't know, and I'm mad as hell about it all morning, but then the call comes from the hospital and now it's something else and I'm not thinking about any of that. I just switched gears. That's what I'm thinking now. They've got Jeremy in the ER there at Resurrection and not only that but he's saying he needs me and that he's in trouble. They're saying he's raving and this don't seem like him but something low down in me believes it nonetheless and it sees him there, lying on a bad old hospital cot, yelling for his mama. This is what you fear.

"Why? What happened?" I ask them on the phone, even though I'd give anything to not know the answer, but I got to, I'm wondering if it's the same again or what, and the woman says, "He's been stabbed, ma'am," nothing about no dope.

He's been stabbed, ma'am—sounds like the movies, maybe a cowboy movie, the way they says it. Of course it ain't really, though, and here I am just all in shock, really it's worse than it could have been, and I say something to Jesus and I get my things and I tell Kevin I gotta leave, whether he likes it or not, because my boy is downtown and in trouble. He sees me crying but I say it angry, too. I'm half-expecting him to fire me on the spot because really he ain't no superior, he's some baby barely older than Jeremy, my boy who's lying down there stabbed (I'm still not believing it at this moment), and here I am fifty-five years old, he don't know how to deal with that, I've even been at this CVS longer than him, and he can't stand how I don't listen when he turns into the Big Man. You can see that glaze come over his eyes that way all men take up the mantle. I turn off when I see it in Kevin because I'm not listening to no one half my age for too long. So now I come at him angry because I don't want him to even start. We're at the registers. Right at the counter in front of us there's some yuppie-ass white girl waiting to buy gum, watching us like we both out of a movie scene.

But Kevin don't turn to her to check her out. Kevin says to me, "All right, Dee," and he says it's okay for me to go and he puts his hand on my shoulder and he says he'll call in Getty or Felicia and he says to hurry up and don't worry about coming back for the rest of the shift, it's fine. I don't say thank you because why would I? I get out of there. Still, it's better than it could have been, and now I'll remember about Kevin.

I go all the way down there in a cab and it's a half-hour before I'm standing there, telling them who I am and who I need to see. I think somewhere in there I tried to call Michael but I couldn't get him. I tried to get my sister but I couldn't get her, either. The world's just coming apart. There's a child standing on the sidewalk out front when we pull up and he's playing with a green umbrella. It's not raining. Here's where things turn murky. Inside they're saying it's too late and that my baby's gone. They had him under but he's gone, now. Some doctor's here and he's tellin' me. I do hear it, mind you. The words come in and they make sense and a part of me understands.

But I won't even get into the pain—that's far too much to say. I got years to go to think about that. Just listen to this, it's on the side, just somethin' I kept thinking on the day my son died: look at yourself next time you hear some news that's so crazy you decide you ain't gonna take it. Look at yourself next time someone dies. You'll see.

The Wildlife Biologist

The summer after my sophomore year of high school, my mother and I took a trip to Chicago to visit my brother James and to give my father time to move out of the house. I knew what was happening; she hadn't tricked me into going on vacation to give him time to pack up his boxes with whatever sad items he thought he might need in his sad apartment on the other side of town. Everything was in the open. We talked about it, and him, during the drive, and I had visions of my father carefully folding his underwear before placing each pair into a cardboard suitcase—soon he would be off on his life as a hobo, immersed in a new and diluted existence. My mother let me drive to and from Chicago with just my temps, even into the city. Even on the Dan Ryan.

We lived in a town in southern Illinois called Farrow. Farrow was fifteen miles east of the Mississippi; the trip was just under three hours, and here is what I learned: My father was leaving, my mother said, because she had asked him to go. She had asked him to go, she said, because somewhere along the line, ten or fifteen years into the marriage, they had fallen out of love.

"It's like a bath you've been in too long," she said. "Eventually you look around and say, 'This is absolutely not pleasurable.'" She shrugged. "So shouldn't I get out? Tell me, Courtney. Shouldn't my happiness be what matters? To myself?"

Clearly this conversation was for her own benefit; I held onto the steering wheel and stared straight ahead. My mother and I did not talk about things like this. But I listened. And as she talked, I realized I had always wanted to have these kinds of conversations with her, to get a sense of the back and forth of her life, to define and re-define happiness, weigh the matters of modern pain in our private ways, but that being her daughter had always felt like being, in a way, the family pet. Pleasant yet inconsequential, and somebody who could not possibly interfere.

They had agreed to divorce once my brother and I were moved out of the house, but my mother—and I only realized this years later, well after she was gone—was prone to cheap revelation, and had decided that one of the two of us out of the house was enough, and that she couldn't wait another two years.

She decided it, she said, watching the very last patch of snow disappear from the front yard over the course of an afternoon. She explained that it was a metaphor about time and loss. I thought it was cheesy.

"He understands. I've warned him for a decade and he's had his opportunities. He prefers Scotch and silence. It's not as though this is a surprise," she said. "It's a rescheduled event."

"Not for me," I said. "Not for James."

"That sounds like the beginning of self-pity, young lady."

"Well," I said. "Yeah."

"I won't have it."

"I'm the one who has it."

"If you could see it from my point of view," she said, and I could hear her blowing air out from her pursed lips, trying and failing to whistle. "Oh my good lord, Courtney."

I did want her to try harder, but not for any good reason.

Summer passed quickly. James decided not to come home, and instead stayed in Chicago, doing an "internship," which I knew actually meant losing his virginity to a Jewish girl named Samantha who he'd met in his summer dorm. He whispered the news to me, on the phone, just as we were saying goodbye.

"She and I," he said. "We've done it."

I waited.

"You had sex?"

"Yeah."

I didn't know what to say, as this wasn't open territory for my brother and me, either.

Finally, I just said, "Congratulations."

Dad did have a pathetic apartment on the other side of town. I had only imagined it that day in the car, but it turned out to be real. It had walls with fake-wood paneling, vertical slats of alternating darkness, one of them bowed and bubbled. He never bothered to fix it. The carpet was indoor/outdoor, and I imagined that if I tripped on my way to the kitchen I would skin my knees. There was usually rotten fruit in a plastic bowl in the kitchen—this summoned images of him at the grocery store, pondering a pile of ripe bananas—and sometimes, when I would come over, I would find three or four pizza boxes stacked outside his door. He had almost no furniture. However, he had a huge television. It loomed, dark and black, alone with the couch in the living room, always tuned to ESPN, muted.

Dad found a new girlfriend quickly. I wasn't mad about it. Was I supposed to be? I don't think I cared. I never cared. Her name was Trish, and she worked at the pet store in the mall. I hardly saw her, but when I did, she was nice, and she asked me about what books I liked to read. I told her that I only ever read *Deliverance*, over and over again, and she smiled and said, "Oh, nice. Is that with Holden Cauliflower?"

"It's for the best, this divorce," Dad said one July evening at dinner. We were alone. He was contemplative—I knew because he had brought out his Jim Croce albums and shown them to me.

"I guess so."

"Imagine if you had to internalize that conflict. Imagine if that was built entirely into your brain."

"That makes no sense."

"This could have stuck with you for the rest of your life," he said, staring off toward his bubbled wall in profound mode. Was he drunk? "It could have led to permanence. This way, our problems are out in the open a little earlier, which means you don't have to get stuck with them yourself. We communicate and relieve ourselves of burdens."

"Are you a psychologist?"

"We're both happier in our new and improved lives," he continued. "That's what's central here. In fact, your mother and I have agreed on this point. Often. Things are cordial between us now. We email."

"I'm not having problems," I told him. "We don't have to always talk about it. I'm not going to blow myself up."

"How is your mother?"

"She knits."

"Knits?" he said, and his eyes went wide with wonderment. "Truly?"

I started to run, I don't know why. I wasn't an athlete, but there was something about the warm nights, running down mile-long abandoned streets after the first pain had come and gone and you'd settled into something steady. I thought about it like a long closed tunnel, like there was a roof over me and walls on both sides—a roof of invisible energy, like the walls of prison cells in science fiction movies—and even if it rained the rain didn't touch me, it just spread out around me as I went. I grew, and one day Dad looked at me angrily and said, "You're taller than me, aren't you?"

I was a cashier at the grocery store, and I was too fast. I used to whip items down the metal runway at a pace that made the bagboys hate me. I was as fast as the laser that read the bar code. Maybe faster. Once, my manager walked by and raised her eyebrows, then nodded with great respect at the work I was doing. In her eyes I could see myself, ten years later, having won all the cashier awards, moving up into the ranks of power-teller elite. I went faster.

I've always had this one problem, with every task in life, and I still have it today, even though I'm far away from that place and even though I'm no longer the same person—but for this. I did not know how to say it then, as I was much, much too young. Here is how I think of it now: I'm stuck in time, and we all are, and it does not matter how much work we do. We can't get out, either way.

★ ✪ ★

Mr. Carpenter had been teaching at my high school for three years when I got into his AP Bio class. Every girl wanted to get into Mr. Carpenter's AP Bio class. Every boy, too. He obviously got high. He was hot. He was funny. He rode his bike to work. He talked like us, he felt like he came from the same place we did. He was usually tan in September because he guided kayak trips in Idaho over the summer. In his class you dissected a fetal pig and learned about electrophoresis. He seemed aware of the existence of the internet. He called us his little lemmings whenever we asked about grades.

On the first day of class, I remember sitting down in his room with everyone else, the tension high as we waited for him to come in from the hall, where he'd greeted us one by one. He was happy because it was the fall. He told us this after the bell rang, and after we made our introductions.

"We think of it as a time of death," he said, pacing in front of his blackboard. He looked up with a sober face. "You English nerds. Tell me what snow means in a poem."

"Death," said a stoner kid in the front, stupidly. Everyone laughed.

"No, no," said Mr. Carpenter, smiling along now. "Jeremy's exactly right," he said, pointing, showing us that he was already remembering names. He was a virtuoso teacher and he cared, very deeply, about knowing us personally.

"And there is a certain beauty to that. But in here, snow is not death. Snow is a product of a process that itself is a product of another process. There's a web of meaning that's different than the web of meaning you find in literature, or even the meaning we give to ideas, to events. There is no right and wrong in nature. Only physical phenomenon. Life changes its habits because of it. The leaves falling from a tree is not death. A squirrel hiding itself away is not death. It's all life."

"Oh my God," Holly, my lab partner, muttered to me. "I just creamed my jeans."

"Now," continued Mr. Carpenter. "Since this is the first day, we have to have a big conversation. A meta conversation. Understand?"

"No," said that same stoner kid, Jeremy. He didn't get as many laughs as he had. What he was only now just understanding was that you couldn't use the same teacher-eroding material on Mr. Carpenter. We didn't want to pick away at him, piece by piece, until he was nothing more than a pile of dust. We all wanted him to survive.

"It means above," said Mr. Carpenter, ignoring him. "It means taking a step back and thinking about the big picture. Okay?" I found myself nodding along with him. He noticed me and picked up on my enthusiasm. "So here's the challenge for you today. I know we have a big test at the end of the year, and I know you all want to do well on that. And we will. I promise. You'll all know enough to get your fives and get your credits at your dream colleges. But for today, forget about that. Here's the challenge: I want you to huddle up with your lab partners, no books, take twenty minutes, and come up with the definition of life."

I noticed that he said "the" and not "a," which was different than what most of the young teachers implied about truth and definitions, no matter what class. They liked to say "voices" and "readings" and "models" and "the situation of the observer." I wondered, then, what would happen if you planted Mr. Carpenter down in the middle of fifth period Theory of Knowledge. I imagined him punching Dr. Masterson right in the face.

We all sat quietly, waiting for more from him. It didn't come.

He gathered up his notebooks and went and sat at his desk. I could see that he was reading a magazine. It had a mountain climber on the cover.

"Do you know?" Holly asked me.

"The definition?"

"Yeah."

"No," I said. "Do you?"

"What about, like, breathing? Or heartbeats? Something about all the systems."

"What about plants?"

"Oh yeah," she said, and snapped a little. Then she frowned. She was wearing a bright yellow shirt with a tie at the ribs, the kind of first-day item that could make or break an entire year for somebody. I thought it would make her. It made her new big boobs look like binary stars.

"What about something having to do with energy?" I said. "You know? Like something that uses energy is alive."

"That's really good, Courtney," she said, nodding. "Let's use that."

I looked down at my hands. "Okay."

We did. When I said it he nodded, then said, "Okay, Courtney. What about a car?"

"What about a car?"

"It uses energy."

"Yeah," I said. "But it's a car. It's not natural."

"So something has to be natural to be alive?"

"I think so," I said, but already I was starting to feel the sinking feeling I sometimes felt in school, when I talked too much and realized, as I spoke, that I knew, honestly, nothing. Usually I wouldn't have said anything, just to keep this exact thing from happening.

"What do you mean by natural?" he asked. My heart now was beating faster and I could feel my cheeks turning red. I realized he wasn't going to stop. "What would you say about a clone? Or a baby born from artificial insemination?"

"I would call those natural." Now I was just answering.

"Why?"

"Because they're based on things—processes?—that already existed. That evolved."

"Okay, so that's a new idea," he said. He looked like he might go to the chalkboard and write it, which gave me a quick thrill, but he decided not to, and turned again, looking down, nodding, thinking.

"Life is something that has evolved over time. Now that might work for a broader definition of life, life in the abstract, but it still doesn't help us situationally. Say we're both looking at a motorcycle." He looked up. "It's evolved, hasn't it? Over the course of generations, different designers have changed it and improved its design. No? So can you tell me a definitive reason that it's not alive?"

"Because it's made out of metal?"

"Your blood has iron in it."

"All those things you just said, though," I said. "Those were people changing it."

"Yes, but I'm not so sure that matters for the analogy. Let's set that aside. Any other reasons?"

Silence. Everyone staring. In my mind I saw the motorcycle parked on the street in front of my father's apartment complex. I imagined him walking toward it, wearing some kind of leather suit, a big helmet under his arm. Somewhere there was a fire decal.

"I don't know," I said, and smiled. "No. I guess I just don't know."

I loved him by October. There was never a moment or a comment, a time his hand brushed my wrist as we all engaged our Bunsen burners. It just happened. It was when I focused on him that the future seemed the biggest, the most real, the most open. My brain felt big. I was never the smart student, but it was as though, from that first day, I had simply decided to set that aside in the same way we had set my argument about evolution aside; suddenly I could do the work. I had never mattered more.

I knew about the love because of my showers in the morning, when I would still be half-asleep, the water coming down over my face, and I would already be thinking about him as I crawled to life. I had had four boyfriends, three if you didn't count a summer hookup with my cousin's friend Phillip from Phoenix, who had come to stay for three weeks and who had talked, a lot, about websites. He had once gotten me alone in my bedroom and had sat on the bed and had said, "I'm interested in romantic"—he touched my hand—"relationships." That was the end.

The other three, the real boyfriends, had come and gone like thunderstorms. They were based on awkward touching, fear, and sex in the dark guest bedrooms of absent parents' homes. I would see these boyfriends—acne-ridden farm kids, really—in the halls, and it was like I didn't know them, that we had never met, that none of us were even there.

In the shower, Mr. Carpenter would come into my mind and ask questions about science. Sometimes they were hard questions that gave me that same feeling I'd felt on the first day of class, embarrassed but excited, too, about what it was possible to think about. To me already he seemed like he might be a failed intellectual, someone who had been forced to settle for high school teaching, even though he'd once aspired to something more, like wildlife fieldwork in an unspecified jungle, and his failure made him all the more tragic and beautiful. I had no reason to believe this, but I had invented facts about him, and I thought I saw it in the way that he walked in front of the chalkboard, I thought I heard it in his disdain for college, and his disdain for the AP test we were working toward. That being smart was something you found when you were alone. He told us that being smart was being able to destroy things as much as it was to make things. And to know which things deserved to be destroyed and which things deserved to keep existing.

In the shower he would also approach me physically. This was much less abstract. It was my mother's shower, the same shower I had used since I was five, when my parents and I first moved in to the house. There was the ornamental tile with the peacock on it, there was the same suction-cupped shampoo station behind the showerhead. There was Mr. Carpenter. In those first weeks, he would be wearing his swimsuit when he entered the shower, as though even my imagination was unhappy with me, and would still not let me go past PG-13. He would kiss me, and then we would shampoo each others' hair.

"How is your father?" my mom asked me, after one of these October showers. "Is he still dating that woman?"

"I think so," I told her. "I haven't seen her in a couple of weeks. He hasn't said anything."

"It certainly didn't take him long," she said.

"I thought you guys mutually agreed to get a divorce, though."

"I can still observe that it didn't take him long, can't I?"

"You can do whatever you want," I told her. I was tired of navigating her brain and heart both. She had had trouble dating. She had tried, even though she'd also tried to keep it from me. One night I had looked out the window and had seen her being dropped off by someone in a red SUV. I had seen what I thought was a goodnight kiss, but I had also seen her storm out of the huge truck and climb down and slam the door. I watched her stomp her way across the driveway in her heels as the truck slowly, weirdly reversed away, like a fat alpha seal sliding backwards, into the ocean, having already eaten its yabbie lobster.

"Is he eating?" she asked.

"No," I said. "He stopped eating completely."

"He was always very good at making pancakes," she said. "At least he can make those."

"He eats stones now. He crushes them in his mortar and pestle and makes shakes with them."

"Now you're just being funny," said Mom.

I got to class a minute late, and when I came through the door, Mr. Carpenter glanced over and said, "Oh, Courtney. We're just talking about something new here."

I went to my lab table and sat down next to Holly and saw what he'd written on the board: Krueger Sport Game Park.

"What is it?" I asked Holly. Mr. Carpenter was talking about elk.

"It's that place between here and Carbondale," she said. "Out in the middle of nowhere. Where those hunters can come on vacation."

"—in our county," Mr. Carpenter said. "Which means tax dollars, which means less ethics, period. Which complicates things even more."

Mr. Carpenter continued to speak about the Krueger Game Park, and as he explained it, I remembered its existence, and people talking about it when it first opened. It was a place you could go to hunt exotic game without really having to hunt. It was a preserve, stocked with deer and elk and antelope and rams and wild boar, so many that it was impossible not to run into something shootable after only ten minutes of strolling. Mr. Carpenter then rolled the television into the room and turned out the lights. I remembered some of the video from the news, years before. A PETA person had snuck in and made the tape. It showed an employee herding deer toward a guest, using a pickup truck to scare them and run them into a trap. Then a man stood up from behind some bushes and started shooting a machine gun. The video was grainy and shaky, and it felt like we were watching porn. The bullets tore into the deer and ripped one line of holes in its side, all in a perfect row, as though someone had glued red sequins from its hindquarters to its chest.

"Gross," Holly said. She had a huge open-mouthed frown on her face. I could see that everyone's shoulders, even in the dark, were tensed up. When the movie was over, Mr. Carpenter hit the lights and turned off the TV.

"What's wrong with this?" he asked.

"It's like the cruelest thing I've ever seen in my life?" Holly said, half-raising her hand.

"Because it's a video of people hunting? Isn't hunting a part of our collective history? Isn't it where our history is? Aren't we omnivores?"

"Dudes have like bazookas," said Nick Wesley, a baseball player who sat to the right of us. Holly liked him. I thought he liked her, too. I looked at him and wondered whether he was making the argument out of love for her, or real outrage at the video. I could see how sometimes it could be difficult to keep those things apart, love and thinking. I could also see Nick Wesley blowing deer away with a machine gun.

"So if it were to be more sporting," said Mr. Carpenter, "if it were to seem as though the deer had a chance to escape, this would be, what, less unethical?"

"Totally," said Nick, and that's when I saw him glance over to us, to Holly. He looked back at Mr. Carpenter. "I mean my dad hunts. I've gone with him. It's no big deal, I'm not saying I'm like for Bambi and against everyone who kills Bambi. But these guys don't have to do anything, they don't have to know anything at all. That's why it sucks. It's like fishing in one of those stocked ponds at boat shows. It's like what's wrong with you that you're such an idiot that you think you did something good when you catch one?"

Our project for that week was to all write a letter to the county, expressing our outrage with Krueger. There was a county policy meeting open to the public coming up in a few weeks, and he urged us to attend, and to speak out against Krueger. Mr. Carpenter told us that part of biology was necessarily activism. He told us that it wasn't science anymore, but it didn't matter. He told us that the world we lived in made it that way.

★　✪　★

The first time we were alone together was a few weeks later, for student-teacher conferences. It wasn't supposed to be just me—it was supposed to be Holly and me together, but she was sick. We needed to talk to him about our plant experiment. More specifically, to talk to him about why all our plants were dead.

His office was back behind the lab. It had big glass windows, books in shelves, and lots of pictures. There were a few on the wall of him next to his kayak, sitting on the rocks in the sun. There was one of him in the rapids. He also had a computer that looked like an Atari.

"This kind of thing just happens sometimes," he said. "Don't sweat it too bad. I'm not going to flunk you. You can't control it." He seemed distracted, and he read some of our lab report draft. We were looking at our dead plants, ten of them, each in its own Styrofoam container, curled over and brown. Holly and I had overwatered.

He turned his big brown eyes right to me, and I froze.

"What are you going to do now?"

He sounded like my dad. Maybe he isn't twenty-eight, I thought. Maybe he's more like thirty-five.

I smiled too much. "You mean, like, change the experiment?"

"No," he said. "I just mean finding a way to use what you have here. Were you measuring your water? How good were your notes along the way?"

He gave me some ideas and I copied them down into my notebook. A list with bullet points on my college-ruled paper. I nodded as though I heard anything he said.

When we were through talking about the plants, he asked me how everything was going in class, and I told him fine. Then he said, looking down into his grade book, "You're doing well. Codominance. Tough the first time you see it. And I know that Holly is benefiting from being next to you, too. I appreciate that."

"Thanks."

"You're good at this," he said, leaning back into his chair, closing the book. "You should keep doing this. Are you interested in the sciences? For a career?"

"I don't know," I said. "Maybe. I haven't decided yet, I guess."

"The good thing is that you don't have to for a long time," he said. "I didn't decide to be a teacher until a few years ago. I did a lot after college."

"Like what?"

"You know," he said. "Circus."

"Whatever."

"Just a lot of things I'd been wanting to do."

"Like that?" I asked, and pointed to the picture of the kayak.

"Like that."

He warmed up. We talked for what even I could tell was an inappropriate amount of time. And he said things.

That day I ran. It was cool outside, and I went east, down the road Krueger was on. It was too far away, and I knew I wouldn't get to it, but I went anyway, pulled by the force of the straight line that led to the thing he cared about so much. I fell into the stable place where my legs stopped burning as much and I thought of what he had told me about his time as a guide on whitewater trips. In Idaho once, he told me, one night with his friends, between chartered trips, he'd been drinking, and they were camped on a small island. They needed wood, and there wasn't any, and so he'd gone through the dark to his kayak, paddled to shore, found wood, and had then started paddling back to the island. No life jacket, no light, no skirt on the kayak. Somewhere in the middle of the river, he said, he got pulled into a current, and before he could react, he was heading downstream, pile of wood in his lap, unable to do much in the way of paddling. It was just as he dumped the wood over the side that his kayak dropped down into a hole.

The bow hit a rock that jolted him forward, and then he was underwater, upside down, his legs still in the kayak, pinned against a vertical stone by a thousand pounds of river force. I asked him if he panicked and he said that he had, but that it didn't make a difference, because he could hardly move. But he said then, after he struggled for a few seconds, and after the feelings passed through his mind, he suddenly became extra-rational. He thought: I have two minutes. I refuse to die, here, like this. And so underwater, the current still mashing him sideways, he managed to plant his paddle between the rock and the kayak, and then slowly, hand over hand, pull his legs from the boat and slither around the side, then crawl, inches at a time, up the length of the long rod. The kayak was pinned so forcefully against the rock that it didn't even budge as he moved. "Imagine trying to free-climb up a cliff with a person on your back," he said, and I did, I imagined it. Being stuck.

After seeing it in my mind a number of times, and trying, over and over again, to feel what it must have felt like for those first moments underwater, my running slowed down, and I came to a gas station.

I realized I was at the edge of Preston, the next town down, and that I had run nine miles.

I was exhausted. Instead of running home, through the night, I called my mom to pick me up, told her that I'd gone way too far, and then drank a Sprite as I sat on the picnic bench and waited.

★ ✪ ★

"How is your mother?" my dad asked me the week before Halloween. It was a Thursday evening. I was about to go to the town hall meeting, the one Mr. Carpenter had asked us to attend. We were having dinner. Fish sticks. "I haven't seen many emails from her lately."

He held a fish stick like a cigar, thoughtfully, and then started dipping it into some ketchup with way too much enthusiasm.

"She's fine," I said. "Why don't you just call her if you want to talk to her?"

"That's okay," he said. "We prefer to use email."

My parents both talked about email as though they were not only the first people in America to find out about it, but as though they perhaps had invented it themselves. Neither of them seemed to have any memory of my brother James sitting down with them for hours at a time in front of the computer, trying to explain what it meant to log on to something. I can remember James sitting at the desk, head down, mentally drained and defeated, and both of them sitting in chairs behind him, leaning forward, glasses on, taking notes.

"So what's this meeting tonight?" he asked. "Is that a new sweater?"

"I told you," I said. "Krueger. The Community Center."

"Right," he said. "You're in a saving the planet phase now."

"It's not a phase," I said. "It's me."

"Okay, okay," he said, smiling. He put his hands up defensively. "I'm joking." He reached for a new fish stick, then stopped himself before eating it. "But actually it probably is a phase," he said after a moment of reflection. "I've seen you go through them. I've been here for as long as you've been here."

"You mean on the planet Earth?"

"Cort," he said. "Do you not remember when you were a historian? And then when you were a writer? And then when you were a potter?"

One of my pots was on the shelf above my dad's head.

"I have interests."

"I know, honey," he said. He could see how mad I was. "I'm sorry."

I walked to the Community Center instead of letting him give me a ride. It was a nice crisp October night. I walked past Dalton's, the grocery store where I'd worked. I'd quit just before the start of school. I wanted As, not Cs. I wanted to be the person the teacher thanked in private, not the one he asked other people to help, not the one riding her bike to the store after school, only to be hypnotized by the beep of the machine and the tit-stares of old men buying peanuts. I didn't miss it at all. When I looked at its blue awning I thought about all of the other kids inside, enslaved, mopping and sweeping and facing up cans of tomato paste.

The Center was downtown, a flat one-story building with tan walls and dark red window shutters that looked like it had been imported from 1905. There were three bars across the street from the parking lot—one of them had a line of motorcycles out front—and the library was next door. The parking lot looked full, and as I walked toward the door, I wondered how many other kids from class would come. It seemed possible that Mr. Carpenter would do something dramatic, especially if enough of us were there for him. I imagined him giving a speech from the crowd, standing up, a strong voice of reason, cutting through everyone's greed. I imagined him bringing in video of elk in the wild to give an example of another version of elk-life. I imagined us all standing up, one by one, and booing to drown out the voice of Mr. Krueger and his sons. I didn't even know if he had sons, but if he did, I thought that they would be evil, and albino, and twins.

People were bustling and talking; there was tension in the room. The lights were up high and I could smell popcorn and coffee. I saw Mr. Carpenter sitting by himself in a middle row. I could see the back of his head. His blond hair looked like it was combed for once, and he was wearing a nice shirt.

There was no one else from class.

After a few more minutes of crowd murmurs, two members of the County Board brought the meeting to order and a man wearing a toupee expertly operated a gavel and then thanked us all for coming. "And I know that most of you are here for the same issue," he said, "so we'll get to that immediately, and then any other topic we can address after a break." My heart was crazy now; it's too complicated to know what it was beating for, and how much of it was him and how much of it was the hunting—I think I cared about the deer that got shot—but it didn't matter then. Something was there and its source was irrelevant. It was so easy to feel nothing, all the time, and I held on as hard as I could, because the worst thing, I thought, now, would be for it to go away.

"I think Mary Geller here in the front row would like to say a few things about her proposal to make quite a few interesting changes to the public pool," said the toupee.

There was silence from the crowd as he looked around. Everyone was finally settled into their seats.

"Without further ado, then, I'll let Mary have the floor. She can make her case."

I didn't quite understand what was happening until a half-hour had passed. There was applause, and then a woman proceeded to speak about the tiles, changing rooms, fence, depth, diving boards, lawn, concessions, tickets, fees, special days, lifeguard coverage, chlorine, filters, and leaf removal at the swimming pool in Abraham Lincoln Park.

She had data with her. Data she had collected over the summer. She told us that she had finally tabulated it all. She held up a graph. She had recommendations.

Another half-hour passed, filled with questions from the crowd and conversations about what moneys were available. I remember hearing somebody say, "Yes, but what about other inflatable options? Are we being myopic?"

Eventually the group reached a consensus on the pool, and one of the council-members said, "Well, thank you, thanks everybody. We have a few other issues that we can get to after a short break. Looks like we'll be discussing"—he looked down—"the bike trail, and we have a man from ComEd here to talk about new electricity policies." He looked up, smiled. "Then we'll have an open floor. Thanks."

When Mr. Carpenter stood up, it didn't look as dramatic as I wanted it to look; everybody else was in the process of standing, too, milling about, chatting, gathering their purses and jackets and hats. We were our town being our town. It was obvious to me that they were all leaving, and that nobody was even going to stay for the second half. I felt it coming—it fit so well. He didn't know because he wasn't from here.

"Sir," he said, raising his hand.

He said it loudly, but still, my heart almost broke.

The toupee man noticed, nodded at Mr. Carpenter. People continued to trickle.

"Can we talk about the wholesale slaughter of caged wildlife that goes on at the Krueger Park every day?"

Some people stopped talking, but not everyone. Toupee nodded and held out his hand, and I guessed that his thought was: We've got a crazy.

"That can be addressed when the floor is open," he said.

"Shaun Carpenter," said Mr. Carpenter. "Local biology teacher."

"We received the letters, we are aware of your class's concern. We have you slated for 8:45."

"No one will be here at 8:45, sir," he said a little louder.

We were sitting in a community center in a small town with local politicians, and it was over, wholly, before it had ever started, and I saw Mr. Carpenter standing there, shaking his head a little, obviously enraged, and I watched everyone continue to filter out of the room, a few of them looking back over their shoulders at him as he made his way down his aisle and then up to the front table. I was elated, seeing him fail. I can't explain. He leaned in close to the toupee man and I could see him speaking passionately, and I could see the man absorbing every bit of passion with condescending nods, even as he packed papers into his briefcase, and I thought of Mr. Carpenter stuck in his kayak, underwater, sitting upside down, holding his breath. How he had won then, in his way, and now something that looked so small was so much stronger than him. He could maybe have done more. He might have stayed longer. But when the conversation ended, I watched him stand, look up at the ceiling, return to his chair, get his jacket, and storm out. He never looked at me.

I followed him outside. I thought he might go lean against his car to cool off. Then he would come back and wait for his time.

"It's so nice to see some of our young people interested in the goings on in the government," I heard someone say. The toupee man was behind me.

I kept watching Mr. Carpenter. He did go to his car, for a second. But only to check to make sure his doors were locked. Then he put his hands in his pockets, crossed the street, and started beating up a garbage can.

I continued to watch as he punched the metal can right in the face and got it onto the ground, then mashed it from the top with stomps. The trash all spilled out onto the sidewalk around his feet. It was loud; I could hear him swearing, too. He jumped onto some fast food leftovers.

He kicked the barrel one last time with a huge football kick, then walked into one of the bars.

"I know," I said, turning to the toupee man, who had just watched the same thing I had. "I couldn't stop thinking about that pool."

He was still looking across the street, at the garbage Mr. Carpenter had attacked.

I shrugged. "We have to keep cool in the summer."

I waited. I didn't go back inside for the second half. There was nobody there, anyway. They'd all come to talk about the pool. I could hear a few voices droning through the door behind me as I sat alone on a bench, watching the front of the bar.

It was past 9:00 when he came out. The meeting had ended, and toupee man had offered me a ride home when he saw that I was still outside.

"No," I told him. "I have a ride coming."

He looked at me curiously and said goodbye, and I hugged myself on the bench as the cars all pulled out, and I was left alone with Mr. Carpenter's vehicle. It looked dumpy. It looked like the kind of thing a clown might drive, except in real life, after finishing a shift of clown-work.

He crossed the street head-down, hands in his pockets, hair hanging over his forehead.

He was trying to get his key in the door when I said, "Hey, Mr. Carpenter."

He looked up, and his eyes were glassy. He squinted toward me and said, "Who's that? Gina?"

"It's Courtney," I said. "From school."

"Courtney?" Just as he said it he wobbled a little bit and reached for the top of his car to hold himself up.

"Hey," I said, standing. "Yeah. Your student."

"Were you at the meeting?"

"I screwed up the time," I said. "I was like an hour and a half late. I only saw the end."

He squinted. "Did they talk about Krueger?"

"No," I said.

"No one else from class? No one came later?"

"No."

All through this conversation I half-strolled my way toward him.

"Yeah," he said, shaking his head. "Yeah. I'm sorry. I'm a little disappointed at the moment."

"I know," I said. "Totally. That sucks."

"Are you waiting for a ride?"

"Yeah," I said. "But I don't think it's coming."

He nodded for a long time with his serious teacher face, as though he were thinking of something he could write on the chalkboard.

"I can drop you," he said finally.

For the first time since I'd known him, something told me to move away from him, not toward him. But I was nervous, too. I said okay and went around to the passenger door of his clown car and waited for him to unlock it. Keys in the lock, he looked at me over the roof, and I looked back at him, this time meeting his eyes and not looking down or away, like I usually did. I felt like we might be on a date.

"I've never seen you anywhere but inside your biology lab," I said.

"That's where I spend most of my time."

"My door's still locked."

I don't know why, but this made him stop rattling his keys. His head was still down and I could see the look on his face for a few seconds. I could see him rubbing his eyes. When he looked up I could see how red his cheeks were.

"Courtney, hey," he said. "You know what? I had a couple of beers over at that place. I actually don't think it's a good idea for me to drive you. It's probably not a good idea for me to drive at all, actually." He raised his eyebrows. Responsible again. He was looking at the top of his car.

"Oh."

"Do you live close?"

"Not far."

He breathed once, through his nose, like he was choking back a burp of puke, then looked over his shoulder.

He burped again under his breath.

"Are you okay."

He burped once more. "How far away?" he said, through the exhale.

He said it still looking over his shoulder, and he sounded like he was in pain.

"I don't know. Less than a mile."

"Do you want me to walk you?"

"Sure," I said. "Okay."

He walked beside me, hands in his pockets, up on people's lawns even though I was in the street. We didn't talk about Krueger. He told me about a book he was trying to write, about wildlife and how it didn't fit into the human world, how it had been doomed from the moment we evolved past a certain point. The Terminal Line. That's what he called it. He told me there were some scientists who wanted to bring elephants and lions to America. This amazed me. I imagined them walking down empty highways.

He was talking softly; I could hardly hear him, but I could smell beer and cigarettes and bar smells even though the wind was blowing—it was just oozing off of him. It made me feel like I had been in the bar with him, or that I was a river guide in Idaho, casting about after college, lost like him. He said, after a little speech about the grasslands in the Midwest, out of nowhere, "I actually don't have many friends anymore," and laughed. "Which is funny, if you know me."

I didn't know what to say.

"Teaching is a funny thing," he said. "In a way it's the noblest thing to do. But you can also end up in strange places. Like here. In this fucking place. For example."

"But what about those who can't do, teach?" I asked, smiling.

"Right," he said. "Funny girl."

"You can do, though," I said. "How come people never say that teaching counts as doing?"

"Excellent question," he said. "I like that. But I think if you say that then you have to admit that there are different kinds of doing."

"Okay," I said. "I admit that."

"Doing," he repeated. "This doing question is important."

"Instead of talking."

"People hold their anger about things," he said. "That's what stalls everything in the modern world. You know?"

"Totally."

"I find it strange to imagine how briefly we've been here in terms of the age of the planet. Or just the age of life."

He looked at me, realized that he was floating away into his own place. He smiled and looked ahead again. "This stuff is a cliché to you. I'm a big cliché, right?"

"No. I completely know what you're saying."

"I think I actually might be."

"You're not."

"What I'm saying is that we've barely been here and already we've come to a point where we only ever compromise."

"What about doing, then?"

"That's what I mean," he said. "Doing is the opposite of compromise."

"What about destroying?"

"Haha," he said. "Funny girl."

I felt we'd reached a plateau. We kept walking. Eventually he asked me all sorts of questions about my family, and I told him about my parents, and he nodded and said, "That's hard," and I said, "Not really," and he said, "Okay," but then suddenly the lost moment was back and he was there, right beside me, and his arms were around me, and we were kissing sloppily in the shadows between streetlights. The kiss was wet with alcohol and peanuts—his tongue whipped in tight circles—and I could hear him breathing heavily through his nose, almost grunting, almost a gorilla, trying, maybe, to push me further back, back between the houses, and it was hard not to see him as an animal.

I didn't let him move me. I might have been stiff at first but after a few seconds of feeling his hands holding onto my ribs underneath my jacket I let myself relax more, even though, as it happened, I felt clear adult sense that it should stop for his sake, not for mine. Like he was maybe even younger than me. Like I was witnessing the real self-destruction of a person. Something I had not, up to that point in my life, understood could actually happen, except in books and movies.

It ended as fast as it started.

He stepped back.

He said, "Oooohkaaayy. I am a pedophile."

We started walking.

"We shouldn't have done that," he said.

"I don't think you're a creep," I said to his back. "Hey, slow down." I touched his shoulder.

"That's not what I mean."

"What do you mean? Maybe you should turn around."

He did.

"This isn't normal," he said. "Is what I'm saying. This is not what I would—it's this fucking place." He yelled the last word, and it echoed.

"I'm not going to tell. It's fine. Whatever."

We were quiet then. The wind blew a little and we both looked straight ahead and moved again. I told him when to go, a few streets later, just so he wouldn't have to take me all the way to my door and keep feeling like a pervert.

"How is your father?"

"He's fine."

"We've been emailing."

"Fine."

"He's become very communicative."

"Fine. Then why did you just ask me how he was?"

"It was last week. He gave me the update. It sounds like things are okay."

"Yes," I said. "They are. You are correct."

"We discussed," she said, "very briefly, the possibility of everyone getting back together for Thanksgiving."

I stared at her. "What do you mean by back together?"

"Well, James will be back. We think it might be a good idea to have the family together this first time."

"Why?"

"To help the transition."

"From what to what?"

"From being together to not being together."

"That's totally weird, Mom. It already happened. And that's being together. You're saying you want to be together to help not be together. Don't you see the problem?"

"It's just a thought."

"It doesn't matter if it's a thought. Don't you see the problem?"

"No," she said. "I don't. I see the solution."

It was a Saturday, November 13th, and it was 69 degrees outside. The sky was perfect. It had been like this for three days, and the people of Farrow had reverted to summertime behavior, strolling in the streets, mowing lawns—I even saw a boy eating melting ice cream. In class, Mr. Carpenter had made comments about carbon and Al Gore, but they felt flip and cynical, not wise, not deliberate, not guided, not teacherly—not containing anything about how it was possible for us to do things and change things, for it to not always be stuck this way. For there to be a chance at reversals. For people to actually use ideas to do something. We hadn't talked about what had happened, we hadn't even acknowledged it, but I could feel his attention in class, this new sexual part of him, and I was scared that everybody else could feel it, too. We had moved on to dissecting our fetal pigs; every day Holly and I would haul out our vacuum-sealed bag and we'd lay our pig out on our long tray and take it apart, piece by piece, and try to name everything that we cut out. I lost the pancreas. But I will be honest. Sometimes, in the midst of this cluster of flesh, as he paced around, I would be able to close my eyes and imagine sex. Far more than I had. Clear pictures in my mind.

I looked outside, at the sun and the blue sky. I wanted to be able to love how beautiful it was, but really, according to science, the Earth was dying.

"I'm going for a run," I told my mother.

"You and running," my mom said. "What's going on?"

"It's an interest," I said. When I turned back to her I saw that she was now staring out the window, too, but the look in her eyes made it seem like she was not allowed to go through to the other side.

"Do you want to come?" I asked.

"Me? Run?" She shook her head. "I can't run. I never learned."

"Everyone can run. You don't learn it."

"So you say."

I had found Mr. Carpenter in the phone book the night he kissed me. Carpenter, S. I had never called him and never gone by his house, but I'd looked it up on the internet and scrolled around and even looked at the satellite pictures, at his blurry roof. He lived in a cul-de-sac three miles away. I had his address written on a tiny piece of blue paper, which I'd tried to fold an infinite amount of times before stuffing into a pair of socks in my drawer.

Since it was so warm outside I got into my summer running clothes, shorts and my sports bra, and I put the tiny paper in my pocket, and I looked in the mirror, proud of my stomach, proud I was not my mother and able to run, and to prove the point I blasted down the stairs and out of the back door and through the yard and down the Parsons' driveway and was three hundred yards from the house before she knew I was gone. I didn't hate her so much as I hated the idea that I had to play any role in any story—the story of her and my father, the story of how she was old and I wasn't. The story that made me need my biology teacher for whatever stupid thing I thought he had. It was anger, but I just wanted it to end, too. It would have been easier for him to have never done anything at all. Or to have been married. Or to have been successful. To have somehow been able to better take care of himself. He had just enough imagination to make great failure possible. I was what could make him work.

My hair got all kinked and curled after the first mile. I took the longest route I could think of, through all the neighborhoods, away from any of the bigger streets, away from downtown, as though it mattered whether or not

I was seen, as though people, when they saw me, would know where I was going and what I planned to do based on gait.

Mr. Carpenter's cul-de-sac was called Warren Way. I never needed my piece of paper. When I got to the intersection I stopped running and put my hands on my hips to catch my breath. I could see him.

He was outside, in his front yard, talking to a dark-haired guy who looked around the same age, both of them standing beside a pickup truck. Mr. Carpenter's clown-car was pulled all the way up in front of the garage. I looked down at the ground and breathed hard.

When I looked up he was staring at me.

"Hey," I said, and half-waved.

There was no way he could hear me from this far away. He motioned and I started walking over, hands still on my hips.

He was shaking the dark-haired guy's hand when I got to the driveway. I heard the guy say, "Okay, peace my friend," before he turned. He nodded at me and got into the truck.

"Courtney," Mr. Carpenter said, watching his friend reverse away. Finally he turned to me, once the truck had left the driveway. "Running?"

"Not right now."

"Right. Standing."

"I can't believe how hot it is," I said. I thought maybe he would say something about the greenhouse effect.

He just said, "Yeah," and put his hands in his pockets.

"Who was that guy?" I asked.

"A friend."

"He said peace my friend."

"Yes he did."

"So weird."

"Not really."

"I thought you didn't have any friends."

"What?"

"You told me that."

"Right," he said.

"No, I know," I said. "No one has no friends."

"I think I said many."

"No. You said any."

This made him look at me and raise his eyebrows. He looked skinny, and I almost said, "Have you been eating?"

"So you want some water?" he asked. "You look like you just jumped in a lake."

"I sweat a lot," I said.

"I'll get you some water."

He walked up the stairs to his front porch and I followed him in without asking. He looked over his shoulder when he heard my footsteps, but he didn't say anything, he just kept going. His house looked just like I would have expected it to look; in the living room there was a big wooden table with a hundred books on it and a laptop crammed into the one open spot. There were chairs here and there, but they didn't look very well-used. I heard jam-band music. I smelled pot and kitty litter. There was no TV.

"Nice house."

"I rent," he said, continuing on into the kitchen. "Hey, why don't you just wait out on the porch? You want any food or anything? I have some, ah, squid."

"No," I said. "I'm running."

He disappeared into the other room. Outside I sat down on the porch-swing; I finally had stopped breathing hard. I leaned back and let myself sway, just a little. I could see a bucket full of suds and a sponge next to his car. I thought it was funny that he did everyday things.

"What's all that stuff on your table?" I asked him, when he came back out and sat down. He was a few feet from me, on a plastic chair. "Is that for your book?"

"Yeah," he said. "Kind of. More Krueger stuff."

"Krueger's in your book?"

"Kind of. I've been trying to interview people out there. Call it a summer project."

"The Terminus," I said. "The Terminal Line."

I thought he'd tell me more about it then, but he didn't say anything else.

"I'm so excited for the semester to be over," I said.

"Courtney."

He leaned forward, put his elbow on his armrest and his hand on his chin and mouth. "Listen. Don't take this the wrong way, but can I ask you something?"

"Yes."

"Why are you here?"

If I took every moment he had looked at me and spoken to me directly, I would not have been able to find one when he looked so adult. He was wearing jeans and a white T-shirt, but I could see the little signs; I could see that he had the beginning of pits under his eyes, I could see that one day, maybe in twenty years, his legs would become spindly and hairless, and that they would awkwardly support the gut that he would grow. He would have two children and would care about his pension, and how the teacher's union had made poor decisions regarding his 401K. He would sometimes look sadly at the cobwebby kayak that was up in the rafters of his garage.

"Don't you want me to be?" I said.

He leaned back in his chair.

"We kissed," I said. "You kissed me. Anyway, I'm saying hi and drinking water. I'm a person. Hi."

"That is not fair."

"To drink water?"

"Yes, I kissed you," he said. "Okay. I did."

"So maybe you did it for no reason at all."

"That's not true, either. I didn't. Don't think that."

I shrugged. "I don't."

"Don't think it's more, either," he said.

"I was running," I said. "That's why I'm here."

"You happened to run right to my house?"

"I run all over the place."

"Okay. But we need to talk about what happened. After the Community

Center. That's something that really—it needs to be addressed. I had been drinking. Okay. I was out of line. The power differentials—"

"I was just addressing it. I think it's fine. I don't think it was out of line. I don't think you're a bad person."

"I have more to say," he said. "What I did was—"

"Can I ask you a question?"

It didn't look like he wanted me asking the questions. He wanted to do some long Socratic dialogue on me and show me that he was a moral, adult person, and that I wasn't.

"Fine."

"Are you going to be a teacher?" I asked. "The whole time? For your whole career?"

He snorted, then smiled and leaned back in his chair. "Why?"

"Sometimes it seems like you love it," I said. "Then sometimes it seems like you really hate us all."

"Hate you all?" he said, frowning at me. He shook his head. "That's absolutely not true. Why would you say that?"

"Or like you wish you were us?"

He just stared.

"Just things you say. When you make fun of us for, like, caring about our futures. Why?"

"I want you to be doing it for the right reason. There are so many ways to get pull—"

"I think we are. Or if we aren't, I don't think you know."

"Look," he said. "There are other things going on."

"So?"

"So you being here is not okay," he said. He stared at me for a second, then looked across the street, at his neighbor's house, and then back at his own door. "Fuck, man. A girl from my class is not okay. That's what I mean."

"Courtney," I said. "My name's Courtney."

"This town," he said.

"It's not the town," I said.

He needed it to be done—I could see the failure already and I had to at least make it real, to make all the ideas exist. There was nothing else to say. I set down my glass and I went in through the door and down the hall and into the bathroom I had seen when he got me the water. It was messy, and small. There was a shag bathmat on the tiled floor and a pile of clothes in the corner, next to the toilet. None of it resembled what I'd pictured. I closed the door.

"Courtney," I heard him say from in the hall. "Please get out of there."

"I'm taking a shower," I said.

I took off my clothes and started the water and was under it with my eyes closed before I could think of my dad, or my mom, or my brother James, or how I wasn't the person who could be here, or the person who had made this. The tiles were coated in mildew and grime. I imagined a picture of myself in the newspaper, looking young.

I showered there, alone, for fifteen minutes. He was gone—he had fled—when I came outside. His car was gone. I walked halfway home, where my mother was probably still sitting in the same spot in the kitchen, before I started to run.

Class got sad. There was no other way to say it, or to feel it. When he lectured he wouldn't make eye contact with me. Once he showed up to the lab with a black eye and told us that he'd stood up at a bar and challenged every man there to a one-round boxing match. One week he spent three days showing us the movie *Grizzly Man* and asked us to think about what it meant in terms of what we'd learned in class. He fell asleep partway in. I fell asleep. A few days later he ended class thirty minutes early and said, "I love you all as friends," and laughed to himself and walked out the door. The next Monday, the week before winter break, he wasn't there.

"Mr. Carpenter had a family emergency and will not be back until after the holidays," said Mr. Robinson, the other biology teacher. He had a beard and a stain on his forehead. "We'll review for your final. Who can tell me something snappy about ATP?"

"This sucks," Holly said. "What do you think happened to my husband Shaun Carpenter?"

"I don't know," I said. "Maybe he disappeared into the wild."

"Did it seem kinda like he was going crazy?" she asked.

"Yeah," I said.

We took our finals with Mr. Robinson standing over us, pacing the aisles. I think I got a C. It was cold again, like it was supposed to be, and on that Friday I walked home through the snow, to my mom's house. I made a sandwich and she came in from the living room and sat down and said, "Your father and I have decided to get back together. It's official!"

I kept eating my sandwich.

"That's really good for you," I said, after a moment. "What happened to the bathtub?"

"What?"

I swallowed my bread. "The bathtub you told me about," I said.

"I don't follow."

"When we were driving to Chicago."

"What bathtub?"

"You said the water cools off. You explained this huge definition of love. You also used snow."

"Oh," she said. "That."

"You told me that love dies."

"Did I say that?"

"Yes."

"Something about this going away," she said, shaking her head. "I mean he was only down the road, for goodness sake. We worked out many of our difficulties. We needed a break. You wouldn't—I don't think you could understand."

She laughed to herself, and I could tell that she was far away. She looked at me—I just stared—and she flapped a hand to shoo my irritating skepticism.

"It's reminded us, I think," she said. "That's all."

I didn't change my look. It no longer felt natural to abide my mother's lies, regardless of whether or not she had the energy to perform them.

On Christmas Eve, I was in my dad's apartment, wearing my favorite brown dress, which was now too short for me—it was as though I was not going to stop growing, ever, and I would be like Alice, shooting up so high that I'd eventually blast through the roof—sitting on his couch, watching the big black TV that would soon be moving home, too. I was helping him get a few more boxes of things, and I could hear him humming "Jingle Bells" in the other room; James and Mom were at the house, waiting for us, but I hadn't seen James yet. I was excited to hug him. Of course there would be a glazed ham. Grandma and Grandpa were coming to town, and my dad's brother Stew had flown in from Cleveland for the first time in five years. The family was bonding. The lights were all up and the snow had started at noon. It was freezing.

We loaded up the car in two trips. At the trunk I watched him go back to lock up; I felt the cold against my tights and looked down at my shoes, which were too nice to be here with the exhaust-stained ice. I had always thought there was something unusual, but good, about being dressed up out in the dark cold. I was fancy here alongside the elements and my makeup wanted to freeze into a mask on my face.

When we were driving, Dad said, "This might be the end for you and that dress." He was looking right at my thighs.

I looked down. Strong but at peace in my black tights, I saw. They looked good. But what I thought was: it must be hard for fathers to see their daughters having passed some Terminal Line of their own.

I pulled at my hem. "This will be fun," I said.

He said nothing.

I looked up. "Won't it? Family Part Two?"

"Don't be sarcastic, Courtney," he said. "Sarcasm is a small thing for small people." When I didn't respond he said, a little softer, "Just please not tonight. Christmas and your mother and everything else."

"No," I said, seeing I had hurt his feelings, or at least reminded him of something that did. "I really do think it'll be fun." I tried to make it sound real. "James is here, too."

After a pause he said, "You never know what's going to happen with your Uncle Stew around."

"I know," I said. "Stew's bananas."

The snow was fat, the kind that might be good to build a snowman or a fort, and I guessed that later we would see the colored puffballs of children in snowmobile suits working savagely at the new landscape, driven to make all thought-up places real, terraforming for their lives. My dad was squinting at the road and driving slow. I didn't want to distract him anymore. Besides, what question could I ask? Father, does tepid bathwater eventually become stagnant and unsafe, as we might hypothesize, following a period of conjecture? Father, do you want to be in this car, going in this direction? With me? And if so, will you always love me? Because I am now not so sure, and nor am I a girl. And Father, at what point, precisely, can we recognize a failed life? (I see yours.) And what can we do once we see it? (Little.) These thoughts went through my mind, for real, as I was the empiricist here, but I sensed the wrong word might shatter him. I stayed quiet. I watched the road and tried to help look out for ice or other spots of danger, knowing he was prone to his own kinds of distraction, which was an unscientific and meddlesome thing to do, I know, but I did it. Because the plows hadn't been through, which left ruts you had to follow, but they could hurt you. Where was Shaun Carpenter? I wondered it right then.

"I haven't driven in anything like this," I said.

"You haven't had much chance," he said. "This is your first winter driving."

I agreed. Based on the math of the birthdays, it was true.

He nodded brusquely, kept his eyes on the oncoming cars, happy now we were on to a certain topic. "Well," he said. "Give it time. You'll learn."

I was glad he said it, but there was sadness to it all. He may as well have said goodbye, then, too.

The Peach

Here's a story: summer of 1945, on her way to San Diego to get my grandfather, George Glen Huygens, discharged after fighting in the Pacific for a year, my grandmother Beatrice evaporated.

Her car broke down outside Santa Fe; she walked nine miles before another car came, and by the time one did, she lay prone beneath wavy lines of heat on the side of the highway, eyes closed, lips chapped. This happened. The water in her slowly moved up through her supine and half-conscious body, then up into the air, where it became a part of the weather and the sky. The sun pulled her up and the water in turn rained her down later. The man who stopped was a Bible salesman on his way to southern California.

My grandfather almost died too. It was three months earlier. He got shot by a Japanese machine gun as he was climbing over a ridge on the island of Iwo To. At the time, he was trying to multiply 37 by 88 in his head, no saying numbers out loud. Once he told me he felt three of the bullets go into his chest—thumpthumpthump—and pass through the layers of his body, and that he heard two go over his head—tssttsst— as he was falling. He could remember the medic trying to patch him up and another soldier telling him he was going to be fine.

The soldier said, "Hold on, Georgie. It's not as bad as you think."

Grandpa, eyes wide, said, "Three-thousand something."

They are both still alive.

I am sitting in their kitchen, drinking coffee with my grandmother.

Grandpa's asleep in the back of the house, and has been since I got here. He has taken to sleeping quite a lot. Grandma only once talked about what it would be like for one when the other was gone, but it wasn't very complicated. There were no metaphors. She said, "It will be hard."

I sometimes come here to see them. I stare at a fork on the table. I have no set routine and never tell them when I'm coming. I roll my Toyota into their driveway.

Grandma says, "Have I told you about my test tubes?"

I look up from the fork.

She is wearing a long summer dress, yellow and blue and white, and I look across the table at the wrinkles at her neck. The sun is coming through the window and making a white glow over her head. She's eating a peach. She's cut it into slices and has them on a white plate. The knife is on the lemon tablecloth beside it.

"No."

"When George and I moved here I got the idea into my head," she says, "that I wanted to collect a sample of water from every lake in Wisconsin, and label every lake. It was my way of dealing with leaving Texas and coming home, I think. You can get used to strange situations and strange places. Texas was like that—I never wanted to live there and when the time came to leave I was furious. So much that everything old suddenly appears stranger. Do you understand? And when the idea came to me I thought about all of the test tubes with pieces of masking tape on them as the labels."

"Did you?"

"Not all," she says. "Some, though."

"And did you label them?"

"I did. In the basement of the old house, George built a rack for me, and every sample I took was labeled. You could walk down there and it'd feel like you were in a laboratory. If you looked closely you would see that it was more like the laboratory of a child, of course, but that didn't matter. It was amateur science."

"What did you do with them?"

"That was the problem with the entire idea. Not a problem, exactly, but let's just say that was a limitation of the idea. George and I would go out on the weekend—I'd take the map and circle a lake, and we'd drive to it. We'd camp if we needed to or come back in the evening if it was close enough. We'd have a picnic."

"It sounds nice."

"George thought I'd lost my mind."

"Because that was it?"

"Because that was the whole idea. There was nothing to do afterwards. Still, it was great fun while it lasted."

"But they're gone now?"

"They are," she says. "When the house burned down ten years ago all of them got eaten up by fire. I was here when that fire started, you know. I was in the shower. I got out, got dressed, and didn't smell anything odd until I was in the kitchen. Then I went down into the basement to see and there was the fuse box and some of the old wires in the back storage room, all ablaze. Do you know what I did?"

"Run?"

"No," she says. "I didn't. I took a handful of the lakes inside of test tubes and started pouring them, one by one, onto the fire. I'd turn over White Potato Lake right onto a flame and there'd be a hiss, then I'd take the cork off of Silver Lake and try to splash it onto another hot spot, and it'd be the same thing. Except new flames were coming up. I didn't have enough water. On the second try I came back with more test tubes and thought I'd try to cast a spell, and that if I did it right, when I poured from a tube the whole lake would be in the sky above the house, and it would drop down, all at once, and stop the fire. We had photos, we had the old furniture. So many things. I was crazy down there."

"I take it your spell didn't work."

"My spell didn't work."

Grandma smiles, looking down at what's left of her peach.

Only a couple of slices and the pit. She slides the plate toward me and I take a slice as well. "We lost so much in that fire," she says. "It's amazing to me. You think these memories are inside of you and it doesn't matter. When you lose the things you realize it's not all inside of you."

"Where is it?"

"Hm."

We hear the footsteps then, and we look up and watch the door as Grandpa comes into the kitchen. His footsteps are sliding, scraping footsteps, and when he is past the countertop I can see that he is wearing his slippers. The rest of him is dressed in his usual comfortable fall outfit. Corduroy pants and a white shirt and a cardigan over the top of it. My grandpa's hair is everywhere.

Grandpa says, "It seems my nap has ended."

"We were just talking about my old nutball idea," says Grandma. "About the test tubes."

"Yes," says Grandpa. "That." He has gone to the coffee maker and has begun pouring his own cup. We both watch him as he turns and comes toward the table. He moves slowly. He broke his hip three years ago on the golf course. Also: this has nothing to do with movement, but they had to remove part of his ear in August because of skin cancer. (They got it.)

He puts his hand on the back of the chair and lowers himself down.

"For a brief period of time we had a fabulous collection of lake water here. What your grandmother doesn't know is that I once drank five of her lakes and replaced the water with tapwater."

Grandma stares at him.

Grandpa has a little twinkle in his eye. He turns back to me. "I was working on the sump pump and couldn't be bothered to go upstairs for a drink," he says, shrugging. "Absolutely parched. I saw them and did it. No looking back. This was before giardia," he adds. "I wasn't worried."

"Do you know what you've done, George?" Grandma says. "All this time and I never realized it. How dare you?"

"What?"

"You're the reason my spell didn't work."

Grandpa looks at me, raises his eyebrows, and takes the last slice of peach.

★ ✪ ★

Now would be the time to tell you that somebody's dying, but nobody is. All three of us are okay. We're just here.

My grandmother had another courter at the same time my grandpa was hovering around. This was 1938. The other man's name was Sylvester Caddimis, and he was a big-shot welder who'd made it through the Depression by going to Chicago and doing unknown thug-work before coming home with cash in his pocket—enough to open a shop and set out looking for a bride. Grandma was dubious, but she liked his dark good looks and the shower of gifts and praise that Caddimis had heaped for months. My grandfather, fresh out of college, was in town to work on an engineering project for the summer, and he'd seen her and tipped his hat to her a number of times out on the street. One night there was a dance. Grandma and her friends were escorted by Caddimis and his friends, and they spent the first hours of the evening sipping punch and chatting; the men smoked cigars in the corner of the gymnasium and the women tried their hand at the Charleston. Then Grandpa came in, alone, his hair greased back, and stood far away from the crowds, alone, staring intently at my grandma, smoking cigarette after cigarette, stubbing each one out on the gymnasium floor until a small pile built up beside his shoe. And of course eventually Caddimis and his crew noticed this, and it wasn't long before they'd gone up to Grandpa and had asked him what his intentions were, why he was hanging out in the dark, staring at women.

"You a pervert or somethin'?" Caddimis asked him, and his crew all laughed, and then he poked Grandpa in the shoulder.

Grandpa turned around and punched him once, in the center of the nose. Caddimis crumpled to the ground. Then he stood up. Without a word, he turned and left the gymnasium. The story sometimes includes an epilogue; they say my grandfather hit him so hard that Caddimis just walked directly to his car and drove all the way back to Chicago, nose bleeding the whole way, never to be heard from again.

★ ✪ ★

"Those test tubes remind me of something else," Grandpa says. "A time I went up to the border, not with your grandmother but with a friend of mine, a man named Jack Dawson."

"Oh good lord," Grandma says. "Not this."

Grandpa ignores her and goes on: "He'd fought in Europe and I'd fought in the Pacific and so sometimes we compared our stories or just talked about the war in the way that veterans such as ourselves tend to talk about it to this day. Your grandmother had the flu but she sent me up to get her water from a lake called Pumpkin Lake. Just on the border of Michigan. It's on the map. Have a look for it. You see your grandmother had no interest in water from lakes in the U.P., but as long as they were in Wisconsin, she wanted them. Why that was, Bea, I will never understand, of course. States are a figment of somebody's imagination. Care to elaborate?"

"No," says Grandma. "I do not."

"So Jack and I drive up there north toward Pumpkin Lake. The highways at this time are not good. It takes hours and hours to get that far north. But it's a pleasant time. We talk some about the war, but Jack tells me about a plan he has to start a bee farm and be a beekeeper instead of a bookkeeper. He tells me that it started as a little fantasy during his workday—he saw a bee on his lunch break once and had some kind of involved revelation—but then he figured out that one might actually be able to do it, and so he'd bought some land down in the southwest of the state and was planning on switching over to it after he learned everything he needed to know. Very interesting."

"This is not even the story, George."

"It is in the way I tell it," Grandpa says to her. "Now. If you don't mind, I'll continue with my preamble."

"Please."

"You see Jack had killed a French woman accidentally. She was in her house, and he was shooting every which way, just thinking he was about to die and letting go. Except he didn't die. He shot everywhere. Some tanks had arrived during his meltdown and cleared out all the Germans from the town. But he remembered the beginning of his shooting spree, and so later he went into a small house and found that he'd shot a 40-something French woman right in the head, through the wall. She was lying on top of her kitchen table in butter. An unusually large pad of butter, Jack always says."

"This is unpleasant."

"It matters for the rest of the story," Grandpa says to her. He turns back to me. "So Jack had never been able to escape this. He killed many German soldiers and was shot himself and saw hundreds of men his age shot and blown up on Normandy beach, but he couldn't escape the woman he'd killed. He talked about her all the time. I had a few of my own stories like that but I was never haunted in the same way. I was never in a place where there were any civilians, except on shore leave, and on shore leave, we weren't shooting. And so anyway Jack thought these bees would somehow help him with his memory problem. With the French woman. He didn't know why, but this is why he was so excited, and all the way up to Pumpkin Lake, he described to me how he and his wife would move, how you could deal with whole hives, how much money you could make with the honey. I listened, but once we got close to the lake I stopped listening to him and started listening instead to the sound the engine was making. I say to him, 'You hear that?' and he says, 'I do,' and just like that, the whole car goes dead and we drift over to the side of the road."

"What do you mean by dead?" I ask. "It stalled?"

"More than that," he says. "Everything went out. All the life fell out of it. And just before I get a chance to open the door and go take a look, we both hear this noise, and up in the sky, right over us, a UFO goes by."

I look at Grandma, who rolls her eyes.

"Just goes right by."

"What do you mean? A plane?"

"Like no plane I'd ever seen," Grandpa says. "It was a circle, but without a middle, like a Life Saver. It wasn't spinning. Just sort of hovering. And it was loud, grunting and grumbling like it was breaking down, too. It followed the highway for a little while and then darted off, over the trees. A minute later we were on our own. We both got out of the car and kept looking at the sky. I look over at Jack and say—and pardon me—but I say, 'What in the fuck was that, Jack?'"

"Jack looks back at me for a long time and says, real serious, 'I need your car.' He's white as a sheet."

"'Why do you need my car?' I ask him."

"'Because,' Jack says, pointing up into the sky. 'Hitler had those. Those are Hitler's. He's here.'" Then Jack starts looking around at the Michigan woods, like Hitler and Goebbels and all of them might be hiding in some bushes nearby."

"Just absurd," Grandma says.

"Now there is a base in the Upper Peninsula," Grandpa says to me, "called Kinross. Earlier that year there was an incident. We had all heard about it in the newspaper. A plane had disappeared; there'd been another, different UFO encounter. A lot of the locals now treat Kinross like Area 51, and they say the woods are haunted up there, et cetera, because of it. I'm not sure how far away we were from it then, but Jack shook his head and told me that's where he was going. Kinross. 'The fate of the country may hang in the balance, George,' he said. I told him he was an idiot. He got real quiet, and that's the last thing I remember. I woke up lying in the ditch with an egg on the back of my head. Jack was gone."

Grandma leans toward me. "The man stole your grandfather's car." She shakes her head. "And beat him. Remember those two parts. I find it all very suspicious."

"This coming from a woman who was trying to cast spells to save her house?"

"That," she says, "was different. I knew it wasn't going to work."

"I'm not sure that gets you off the hook."

"But what happened?" I ask.

"What happened is simple," Grandpa says. "I got up and started walking south. Twenty minutes later I got picked up by a truck that took me to Lena. I sit around there for awhile, then hitch home. I come in, stained, starving, carless. Your grandmother is in the kitchen and takes one look at me and says, 'Where is my Pumpkin Lake test tube, George?' and I say, 'I've been robbed.' I tell the story to Grandma and she calls up Jack's wife and tells her what Jack did and I don't try to stop it because I know there's nothing I can do. I eat, sleep, shower up, and mow the lawn. Next day I wake up and I see my car out there in the driveway, and I look inside and I see that there's a full tank of gas, and so I drive over to Jack's house and knock on the door and he opens it in his bathrobe and says, 'I didn't find him.'"

"'Who didn't you find?' I ask him."

"'Hitler. Aliens. The UFO. Anything.'"

"'Where did you go?' I say."

"'I drove around all day,' he says. 'I found nothing.'"

"What I believe," Grandma says, looking at Grandpa, who is looking down at his coffee cup, having finished his story, "is a little simpler." She turns to me. "And it has nothing to do with any UFOs. I think they got drunk at some bar and had a fight."

"An interesting side note to this is that Jack did actually go south and start that bee farm," says Grandpa. "We've been there."

"Lots of bees," says Grandma.

"Exactly what you'd expect," says Grandpa.

I think of the French woman. What ways can you put together a whole farm to her lying there in the butter in 1944, and then forward again, to a UFO flying overhead? Jack is the one who knows.

★ ✪ ★

"Is everything okay?" Grandma asks me. We are alone again; we've moved to the backyard, and I am watching her probe one of her flowerbeds for weeds, walking slowly alongside the black dirt like a cat, looking down. Grandpa is in the garage, working on his birdhouse. "Now?"

"What do you mean?" I say. There are many ways to answer this question. The word "no" would probably work for all the different ways.

"You're sad," she says.

"Obviously I'm sad," I say.

"I know," she says. "That's not what I meant. But I've been under the impression, these last months—I've been under the impression that you've been feeling better."

"I'm just visiting," I say.

"And your marriage? Is that it?"

"I'm visiting."

"I see," says Grandma. "I see. You know we appreciate it. That's all I'll say. I like to think of us as some kind of tonic for whatever happens to you. We're always here. It doesn't matter. That's a nice thought." She smiles to herself. "Did you know that George and I—please don't tell this to your mother, because I truly think she was too blind to notice at the time—but George and I had our share of problems, long ago?"

"What problems?"

"We both had an affair," she says. "One each. We have never once discussed it and I am sure we never will."

"But how did you—"

"I felt it," she says, "and then he felt it."

"Felt what?"

"We have been married for 70 years. If you can believe that. Can you?"

"Yes."

"After 30 years you begin to feel things. You'll see. If the two of you stay together, you'll see. You move through all the lonely periods and the angry periods and the resurgence of the old romantic periods, and then you enter something new. It does feel like moving into a new home. At first like a vacation, then you realize you're staying. It's very hard to describe. Needless to say, secrets are no longer possible. George would walk in and I would see a thundercloud over his head from the time he came through the door until the time I saw him climb into his car the next morning, out in the driveway. I could really see it there. It had little lightning bolts and everything. It was gray. Obviously." She raises her eyebrows at me. She is mad at me for saying "obviously" to her before. She hates it when people say "obviously." I do, too.

"What did you do?"

"I waited. It stopped. Then I got my own thundercloud. And I told myself that I would stop mine, and I would wait and see if a new one appeared over his head, and if so, that would be the end."

"Who was he?"

"Just a man."

"Who was she?"

"I don't know."

"And the cloud never came back?"

"No," she says. "It never came back."

We make our way past that bed, to the three apple trees at the edge of the property. "Too late for these, I think." At our feet there are many rotting Macintoshes in the grass.

"And that was it?" I ask. "That was honestly it? You both knew and no one has ever said anything out loud."

"I suppose it's not fair to assume that he knows. Maybe it's not even fair to assume that anything happened. But fair is not the appropriate word, considering we're speaking about the truth."

"Fair doesn't matter in the least," I say. "Besides. None of this is what my problem is. We're not going to be together in 30 years."

"Yes," Grandma says. "Your mother told me."

"So there you go."

"What happened to you both—it's only nature."

She leads me around the side of the house, and then we drift in through the garage and find Grandpa sitting on a stool at his workbench, leaning over what looks like a nearly-completed structure. A birdhouse. The birdhouse is stained a dark rosy brown.

When he hears us, he looks up, smiles at us, then nods at it. "Now. Would you not be happy to reside in this place?"

On the way out the door, Grandma hugs me and gives me a new peach. She says, "They're good, aren't they? I got them at the farmer's market but I have no idea where they come from originally."

"Thank you."

"Please feel better," she says. "Please don't—please understand how different anything can look."

"It's not that," I say. "Not exactly."

"No? Then what?"

"I honestly don't know."

"Then maybe you're fine," she says. "After all."

We say our goodbyes. I go out to the driveway and stand beside my car and look at the peach. I run my finger across the light fuzz, then scratch at the skin, like it's alive, a little curled up animal, like it has an itch and can feel. Peaches are the strangest things, aren't they? Like with the right words, sung as an incantation, you can wake them up and they'll grow.

The Cop

I know something's wrong with him just by looking at his eyes—I can almost feel the shit this guy's done, it's all bound up in his face, the way he walks. I've heard guys talk about this sense but it's just the last couple of months where I get flashes like this and I can't say I've ever done a thing to act on them. What the fuck are you gonna say to the judge? Your honor, I felt the crime on him and took him down?

But this time I walk past him and not ten seconds later the radio blows up with the 4-1 and I turn on my heel and I'm running back toward the guy before dispatch is close to done talking.

I find psychology amazing. Maybe I even would have done it, somehow, if I didn't do this. Because later, after I tackle the guy—this after he looks back and sees me coming and starts to run—I see that he's got on this cream-colored scarf with some maroon stripes and right below one of those stripes is a speck of blood. He's sitting down cuffed not saying anything and I've already got the knife and I'm waiting, so it's no surprise, but I notice that speck of blood and I wonder if that's what I saw, really, when I passed him, and if all this about moods and ESP just comes down to noticing the world a little better.

Dispatch chirps up and it sounds like whoever it was this fuck stabbed is not well. Not well at all.

I look at his eyes. He heard dispatch. But all I see there is calm.

Hair University

I live in the same neighborhood as Phil's brothers. My embarrassment about this comes from an idea I got into my head when I was a student at the SSTD: Grayson (all of America, actually, perhaps even all of Earth) is separated into two halves. One half, the real half, is the north side. That's where the artists, workers, and minorities live. Honest people. The south side is where all the white people with information jobs live. They are by definition dishonest. The south side is therefore not real; satellite televisions and hybrid, Bluetooth-wired vehicles work in concert to create the simulacra, occupy the space where reality is supposed to be. Inside of here, we are all dying. We don't even bother to get out. We don't know. I occupy this space, too. And in the end, it could even be considered a zoo, or some kind of wildlife sanctuary, but for the fact that there is no one watching us, and we've built it ourselves.

Well.

It sounds like something someone at college would think up. A person with not enough income, which is what I was for the first half of my life. But after the final book in the trilogy was published (mixed reviews), and I was through with the conventions and the readings and the honestly hot sex with girls dressed like Vyborgs (ask me some time about the underworld of softcore SF porn—I will tell you the truth), I got it in my head to move back to Grayson to relax, recharge my *creative batteries*, escape the east coast, and escape city life. Besides, I was not respected in the New York literary community. I knew one writer of self-help books, Chester Chalky, a diabetic man who chewed Nicorette Gum and wore only Under Armour athletic clothing, and whenever we got together for a drink, he could not keep himself from chuckling and drawing attention to bad sentences I had long ago written and my lack of premier publications.

So. When I was 38, looking for something new, I moved back to Grayson, my hometown, and bought a palace on the south shore of the river. Very cheap, considering the size and the waterfront. Such are the economics of a dying Midwestern town in the midst of ongoing, postindustrial collapse. There was a long pier. There were two large, rectangular, useless brick pillars on either side of the driveway. These were beautiful pillars.

I remain comfortable with this decision. Except when I see Phil's brothers on their evening strolls.

I don't think that it was an idea in the traditional sense. Anthropologists tell us that cultural rituals like these strolls simply evolve; at first, they are functional. For example, someone needs to walk the dog. But they begin to take on a significance of their own, and have a meaning of their own, and pretty soon, the dog isn't even there.

Every evening, you see, Phil's brothers walk down the street together. One of them—Henry—smokes a pipe. Usually they talk. If you live anywhere near them and wait quietly on your porch sometime around dusk, you will probably be able to hear the soft murmurings of their disturbingly sophisticated conversations carried on the evening breeze. I often see them from my kitchen: four stout, hearty silhouettes, strolling, each with a strong puff of thick, curly hair surrounding their heads, the silhouettes of their hair glowing beneath the pink light of sunset. I once saw them with their arms interlocked at the elbows. Discussing the family. Discussing their marriages. The International Monetary Fund. Their kids. Tiers of String Theory. Life. And of course Phil is not, nor has he ever been, with them.

Phil's much younger. He's much, much less successful.

He has much less hair.

And yet you can tell, when you see them, that they are nevertheless a complete unit, cohesive and fully-formed. Phil's absence is unimportant.

It's hard not to shake the feeling that this exclusion is at the root of my old friend's troubles. I want to help him, I really do, but tonight, as I again stand in my kitchen and watch them go by, dishtowel in my hands, I realize that they are much too intimidating to confront, even for someone successful like me, and that it would be best to leave them to their walk. These are large, physically fit, overpowering men we're talking about. People who have never failed in life.

No matter how I try, I'm only ever at ease amongst the skinny and the weak, those with emaciated quadriceps and hamstrings. I like people with bad hair who are hunched over, not people who have never felt the tendrils of the neurotic anxiety octopus first tickle, then clamp. (Who also don't have emaciated quadriceps and hamstrings.)

I look down at my dog and tell him that I'll have to find another way to get Phil inserted into the group. Then I go out back to light up the citronella candles.

★　✪　★

Phil wants to undergo a dangerous experimental follicle procedure at a place called Hair University. The risk, he says, is full-body disintegration. I'm against it.

He's sitting across from me, staring down at a translucent red cup full of orange soda. I have trouble not looking at the top of his head, which is, of course, the subject of our current conversation. Yes, I can see a little bit of whitish scalp, it's true, but I would not go so far as to call him bald. Yet.

If anything, "balding" seems more appropriate.

But even that might be going too far. He's got a lot of strong, sandy-brown hairs up there. Thick ones.

Quite a bit of swirl, too, and it will probably last. I've just got a feeling.

And don't even get me started about the thickness around the sides.

Overall, I think that there's great hair-fortitude here, and I have just said as much to him, and he has denied it, and now things are tense.

We stare at one another.

We are in a booth at Paco and Paco's Fine Dining and Fish Fry, a ragged place that has been in Grayson longer than I have been on Earth, and one that will (I hope) be here long after I'm gone. Paco the Younger is a fine-looking man with the musculature of a Belgian cow who is not at all Mexican and looks pretty white to me, but I have no problem calling him what he wants to be called, because I like to think of myself as a liberal person, and maybe it's really his name, anyway. I have never seen Paco the Elder.

"In life we must take dramatic steps," Phil finally says, but to his soda. There is failed dignity lurking in the background of his voice.

"This is not a dramatic step," I say, talking as calmly as possible.

The dark table is made up of parallel wood planks of different hues, enthusiastically varnished, and, of course, covered in today's layer of grease and granules of salt, so it takes me a few tries to find a comfortable place to rest my elbows before I make my point. The whole restaurant smells like a combination of the South Street Seaport and a donut factory.

"You've misunderstood the idea of drama," I say. "You're not going bald."

He looks up and holds on to me with his blue eyes. He's not blinking, and I am uncomfortable. His face shares a remarkable resemblance to his brother's faces, even though he's going bald.

"Mutability is the first source of drama," he says. "We must do what we can to corral it. Wordsworth. Have you heard of a man named Wordsworth?"

"Please," I say. "Listen to yourself."

"Wordsworth the poet."

"Please."

"Everyone knows that. You're a writer. You know that."

"Phil," I say. "I'm not that kind of writer."

He shakes his head, looks over his shoulder for his fish sandwich, which has not arrived. Paco the Younger has disappeared into the back room. I look around impatiently, too. Some of his interesting hot sauce knowledge could really break the tension right now.

"How is it you could be accidentally disintegrated at this place?"

He rolls his eyes. "I don't want to talk about it."

"Don't you think you should?"

"Anyway," Phil says, "that's not even the biggest risk. I haven't even told you about the Hair Monster."

"I don't even want to hear about the Hair Monster."

I wonder to myself what the fuck the Hair Monster is. For the moment, all we have to cut through the atmosphere is the music coming from the black rectangular speaker haphazardly mounted in one of the ceiling's corners. I feel as though the old woman sitting beneath it is in danger, but I say nothing. The music—it's not salsa. I can hear toms but then again they might be something else completely.

"Listen," I say, thinking about Phil's whole body lighting up like the phosphorous in a light-bulb, then turning to dust. "It sounds too dangerous." Or would Hair Monster be down in some maze, lurking like a Minotaur? But I'm getting tired, and I don't sound convincing. I'm also starting to wonder what he would look like with his hair back. He'd probably look pretty good.

"That's because I just told you it was dangerous," Phil says. "Hair University cannot guarantee my safety. Hair University is not subject to FDA or ATF restrictions. That's why it's on a small Caribbean island."

I can tell now that he's mimicking something he's read in the literature. I saw it all over at his apartment: a pile of papers, workbooks, DVDs, and charts more substantial than my own current research project, which has to do with the vaginas of extraterrestrials. (Whether or not they're there.) This I noted with extra attention that last time I paid him a visit. Phil is not much of a researcher, or a reader, or someone who thinks anything through. For him to be preparing is a meaningful development. It's like a horse reading *The Celestine Prophecy*.

"So why would you choose to do something so dangerous?"

"I'm a Norwood Six, Danny. Six." He sips his soda dramatically. "Don't talk to me about dangerous."

He's recently explained the Norwood Scale to me. Basically—and I'm assuming this was all thought up by a man named Norwood—there are varying degrees of baldness, and along the continuum are Norwoods 1 through 8. There's even a 3A, which denotes, I believe, a very specific pattern of hairline-regression combined with crown-thinning. Different enough from Norwood 3 to get its own subcategory. Not unlike how you might measure cancer. What are you? I'm a Norwood 4. I don't know whether this Norwood hung, shot, or drowned himself.

"Your life will never be endangered by this condition. Yet it will be endangered by this procedure," I say. "Analyze the logic."

"What you say depends on your definitions of several terms."

"It's not worth it," I tell him. "And you don't exactly have the money, either."

"You have the money coming out of your ears," he says. "And you care about me. And you can't not give it to me."

"Yes I can't. You have a family. They can help you."

"I have four brothers who don't talk to me and they all live on the same block on the other side of town."

"That's a family."

"That's a fraternity."

"I don't have a family like you have a family."

"I don't have a family like you think I have a family."

"You're a part of that fraternity."

"I'm not," he says. Glistening eyes. "They don't let bald people into that one." I swear that I see a full tear forming, but he rubs it too fast for me to actually tell.

"You are superficial," I say.

This conversation is coming to a close.

It's true, all of Phil's brothers have quite a bit of hair. Fine. As does his father. Fine. As did his mother, and all of the grandparents, and all of the ancestors, all the way back to Homo Habilis. Phil's thinning is a genetic anomaly; to him it is tragic precisely for this reason. He says that had it not been an anomaly, had it been expected, he would have been able to deal. But there is something "extra-stingy"—his words—about rolling the dice and losing. Especially since he didn't even get to literally roll, it was done instead by chromosome arms wrapping around one another. I have been spending the last forty minutes—first in the aisles of the hardware store, and now here—trying to convince him that nobody in the whole town has ever noticed a thing about it, and even if he was completely bald, nobody would care, because deep, deep, down, nobody cares about baldness but bald people. Women, in particular, only care about bald people who care about their own baldness. They don't like them.

He shot a terrified look at me and said, "Liar," when I said that, back when we were getting some keys copied. "It's the ultimate untrue nice thing to say. People do care. A lot."

When Paco the Younger finally shows up with the fish sandwiches he sets down the plates, wipes his hands on his white apron, and pats Phil on the shoulder. I am being intimidated by the veins on his forearms as he asks Phil how things are.

Phil tells him about Hair University.

We wait, and Paco nods his head to the unidentifiable music. I imagine that he is thinking about fish.

"What?" says Paco.

"H.U."

"Some college or something, bro?"

"I just told you," says Phil patiently. "It's an institute for the study of hair and all of its materializations. It's the twenty-first century. It's time for baldness to be eliminated outright. What the fuck is technology for, you know? If not this?" Phil is fired up.

Paco must be ten years younger than us, but you can tell that he looks at Phil and me like little brothers, lost and wayward people who don't understand that the world is not a complicated place. He believes (I admit that he might be on to something here) that it's impossible to be as stupid as we are as long as you don't think.

"You do look a little thin up there, buddy," says Paco, grinning. And then, to my horror, I see him actually touching Phil's hair, moving around individual pieces as though he's looking for a lost button in a shag carpet.

"The thing about H.U.," Phil says to me casually, as he's being examined, "is that it's a place where people understand that something like this hurts.

Emotionally. In many ways, that's more important than the technology. AIDS, death, terrorists, hairlessness. It all leads to the same thing. It all leads to emotional problems."

"Death?"

"Well," Phil says. "For other people. Who don't die."

I don't understand why he isn't freaking out and slapping Paco's hand away. He is usually most neurotic about touching.

"Why are you so comfortable?" I ask.

Phil shrugs. "I've come to terms with some things. Your characters aren't the only people who have stupid-ass epiphanies."

"Yeah," says Paco as he finishes his examination.

He again pats Phil on the shoulder, and this time squeezes the muscle beside his neck. He leans real close to my face. "He's come to terms with some things. Leave him be." Then he turns his neck and stares right into Phil's eyes. "You guys want any hot sauce, or are you gonna be assholes about that, too?"

★　✪　★

I hit the big time about three years ago with *The Gesticulating Rock Cycle*, and since then I've been doing some thinking. Here's the deep part: loneliness is an important part of life, an important time during which a man cultivates his soul and grows and gets to know himself. Suffering. A prerequisite to the complete package. You learn to cook, you learn to clean, you learn to take care of yourself. You set your own schedule. You live for you. You get a good exercise routine going. And buried deep inside of that lonely guy, like a vein of invaluable Manacodavian Ore, is the true stuff of existence, a swath of magic. You need to get down pretty far and do the legwork, the real exploring, but once you've done it, then you're in for something stellar. Real heart.

That's me, that's my theory, and I think, so far, it's working. Its predictions have been accurate, this theory. I've got my place, my porch, my backyard. A nice little ceramic dog. I'm feeling things out. I'm not sure I have a real heart, but maybe. I could use a woman.

Phil, though. Depression's not right for him. He's been bumming around town for too long. He hasn't gotten out and seen the world. He doesn't know what loneliness is. Not the real kind. And I can tell that he doesn't really want to, that this narcissistic hair impulse is predominant and unmovable, some boulder he will never be able to move. So he's never going to learn.

The doorbell rings, and I walk through the kitchen to the front door. When I pull it open, Phil is standing in front of me, his jaw set. He is wearing a stocking cap, and it is too warm for him to be wearing a stocking cap. Bald people, I think.

"I drove by them," he says, storming past me. "I just drove *right* by them."

"Did you talk to them?" I ask, closing the door when I realize he's not coming back to do it.

He has become distracted by the painting on the wall. He is leaning very close to the frame.

"What the hell is this?" he asks.

He turns and looks at me. "You know you're just as sick as everyone else, right?"

"It's a girl," I say.

"What's that?" he asks, tapping the tip of his finger on the glass. He looks at me again, now with a stupid grin on his face.

"That's a big...phaser," I say.

"Oh?"

"Let's go out back and have some gin and tonics."

"And what's that?"

"That's her holster."

"Am I right to say that she has haphazardly strewn it in the corner of the room?"

"Artists have to balance colors and light."

"Have we just entered her room, Danny? Should I think of this as a first-person perspective? Have we, as the observers of the painting, just stumbled in on this lovely and, might I add, sexy space-lady undressing? Would you call this alien erotica? Because I might! I might!"

FIGURE vb7009: "THE THOUGHT OF A FOREIGN CARESS BEFORE THE BATTLE OF §Œʃ∑θΓ" BY G.W. GURGLESMITH

"That's the color and light being balanced. Right in the corner there."

He puts his hand on my shoulder. "I feel sorry for you and you feel sorry for me," he says. "That makes for a good friendship."

He is very right about that, I realize. We go out back. After I bring him his drink he remembers that he is angry about seeing his brothers.

I let him bitch.

After he's gotten it all out he turns his head and says, "Shit. Anyway, I'm doing it. I've decided to do the experimental procedure, Danny. Anyway."

"Fine," I say. "I don't care." I'm still smarting about his critique of the painting, which I just put up yesterday. It took me six months of cajoling the artist to get him to sell it to me in the first place. And then this fat, bald, nearly-unemployed, manchild basket-case walks in and tries to kill it to feed the monster of his neurosis.

I think about dropping my line about narcissism and the boulder, but I'm sure it will be lost on him. I also can't remember the exact wording.

"Good," he says, nodding. "Good. I know you're just saying that, buddy."

"And now I suppose you've come here for the money," I say.

He's quiet.

"How much?" I ask.

"I need around eighty-five thousand, even though it's not entirely clear from the literature—"

I have drunk the whole lime wedge from my gin and tonic. Very soon after I get his attention with my waving hands, Phil is slapping me hard on the back, and I'm leaning forward, trying to push, and reaching down into my throat, trying to catch the lime by a little stringy piece of lime-meat, and I am also holding my nostrils together with my other hand, trying to create the pressure I need to launch the thing free. I believe that Phil is also behind me, attempting some creative interpretation of the Heimlich maneuver. He hurts me.

We remain locked in this mortal embrace for about twenty seconds. I begin to wonder if I will die.

Then, just like that, the whole thing slides down, and I have to slap at him to make him quit with the slaps.

"Stop it," I say. "Stop it." I breathe once, afraid that the lime wedge has fallen into one of my lungs, doomed to rot on the floor of the cave like a lost spelunker. How terrible.

"I'm okay," I say.

We both sit down again.

"What do you think would happen if you had a lime wedge in your lung?" I ask.

"I don't care," he says.

"Do you have any idea how much money that is?" I ask him.

"Yeah, Dan," he says. "It's eighty-five thousand dollars."

"I mean in relation to the economy," I say. "To other things." I am talking to a man who has made six dollars an hour at the grocery store for the last eight years.

"I don't know," he says, after a moment of thought. "A really nice car?"

"More."

"A house?"

"A little one," I say. "Yes."

"But don't you see how hair can be a house?"

"No," I say. "I can't."

"Hey Danny," he says.

"What."

"What's it like to be so successful, buddy? Remember how you and I used to be...kind of...on the same plane?"

"I need another lime. Get me another lime, please."

I don't get up to get more limes. Instead, I close my eyes, not able to believe what I'm about to do. He has tapped into my central guilt reservoir. There is a lot in there. I have done terrible things to several people. A lot to Phil, specifically, as tends to happen with old friends. A lot to other people, though. The difference is, most people don't know how to tap into guilt in order to manipulate me. Phil knows.

"Phil," I say. He looks over, bright-eyed. "Let's say, for the sake of argument, that the trilogy has recently been optioned for an astronomical amount of money, and that I can afford to lend you what you need. If it means happiness. For you." Look for my work in theatres in 2013, by the way. They won't let me make a cameo. Too stilted.

"Okay."

"Can you answer some questions for me? A few preliminary questions?"

"Yes."

"Why not a more traditional, less risky form of hair regrowth? Like the medication? Or Rogaine? Or even transplants? Or plugs? Where they put new follicles back up on the top?" I've been doing a little research. "The surgery has improved quite a bit in the last few years." In my research I read that Terry Bradshaw, Pittsburgh Steelers quarterback, had attempted plugs in the early-80s, but they had nearly killed him via pus. Pus got trapped in his scalp. Things have changed since then.

"Hair University offers complete and permanent regrowth. You go back to around seventeen, hairwise. That other stuff is nowhere near as reliable. This is gene therapy, we're talking about. This is not cosmetic stuff, Danny. This is the nuts and bolts. You know about all that stuff."

"Seventeen?"

"Seventeen years old," he says. "That's what I want to be."

I have never seen somebody so much in earnest. And to hear him say it like that, I realize that it's not very complicated. This is not about hair. Paco would appreciate how simple everything has become, and all just because I haven't let myself think about it too much. Phil has a wonderfully kind face, with round cheeks, and his soul is mangled. Time for his friend to step in.

He needs a roof.

We're talking about mortality.

We sit.

There are no mosquitoes around because of my citronella candles. Am I right now inside or outside the simulacra bubble? And what have I ever done that's really worth anything?

Since Hair University is on a small hidden corporate island nation in the Caribbean, Phil informs me that it will take a few days to solidify his travel plans. I have to drive over to Minneapolis to sit on a panel and to give a reading, so I get him to promise to have one more fish sandwich with me at Paco's before he leaves. The moron is so excited he can hardly breathe.

The conference is at a swank downtown hotel in Minneapolis called Le Meridien. My reading is typical; a couple of yells, a couple of crying babies, a couple of screeches in Affruld's special high voice which can disturb nearby gravitational fields. I read from a quiet chapter in the middle of the second book, one in which Affruld, who has just lost the love of two women, his mistress and his wife, contemplates throwing himself out of the airlock; he believes, irrationally, that all the pain will be unable to keep its grip on him as he floats away and suffocates—this is linked to his theories about God, space, and suffering. The crowd always wants me to go right to the Barrel Organ showdown, and to stop messing around with the pathos and the internal struggle bit, but I'm no pandering whore. As I'm reading, and I see the disappointment on their faces, I think: bear with me. I learned about pathos when I got my MFA.

Afterwards, during the reception, a grizzly, skinny old man ambles up to me with a smile on his face and pats me on the arm.

"Nice work," he says. "I like that chapter. It shouldn't have to be about the exciting stuff. Don't pay any attention to them."

"To who?" I ask.

"To that group making the catcalls. Or the fuckers who were hissing."

"I thought those people were doing Affruld's screeches. Like an homage."

"Well," says the man, nodding. "Don't pay any attention to them."

"I couldn't," I say. "I didn't know they were insulting me. Are you sure?"

"Good," he says. "Good. From one writer to another, though." He leans close. "You think maybe you should lay off the adjectives? The big words in general? These people don't care about that. They already think you're smart. You don't need to impress them like that."

"That's not always why writers use larger words," I say. "Sometimes you need an exact, perfect description."

He says nothing.

"I use too many?" I ask.

"Coxcombical and flagitious aren't crystal clear to most genre readers. Especially when you're describing a pair of pants."

"I was trying for something with the pacing," I say.

He nods amicably, pats again. "Don't take it the wrong way. I liked everything else about it. Good for you."

"You're a writer?" I ask. "Do you write science fiction?"

He holds out a hand. "Norman Kletz."

A big idiotic grin washes over my face. "Norman Kletz!" I say, pumping his hand up and down too hard. "I know your books! I own all of your books! Of course I know who you are!"

"I know you know who I am," he says. "Everyone does. I'm not being humble. I don't want these idiots to know it's me. I'm too famous for this convention."

He's right. Not only that, but he's a famous recluse. I've read maybe twenty of his books, and have never once seen a photo. All anyone knows about him is that he's a humanist and he likes to bowl.

"We're on the panel together tomorrow," he says, after I've released his hand. "Just so you know."

"The panel together!" I cry, taking his hand again. "The panel together!"

"Let go of me," he says. "Let go."

I apologize for my groveling, and Norman Kletz waves it off. "What are you working on now?" he asks.

"A short story," I say. "About aliens who don't know how to fly their own ship."

"Why can't they?"

"Too stupid."

Norman Kletz nods.

"You like the concept?"

Norman Kletz says, "Eh."

"I do it in a new way, though."

"Sounds great, kid."

Late that night, long after I've fallen asleep upstairs in my room, I get a call from Phil. He tells me that just before five o'clock, his brother was pulled into one of the paper-pressing machines at the plant, and was declared dead on site.

"Who?" I yell. "Which?"

"Sandy."

"Sandy!" I try to taste the word. I can't remember which one Sandy is. I am weeping.

"Calm down," he says flatly. "It's no big deal. They got him out and untangled him from the cogs and everything. But now no one's talking to me because I said I can't go to the funeral."

I catch my breath and wipe my nose.

"Why can't you go to the funeral?" I ask.

"Because I'm going to Hair University. You know that. You're paying."

I get out of the bed and pace, very calmly. I sit back down on the bed. I sip my water. "You can't go to Hair University," I tell him. "Your brother died. Do you understand the difference in degrees of importance?"

"No," he says, obviously angry. "No, I don't, Danny. That asshole tortured me growing up. Why am I supposed to go? Because I'm supposed to have loved him? Well, I didn't. I don't. I only loved my hair, Danny. And it left me. It divorced me. And now I'm going to get it back. And I'm not going to Greg's stupid funeral."

"Sandy's."

"To Sandy's stupid funeral."

"He's your dead brother."

"Do you have any idea how hard it was to make the travel arrangements? Do you have any idea how long I would have to wait if I backed out now? The shots! The visa alone—"

"I'll withdraw my financial support."

"The check already cleared, miser," he says. "They're waiting for me. I have to go."

We argue for about ten minutes, and in the end, I essentially tell him that he's psychotic and juvenile, and he says, "Juvenile! Yes! Ha! Affruld would know much better! Thanks for nothing, friend! Thanks for one more nice sting on my way to finally do something important!" And he hangs up on me. And it's the last time I ever speak to him.

And I don't fall back asleep.

Throughout most of the panel discussion, I am quiet. Usually I would be trailing after everything Norman Kletz says, trying to impress him with my autodidactic knowledge of astrophysics or my organic feeling for narrative, but I can't do anything but stare at the blank piece of white paper on the table in front of me and think about Sandy, whose face I can't even picture, getting sucked through a piece of machinery by his shirt, and subsequently losing all of his skin.

Norman Kletz, for a recluse, is extremely articulate and charismatic. He looks everybody in the eye and cracks jokes and takes pains to understand questions before he launches into their answers. He never talks for too long. He winks at people and knows everything.

There is only one question directed toward me, and when the woman begins asking, I smile and watch her, and nod as she speaks, and when she finishes speaking, I realize I have not heard a word she has said, distracted as I am by images of Phil, with hair, smiling down at his brother's dead body.

I ask her to repeat the question.

After she does, I say: "That depends on whether or not you, as an audience member, sympathize with the Dregtallers as a marginalized species. It's an important distinction. You have a choice. An aesthetic choice, if you will, but an important one nevertheless. If you will. This goes back to my earlier arguments about the audience participating with the aesthetic of the piece via a kind of…mental interplay. I've thought quite a lot about this issue and I'm prepared to speak at length. Are you ready for me?"

There is silence. The woman looks confused. I am suddenly unsure whether she asked about Dregtallers at all.

"I think what Danny is trying to say…" says Norman, and the muscles in my back relax, and I let him take over from there. I don't listen to what he says, either. I touch the paper. I imagine a whole roll on a big spindle, all of it red and brainy.

Whatever it is that he says, everyone loves it, and they clap, and the moderator comes out and calls it quits for the panel discussion.

And then when we're all walking off the stage, Norman Keltz trips and falls down the stairs.

My heart breaks while he falls; I hear it tinkle. It is the fall of an elderly man, nothing more than a muscle failing to respond with 100% correspondence to intention. He rolls, he hits his head. People gasp and scream.

I run around in circles down on the floor. Keeping people back. I am too afraid to actually look down at him, too afraid that he has died, too, but I can hear other members of the panel talking to him, and eventually I hear him weakly discussing the various pains he is experiencing.

An ambulance comes, and the conference is over. I don't talk to him again. All I've got, now, is the image of an old man falling, someone frail doing what it is that frail humans do, which is significant to this story simply because it is another one of the worst things I've seen. (The red paper, for example, but the worst is at the end.)

Human beings, you see, fall apart all the time. In many different ways. That is the central theme. There is no need to disguise it.

It takes me six hours to drive home. I have no idea what he broke.

★ ✪ ★

Phil, of course, has already left when I return, and the next day I stand amongst the hundreds gathered at Sandy Beloit's funeral. His wife and his two children stand beside the coffin as it is lowered into its hole. One of his sons is distracted by a bird in a tree. I catch a glimpse of Phil's father weeping into the arms of his wife. (Going on 90, amazing thickness.) I wonder whether or not Phil is over the aquamarine sea somewhere, perhaps riding a hovercraft, rapt with anticipation, a hero with his own living dream. I wonder whether he will end up with long blond hair, Fabio-like, or if he will concentrate on something more dense, something respectable. Something perfect.

After the service, at the reception, Phil's brother Georgie comes up to me and gives me a margarita.

"Sandy would have wanted you to have it," he says.

"Really?"

"We think so, yes."

"Thank you."

"So listen, Danny," he begins. He is packed inside of a suit too small for his large frame, and is obviously uncomfortable. He yanks at his tie and sips his own margarita as though the crushed ice will give him some relief from the pressure. "You're Phil's friend and everything. We were just wondering if you knew what was so important that he had to miss Sandy's big day here, so to speak."

"He didn't tell you?"

"Ah, no, no he didn't tell us. He just said that he didn't feel like coming."

"You know that he's left the country, don't you?" I ask. "For a dangerous hair procedure?"

"Dangerous hair procedure?"

I explain Hair University. I try to explain the Norwood Scale, but Georgie frowns through most of it. I mention the Hair Monster.

After I'm through, he says: "He went to stop balding?"

"Yes."

He only looks back at me, margarita suspended in the air between us. I start to talk. I don't know what I'm saying, really, but I talk about hair and roofs. His face sags more and more. I think that he's going to cry, but he doesn't. Instead he nods along as he listens, and I think: Go Danny, keep talking, just keep talking. People always listen when you talk. And he's not going to understand this, anyway.

Confused Aliens

I am delivering a speech on the bridge concerning happiness, duty, and morale. I can't quite put my snurf on it, but some of the crewmembers have looked a little apathetic lately, a little glassy-eyed—the speech is directed at them, yes, but I'll be honest here, I'm putting on the show to pump myself up, too. You know that thing about how if you smile enough, it makes you actually feel good? That's what I'm going for.

As everyone knows from previous episodes, I suffer from free-floating low-morale, and the last few weeks have been pretty dark, plenty of gloom-and-doom, bedroom-and-cookies-and-molting time. Pathetic. If I'm being really honest this could easily be the beginning of another full-blown breakdown for me, which would be just fantastic, just great timing, considering everything else that's going on with outer space and the universe right now, but as Admiral, you're not about to admit you're on thin psychological ice to a crew of disparate, idiot extraterrestrials who rely on you for everything. The mission to Belvetron IV demands more, demands the best that we can muster, not simply for morale, but for the future of the universe. (Theoretically.) Before us, the small yellow planet looms like a nugget; we are in position; the orbits are beneficial. The scanners have reported high population density and a technologically advanced race of intelligent, sensitive beings. They are not yet space-faring but we feel good about dropping in and saying hey. We ran the numbers. They're ready for us to come in as deities, at least. We've been chatting for about a week, sending down some feelers into their electromagnetics. We just now beamed their diplomat up. We are prepared to open a real dialogue, to greet this dignified civilization, to learn from its history, to welcome it into the greater intergalactic community. Maybe we'll do a little mining. We share in common our existence. As conscious beings we are linked by our loneliness and by our questions of **BLAH BLAH BLAH BLAH**.

What small comfort we have comes from knowing we are not alone.

I say this to the crew. I say these things in an interesting manner, with decent gravitas. Everyone is interested at least, and near the end I start to feel okay. And as I turn for a final flourish, sort of a sum-up-the-major-points kind of spin-move, my tail sweeps across the weapons console, and the computer whistles to inform us that I've accidentally just shot the big gun.

"Oh," Gleegluk says. "Okay."

"Whoops," I say.

We all watch the viewscreen as the cannons fire and the little yellow planet explodes into a million pieces.

"Whoopsy, Admiral," says Gleegluk, nodding gravely. "That's a whoopsy. There goes Belvetron IV."

My personal morale once again plummets. We are bad at what we do, and honestly, we don't know how to run the ship. We try, but usually we make mistakes like this. It's not because we're immoral or lazy. It's just because we get confused. We make mistakes. There are so many shiny buttons. You would never be able to guess what they all control (even though we try), and of course there is no instruction manual. We have many different body types, and I do not think this ship was designed with any of them in mind.

After everybody's calmed down and digested the deaths of seventeen billion conscious beings, Smellvamp asks, "What should we do now?"

"Well," I say. "We could use a new mission."

"What kind?"

He is gazing back in my direction like I know.

"We'll retreat, how about?" I say. It feels good, trying it on for size, and I nod. "Yeah. I order you to retreat."

Smellvamp looks at his control panel.

"Not sure how," he says.

"Press the green thing," I say. "Then pull that thing there."

He performs the two actions in reverse order and the computer announces that all of the emergency life capsules have been jettisoned. The viewscreen shows us several close-up shots of the small gray pills drifting off into empty space, their boosters glowing orange against the vast blackness and the starlight.

I leave the bridge. The mess hall is nearly empty, and as I snorfle my paste I blame myself.

SILLINESS

Pangea

Dr. G. and the other fine mental health care people have suggested
a journal—some might call it a log—others a letter (if we mail it to the
company I admit I like that idea)—something along those lines. It's helped
already. It's prompted me to make a choice, and you know what? Choice
happens to be the answer. I have it right off the bat. Dr. G., who is you
are lovely, gorgeous, talented, smarter than I am, I appreciate her beauty.
Your beauty, it's powerful, I feel as though me-being-in-love-with-her may
very well be one of her strongest therapeutic strategies, almost a form of
anesthesia, or even better, she is a soporific or mushroom, a sort of doping,
pleasurable undercurrent of Dr. G. eros with us in the room, the pull toward
beauty, the urge to become beautiful yourself when you're around it, like
an angel, say Gabriel is sitting in the corner but he's invisible, one of the
possible candidates to answer the burning question of whether not being
alive but staying alive is a smart choice, which I seem to ask too much...
questions...I've answered the central question of the journal exercise. The
question on the prescription pad note she gave me (I thought that was cute
to hand it to me like it would be a prescription for Xanax but it turned out
to be an assignment, cute not sexy, an index I think she is also continuously
calculating during our sessions, but one problem is this came from *What
About Bob?*, didn't it?) is: WHAT DO YOU LOVE AND WHY, JERRY? That's all she
wrote on the paper. WHAT DO YOU LOVE AND WHY, JERRY? I have never known
where I'm going, most people just go forward and don't, that's okay you
say. WHAT DO YOU LOVE AND WHY, JERRY? I feel proud, a real, authentic,
embarrassing swell of super pride, about the skill of being normal, developed
for so long, right, but no, I actually mean something specific: I mean life, my

job, my family, mortgage, etc. I smoked cigarettes in 1976 for three months but quit because I realized they were not for me. Is that the information you want? Now? Afterwards? There was no question on any form that could have solicited the answer. You say it, I respond to it, yes, that way: In daily life I commute, I drive, I honk, beep, get angry in the morning, probably that's caffeine addiction because it goes away eventually, I have trouble properly organizing and arranging closets and keeping them organized if I do, by some miracle, gather the energy required on a Saturday afternoon and go to the store and buy the basket/organizer units and put them all together and put all the shoes in the bottom, hats in the middle. My shoe size is 10. Cats? I like you. Chesterfield, ours, I believe I truly do love him in the same way I love my wife. Yes. That's the same human heart. If you are a romantic it is. If you are me, it's not. Think mundane-man thoughts most of the time but then I can be casually strolling down the street, on my way back to the office—this happens to all of us, I know, but I feel it's important to draw attention to how I notice, I think that characterizes me better than other details—and this stroll is downtown Chicago, say I've been eating at The Berghoff, eating a hamburger in a crowded room full of people like me, suit-types, businessmen, neither successful or unsuccessful people, the middle unexceptional mass, just letting the bacon cheeseburger slop down all over my face, crazy, my napkin, grease and ketchup exploding, probably on my shirt, sitting at the bar because I go to lunch on my own, always, and now I'm walking back after this unholy gluttonous orgy of consumption as though nothing has happened, or I did not leave a part of myself back there, can still taste the luxurious grease, still dream of dying with bacon melting in my mouth, hot bacon, just finished, still dripping, salty, there is no other taste like that, I not only have what is clearly a unique thought that is indisputably my own and therefore something I should be proud of, proud of as a thoughtful and introspective human being, I mean, an example of how I'm special now and then, in my way, it's not vanity, nor is it the most important thing, it's just what we all are, I can even stay with it long enough to get back to my desk and feel happy about it for a few minutes, cross my feet, think more, say, Hey Jerry, okay, there's a little insight, once in a while the clouds part and I catch a glimpse. Yes it all fell apart that night. For all of us the lightning bolt strikes. I believe that. I've always liked that. So things like: here's life in our time, everyone (I am thinking this as I walk down the street with the hamburger grease on my face): do you know the sense of wandering? It's astounding to me that I can walk, bleary-eyed morning-man in pajamas with hair sticking up, erection, the upstairs carpeted-hall first, then climb down the stairs, wander to the kitchen, make the coffee, pour pour, shake shake, and yet here we are, Dr., wanderers, crestfallen nomadic creatures who've sprung from nothing but the wet lush mitochondrial muck in a thunderstorm, give it a lightning strike for good measure because maybe that's how it happened, and zip, zip, zap, magic, the supernatural, wonder, we're on multiple, interlacing, simultaneous complex metaphysical paths just as thinking beings with freedom must necessarily be—read a book about consciousness sometime, okay? The many of our outside lives combined with the many of our inside lives form a net or a tangle, crisscrossing swath, yes it has meaning, it's premised on amazement, however it's bungled, however you hold the key, however it's chronically misplaced—and astride or within or on top of or whatever these deep routes we get stuck, we get trapped, we get chained, right, and we're stricken by...they are ours. Each one of these paths, routes, strings, secret lives (apologies, metaphors, but this is real, here, this isn't refined, you overestimate me) is absolutely ours. A little exciting, a little liberating...yes. Or: proprietary, banal.

That's the idea I like, that's the story of the bacon grease. And who else can say that? My wife? No. My son? No. But yes, too. It happens to them because they're like me, like you, the people. To pandas? I saw a miraculous and awesome picture of a panda cub. It looked like a Fraggle and then I thought, Ah, no, Jerry, Fraggi look like panda cubs, you have it flipped. Do they walk simultaneous paths and have tangled nets? Either Fraggi or pandas? No. So we are doomed. Now there's a worthwhile question. WHAT DO YOU LOVE AND WHY, JERRY? WHAT DO YOU LOVE AND WHY, JERRY? BESIDES ME, AND MY UNBELIEVABLE YOUTH AND BEAUTY, WHICH YOU SHALL NOT HAVE? My answer is the burning moment of choice that is our only inheritance as conscious beings. Does this mean I can quit now? Smiles all around, from me to you.

I've given one superficial answer and the point is the exploration, I get that, I agree with that, I'm not this oppositional, a defensive patient who thinks he knows better than science and expertise, in fact I've always been beholden to expertise, probably always believed in my secular, well-organized-for-supply-side-economics beliefs too strongly, too adamantly been the science promoter at cocktail parties who himself has no real understanding of even the basics of science, Hey listen to this thing I read about quantum physics, so interesting, too often grinned and shook my head at the barbarism of those who expressed slight skepticism as to the findings of this or that study which, it would no doubt turn out after a little investigation, was funded by whatever interest it endorses. I'm with you, my healers, science is both true and false and as a truth-gathering device perhaps no more accurate than Shelley drunk and screaming in a tavern on a good night, talking about oceans or something, normal nineteenth-century bourgeoisie upset and disturbed by the volume of his rant, I love the thought of him there, scaring people kind of badly—short, ecstatic, drunk, aware, but you're not him, you're science, it's okay, I believe you're at work to make me better and "bring back my heart," get the suit on me, get the case in my hand, get me up out of this very dangerous psychological state I seem to have dropped into, tee hee, get the lover of competitive sports operating properly once more. When was the last time Tom had someone to play catch with? I should have built a robot for my son before I lost my mind. It could have resembled me and done most of what I used to do. I'm working in tandem with you to solve my problems. Not one of these difficult ones who screams.

Open it. (Of course none of you have problems, nor could you ever, ever descend to where I'm floating, we accept that premise.) But here's a sure thought, if we are at the very least trying to snatch up certainty by using this exercise: I'm not going to be "getting better," which is a problem, it will frustrate the insurance companies along the way, not to mention my wife, so maybe we should not after all submit this as evidence to the company, because clearly I am keenly aware of the stakes, and this undermines psychosis, so far as I understand it, but the ways in which our world is meticulously organized to hurt the weak, to crush them after being crushed already, like the second time you step on a spider even though you're certain it's dead just because you hate it so much and hate the idea of it making a miraculous recovery, because then it could crawl on your face while you are napping, you stomp down harder the second time, you twist your ankle a little bit to rip it apart more and be sure, you grit your teeth, and also the way we are organized to take from the gullible because it's statistically advantageous, to entice all those who don't know any better, and because I am keenly aware of the stakes or I have a feeling someone, somewhere, will try to use that against me, so therefore no. I want what I can get. I like robbing, cheating. It—the thing, the incident, the stimulus, the vision, the event, the lightning—happened, I changed, my mind changed tremendously in a second, and I have never been one to believe in these moments that change people. I don't believe in epiphanies. So there, you arrogant mothers! Did I have one? Unclear. I saw all the continents sliding apart. It's physical. You know! Brain cells moved and twisted around. I'm the skeptic yet I've had what they call a mystical spiritual event and I don't believe in them. Where does that put me? Crazy. Or them? Or you? I mentioned choice. A choice. One that made me happy about the writing so far. The choice is I don't want dates as in our record of time. For me. I won't try to force that idea on the world. The airlines would be in trouble. It sounds trite and twee. It sounds like a choice about the font. Formatting... design...pop-out planets...what colored paper...but it means more, which I'm sure you'll see if you reflect for just a moment. I don't want to sully the things I decide to write by locating them in our baby-human-sphere or on the plane (as in slice or layer or strata, not flying machine) that claims we control the universe, human beings trying to place themselves, over and over, on the map that is no map or on the diagram that looks strong but which has been initially sketched on a blank piece of paper that is no longer there. Remember our crestfallen nomadic wandering ancestors. That was also their situation as they spread out away from Africa, their hearts laden, walking billowing weeping sadness, each one walking east up through Asia like he or she were Frodo when he has that ring around his neck and it's become heavy, not to mention a goblin and servant constantly adding stress to the situation. I feel so sad for those people. My god! Let's put our cards on the table here and admit that all that's happened to me is that I've done it, I've admitted it, while most don't: we don't know and we die. Wagner says yearn then die. Is it true? I walked out of that opera feeling Wagner was a child. But what does that mean? We don't know and we die, we are here, rodents at best, we are asked to go forward, go down the road, be civil, find the right endpoint, be good, be all right, be calm, have skills, be alone, love some, die, nurse our mothers and fathers at death, stare at the toys of our mind—limited powers of perception, analysis, comprehension, imagination, flawed memory, susceptibility to toxicity, and (my favorite, somehow the most tragic, pathetic, embarrassing, real) susceptibility to skull injuries—go out, do your work, get through it, do a day, do another, we call that a week, a month, try to stay safe, just go do it, yes you'll age, we don't understand that, accept it, don't let that stand in your way, you have places you will go, you have happiness to achieve, you have friends who will drink a beer or two with you, we can all go bowling every month, you have humanity to consider, you have primaries you have to vote at because your opinion gets used to decide important policy measures by proxy vis-à-vis the individual you elect, you have dignity to uphold and explore and trade away, sex to have, go do it, go down the road feeling bad, about which there is a song. We're asked to do all these things. What are we told? Nothing.

    I hate that.

I'd like to say the previous entry was inspired by grapefruit juice. My glass is here at my side. Me, my glass, my glasses, a table, a notebook, a pen. Here we all are. Reading the entry, I'm for the first time (in my life, I mean, with regards to any record of me, in any medium, ever) feeling this feeling that yes, pretty close, I do feel that way. Still. Days later. For once it is not a shifting, disgusting mountain of unidentified emotion burbling below the layer of trash that floats atop my consciousness and serves as my "personality"; for once it feels whole. Cohesive, firm, strong, permanent, alive, raw, honest.

It's okay. It's an okay feeling. Does this mean I'm actualized? Or dead? Jane came to see me. Prompting this entry. Yesterday, she was here. She cried. I didn't. Consoled her. It's amazing; it would be impossible to tell which one of us was the psycho, given a photo. Minus my mustache. You have to be insane to have a mustache in this day and age. I should have known—I should have known some storm was brewing within me the day I shaved the beard and left the mustache. I had a vision, life called, I decided to act. Closed my eyes and saw a sort of glorious me, Tremendous Jerry, shirtless, no chest hair, probably forty pounds lighter, muscles, all of that, standing I think on top of a mountain or a cliff with a flag? With the wind blowing? Hair waving? One leg up on a boulder, knee up? Very close look and you can see on the waving flag that the flag has a red background and then an image of me standing on a cliff holding a flag. And I had a mustache in this, and in the little one. (You're wondering if the flags and the images within them went on forever, smaller and smaller? Don't know.) Just one of those visions, this whole thing was, but now that I reflect I see too that it was a precursor to the big one, but then it felt more like a daydream. No biggie. I opened my eyes and there I was in the mirror, and a wonderful feeling of power came over me, this sense that I could truly go to that mountain. I have no interest in it but they say *Finnegans Wake* has a sleeping giant and this is a tremendous metaphor for humanity, they say we haven't even woken up yet. All this sadness and we haven't even woken up. Imagine that. Imagine, say, being an amiable young lad walking through a field in the easternmost regions of Europe sometime in the thirteenth century and looking up and a Mongol with a ten foot pike comes around the corner on horseback, screaming, he goes, "Ha!," and he drives his huge pole right through your heart, all the way, and you go down to your knees right there as the rest of the army sweeps up toward your home, and your last thought can be about how they will definitely be raping your wife and sisters and mother and killing them all or maybe even enslaving them? Imagine that young man also finding out, later, like when he's on the spaceship loading dock waiting in line, that he existed in an era that would be looked back upon as prehistory, and that **real** human life wouldn't begin for another two or three thousand years? That would be an annoying thing to find out. I feel that way too! What is the death of a child? I could use Jane's Nair on my testicles. I don't know. I could maybe get all the way to that vision and make it be and I'll tell you what, it would be a significant thing. It's the principle of this I'm concerned with, not the actual vision and the mustache, the principle of formation in the mind then moving forward and doing, being, it becoming something you have done. That was two weeks before I saw what I saw on the street. Another one of those walks back to the office. But it makes…it makes no sense, if that's the case, because I already had the mustache, and if the mustache was evidence of approaching mental problems, how could it have been that I saw what I saw after I went with the mustache? Should be opposite? They say what completely did in Nietzsche was seeing a horse beaten to death with a whip. I found this to be interesting because this is the thing Raskolnikov dreams about in *Crime and Punishment*, but then I looked up the dates one evening and Nietzsche saw his horse two decades after Dostoevsky wrote *Crime and Punishment* which means the art predicted the demise of the philosopher somehow. But how could that be? You, Dr. G., would probably say that Nietzsche read the book and was moved by the image, remembered it, and as it was probably a common thing to see a horse beaten to death in the streets back then, he saw it during a period of instability, later, recalled the moment of reading the book, and it all came together like the lightning bolts we've discussed, and he went nutso. That would be a reasonable explanation.

I don't talk to Jane about things like this. I don't dare. Almost any word that comes out of my mouth makes her cry. I can say, "Hello, Jane," and she'll crumple as though I've hit her on the top of the head with a ball-peen hammer. You'll see the energy and life go right out of her, she'll fade out. Yesterday I was even wearing normal clothes. In the picture—the picture of us, talking, the one you could look at and not, except for the mustache, be able to identify the psychopath—the picture would be from the side— you'd see the flat surface of the table, you'd see my right arm and her left arm resting on it. This is tremendously sad to me. This photo—and in fact any photo of any human being smiling, ever—absolutely unbearable. We have no reason to smile, ever, and to see a photo of people smiling is to see a photo of people confused. Terrible sadness! Imagine if we were in a movie. Imagine if this was an important scene. Jane's got her face in her hand, holding it, and I'm reaching across the table, comforting her. Take one guess what we have been discussing. No. No. No. No. No. Yes, that. Also, electroshock therapy. There's one person here for it and one person here against it. I say, "But I'm not sick," and she says, "Jerry, you are. How do you know? If I tell you an important symptom of your sickness is that you can't tell that you're sick, what do you say to that?" "I say that's a good way to manipulate somebody," and her response is to ask, "Well, do you trust me?" and I say, "Yes," and she says, "So when someone you love is telling you that you've lost sight of reason, but there's a way to regain it, how can you possibly say no to that person, Jerry?" and I tell her, "Look. I can't. I'll do it. For you. At the very least, it will help with insurance. But put this down for the record, because who knows what I'll say afterwards: I'm not sick at all. It's obvious to me that I'm not. Because look, Jane: I can say the same thing back to you and there's no reason we should believe you over me other than the general agreement of everyone else in the world that I actually am crazy." "I think that's a significant difference," Jane says. "You would think," I say to her, "but they're not right, I don't think. I think I'm right. But I'll let them electrocute me if it makes you happy." "It doesn't make me happy." "Has humanity ever seemed more foolish to you?" "What?" "When it comes to a treatment?" "What do you mean?" (She's crying.) "It's trial and error," I say. "It's like watching Tom trying to put his blocks through the holes when he was a baby. The different shapes? That's what sending electricity into someone's brain, hoping it will sort itself out, is equivalent to." "They say it's effective, Jerry. I wouldn't—" "I'm not being fair," I say (warm tones). "I'm sorry. I'll do it. And you're right, I know, they do say it works." "Please stop talking about Tommy when you're looking for examples." "Why would I stop talking about him?" "Don't, Jerry." "Don't stop or stop?" "Please." "I'll do it," I say. "Okay. I'll do it. Please don't cry." Do you know what I am thinking about throughout most of this conversation? Fucking her. Fucking my beloved wife in an insane asylum. We could, I think; it's not as though I'm handcuffed to the wall in a straitjacket here. I have my own bedroom. I don't think it would be a problem. Jane loves me and thinks it would be a good idea to do some electroshock therapy, so we'll do it. Let's do it tomorrow. I am agreeing to do it tomorrow. I will sleep like a baby. I am in bed already, in my PJs. This could become a story of redemption but I don't think so, and either way, the journal can't continue, Drs. For one thing, Dr. G., I've admitted I love you, which makes this a document I will pretend emerges from my "temporary" episode no matter what, but also Jerry is simply not the type to write in a journal, as though he thinks his own or anyone else's innermost thoughts, coherent or otherwise, need to be recorded. I would like to die with one strip of bacon in my pocket. Have you not been listening? Because for who? For the record, the thoughts and feelings do not die or go away once they are articulated, guys, smart guys, so there goes that whole idea, and if we throw that out we may as well just dump all of it. At what other time would I have the confidence to make such an assertion? I feel godlike today and I'll be sad to see it go. The day, the state. I'm tired of writing. Dr. G., it was a good assignment and a good thought and I'd like you to laminate these pages and place them on your wall. All of them. I will stop by around Thanksgiving to check. The moment on the street had no horses being beaten, as we no longer live in those times, and in fact there was no haiku sensory moment that brought it on, no little cookie, just the bacon juice slathered on my face and the bright sun and the blue sky and suddenly my whole sense of time just dropped out of me. I smelled hot dogs, then. They'll laminate anything at my office. They have a woman and it's her only job. She has an office, a desk, a big-time laminator, and the will to do it. You stop in there with anything. She'll laminate three-dimensional objects. So I'm on the street and I stopped walking and I saw them: I saw the people, the nomads, walking, moving, migrating. That's who I saw. Us. Chicago fell away and with it went the buildings and the Loop and the people and I could see them, I was on Pangea or whatever it was, actually no, I think Pangea was long before because they used the ice to get across the water, didn't they? And feel it: the continents breaking apart and shaking the ancient spectral dust of our Earth. See it, even: from above, those shapes we know and were taught, and they slide. They slide. Interlocking parts. A big puzzle. The times are mixed but that doesn't matter; they were with the beaten horse as well and my whole sense had dropped out. I feel it. I can feel it right now. It was Pangea, the land was all together. And I stood very still and watched those lonely people walking. They said: We must keep moving, Jerry, at least, to see what else is out there. I said: Why? They said: We're just going, we're just doing it. Do you understand? What else can we do? I said: I loved them for this choice, I did. I love you, everyone. (I'm standing there, arms up, yelling it at them as they go by.) Nothing to do but walk, so walk. The land was still together, they were heading out, moving on, and I loved them for this choice. There's your answer. Take it. That's all I've got.

The Abacus

I knew when I woke. The eyes on that day. Different. The way I've always felt it, it's like a mood, but no, nothing so crass as anger.

Sometimes you are involved with the questions of accounting and I do not know why, but I am one of the accountants—I have been chosen as one of the accountants and I am certain there are others, but I have never thought to seek those others out, as I believe they are hidden and supposed to be hidden and that is fine.

I am an accountant.

A day begins and finally some quotient most are not privy to has leaned too far and I am sent out to do the computations. What can't matter is who. And I am not one of those who seeks out my types and in truth I get no pleasure from it, so far as I can tell. I get pleasure from the normal things. Like cake.

But do you know? Today I am standing on the corner, I am in the Loop,
it is a day of the week, I don't know which, but I am just watching.

I have my coffee and my place of work is not far and they think I am at the dentist. And do you know?

It dawns on me that today, unlike the other days,
I will be captured.

Sad.

A great melancholy dawns on me at the thought, but it doesn't last.
Not too long. This is not my choice.

Calm comes. I am on this street. I am here, now, at this moment.
But do you know?

There are people—there are so many people. Just crossing. Just passing to and fro. They are animals. As am I. Chicago is the zoo. This city. But I know better.

There is something about imagination, too.

There is danger to what can be imagined, which is me.

I am the abacus. The bead slid. And I see my bead.

A young man.

I start to walk.

I follow him and watch his backpack.

Why not?

It will be my X.

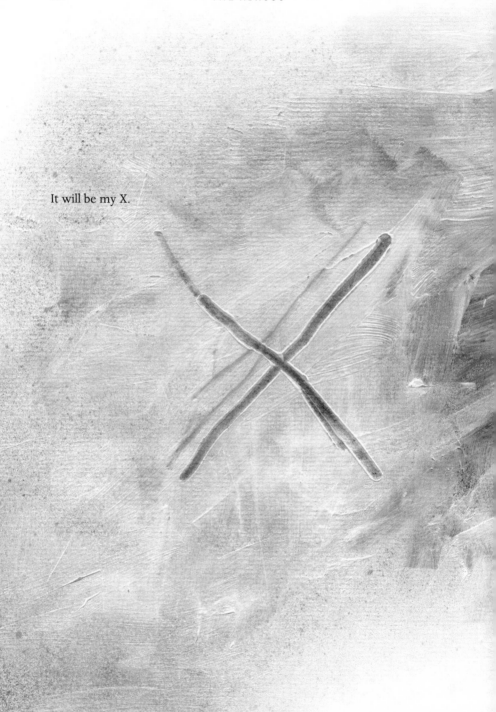

People Like Me

I've broken the house into quadrants and I've drawn these quadrants on poster board and I've taped this poster board to the kitchen wall. There are different colors.

The first two weeks were all basement. I went down and cleaned out the boxes and burned the cardboard in the backyard. I got down on my knees and scrubbed the concrete. I scrubbed every cobwebbed, grimy corner. I cleaned the exposed pipe in the ceiling. I laid carpet. I pulled the washer and dryer away from the wall and got all that crap underneath. I tilted the machines on their sides and cleaned them, too.

When the doorbell rings I am standing in front of the blender. I am wondering whether I should take it apart and scrub its parts. Within a blender there will most likely be difficult-to-manage and very small pieces of metal. I have steel wool, I have my cleaning agents. Lime-based. Do I need tweezers? The house is sparkling, but what about the inside of objects? You could do surgery on the kitchen table. But could you do surgery inside of the washing machine?

Lanie's at her brother's. She wants me to go to Anger Management. Either that or we're done, she said, and I asked her if she honestly thought me talking to some people in a high school gymnasium about, oh, I don't know, bayoneting (in the face) the man who jumped on me from the roof of a bungalow in Hyderabad was really going to make the difference. Will that unburden me? I asked. She said Yes, it might help. You'd be surprised. At least it's something. I said: You realize that is not a hypothetical example, that's me drawing from an actual well of actual examples, and the well is full of them, and she said Yes, I do realize that, Aaron. That is the problem.

But I go on.

The bell rings, I stand in silence, I look at the rectangular buttons, I think, I go to the door. There are two men. One I know, one I don't. The man I know is named Wesley Chambers. He's my direct supervisor for my final two jobs at ICS. He's softer-looking than he actually is. I once saw Wes kick an Indonesian kid in the teeth so hard his neck clearly broke. Crack-crack!

Right now, Wes looks like a well-to-do, manicured lawyer in his civilian clothes. About ten years younger than me, he has a boyish face and an expensive-looking haircut. He's wearing a black peacoat and underneath I can see a collared shirt and tie. He's holding a bouquet of very, very ugly flowers.

The other guy I don't know.

"Wes," I say, nodding, holding on to the side of the door. "Other person," I say to the other man. "What can I do for you gentlemen?"

I look at the flowers.

"Or how can I help those?"

"What's up, man?" Wes says, eyes wide, hyperactive. Somewhat menacing, but in a nice way.

"You're at my house," I say.

"In the neighborhood," he says.

"No you weren't."

"Thought we'd give it one more try."

"I see."

"This is Norman." Wes jerks a thumb at his buddy, then looks past me, into the house. "Lanie home? Can you talk?"

"She's not home," I say.

I have never once mentioned Lanie to him, but it's not a surprise that he's saying her name like they're friends.

"You wanna invite us in?" he says. "It's colder than cold. I know it gets cold in this city but this is the mega for a dude from California. Hahaha. Right? Haha."

He really talks like that.

"Come in," I say, and step back. "Take your shoes off."

They don't complain. Wes says, "Haha." I find a vase for the flowers as they take them off, then they follow me into the kitchen. As I cut the stems on the butcher block I ask them if they'd like something to drink. I suggest various lethal chemicals.

Wes, still bright-eyed, says, "I actually don't drink." He smiles and points. "You didn't know that about me, buddy?"

"I didn't," I say. I look at the other guy. "You?" I ask.

"I like lemonade."

"I don't have any lemonade."

"No thanks, then," he says. "Nothing."

I get a beer for myself and I sit down.

"How's the time off been?" Wes asks.

"What do you want?" I ask.

"What do you think I want?"

"Do you think I went through all of that just so I can come back?"

"No," he says. "I don't. But this happens, you know? I was talking to Chuck"—Chuck's the founder—"and I was telling him about you. He knows about you, Aaron. You know that? That he's personally been through your files?"

"No."

"I told him what you said and how you were done, all of that," Wes says. "But I was telling him about how good you are. I told him about that village. The way you set fires, in general? Dude. Talent. You have talent, is what I told him. Inborn. I told him we needed you for a lot more things."

"You don't."

"We want you to consider a different position."

I look at this other guy Wes has with him. Something is wrong. Unlike Wes, he looks like a soldier. His face is a rectangle, he's got no neck (a very small leathery one, but almost none), and he's got a scar on his forehead. He doesn't look like a frat-boy, like Wes. He looks more like a gladiator you might run into in a cage underneath the Coliseum. The kind of man who could eat you if you ended up in a life raft together for over ten days.

"Did you bring Norman to romance me?" I ask, because the way this other guy is staring is doing a number on me. My armpit-hair has begun to collect cold droplets of sweat.

"No," Wes says.

"What?" I say. "What, then?"

"Aaron," Wes says. "Look. We have four new contracts. Shit you wouldn't believe. Two in Europe. I don't know if you've been reading anything in the papers lately but ignore it if you have. They're saying one thing and throwing more money at us at the same time. New president? Doesn't fucking matter. All the same." The papers say ICS is in trouble—at least it appears to be. Congress is upset about what they are, what they do, where they've been. The Katrina things. Just a little while ago some journalist found out about their submarines. They'll figure out the field-nukes eventually. Long story short, there's been some public outrage, it's true, even though I haven't been paying much attention and I doubt it will come to anything. People want ICS to exist and don't want to know it's there. People prefer it to be private. Besides, none of my problems with ICS have to do with what people think of it. My problems have to do with what you end up thinking once you work for them. I am therefore the embodiment of my own problem.

"Come back. Three days. One job. Eighty-grand. That's it. Then you can decide again." He turns both palms up. "It'll be like restarting the computer."

I stand up. "Don't come to my house anymore, okay Wes? Your metaphors suck. Also, I don't have a computer." Lanie took it with her.

Wes looks disappointed. He is mercurial and dangerous and can make his face appear to be whatever he wants it to be. He's a chimera. I'm sure he'll therefore be successful once he quits, too. He'll be a lawyer or a businessman, whatever. And I do think he'll quit one of these days. It will get him. It probably already has. There are basically three types who work at ICS: Meatbrains, Pros, and Whiners. Meatbrains like to blow shit up, kill people now and then, and have a good reason to use steroids. Pros don't give a shit one way or the other. They're like robots. They do the work, they get paid, they do more work, they get paid, etcetera. They are likely to be old and have fought in places like Granada. And third, people like me. Whiners. Whiners are the dumbest. We hate ourselves and love it all at the same time. We crack jokes and cry in the woods by ourselves when no one is watching. We're the ones all the movies are about. The humans. Foolishness. For a while I thought Wes was just a Pro, but looking at this face, this look of disappointment at my prickliness, practiced and convincing and totally natural here in my kitchen, I think to myself no, closet-Whiner. Pros can't even fake emotions, which is probably to their credit. Pros don't really understand what emotions are, or what they're for. To Pros, emotions are like spleens.

"All right," Wes says finally. "But we'll be around for a couple of days. Call me if you change your mind."

He stands up, his friend stands up, and magically, we're a circle of jackasses standing around a table.

"Should we kiss?" I say.

"Two days," Wes says. "We'll be here for two days."

"Just hangin' around?" I say. "Not a lot goin' on?"

"We have business."

"Right."

"Where's Lanie?" Wes asks. He's not smiling or chipper now.

"Out," I say.

"Mm."

"Justin?"

"Out."

"Mm."

He nods to himself, looking across the room at the flowers he brought.

"Make sure she gets those," he says, pointing. "Those are money flowers."

"Money flowers?"

"It means fantastic."

He turns and leaves the kitchen like he's walking out of my office.

I follow them, watching the back of Wes's black jacket as he takes his slow steps. I look at his black socks. The other guy's got big gray wool ones. Just what a Pro would wear. Wes slips his shoes on standing up, but the other guy has to sit down to pull on his boots. I find it oddly satisfying, watching this badass mercenary robowarrior dude down there on his ass.

Wes puts his hand on the doorknob. I put my hands in my pockets. The other guy stands up.

"You know what, Aaron?" Wes says.

"What?"

"It's really, really clean in here."

A couple of times since she left I've gone out by myself to whine in a lonesome, sorrowful manner, and I like how the snow looks now. After a few minutes I find my boots and my coat and lock up and start walking down the street. The sky's yellow, the flakes are coming down. There's a dive bar maybe twenty minutes away, but not long into the walk I start thinking I'm hungry, not thirsty, not really interested in sitting in front of a bottle and staring up at a TV screen for an hour, so I go a different way, crunching along down the sidewalk, hands in my pockets. What I would very much like to have is sushi, I don't know why, as I'm not a sushi person. I'm all turned around because of Wes and his buddy. Eighty-grand is a good year's salary, not a weekend. Some of the adrenaline is lingering in my stomach. Eighty-grand is a cabin in Wisconsin. Or another year or two of not working if I save, if I'm smart. Shit, man: all of college for Justin. His buddy, I am now starting to worry, was from IIS, the intelligence wing. If that's so then I might as well shoot myself now. I concentrate on the cabin.

There's a place called Tamaraki. It might not be called that—it's called something like that. I've been to it twice with Lanie. It's a little unusual for me to be showing up on my own, it seems, but there's something to the idea of sitting at that well-lit, clean wooden bar, by myself, with all the chefs cutting up the fish, that grabs me.

Then, during this brief fantasy, I catch myself. I don't care about sushi. I am experiencing instinctual counterintelligence. I'm outsmarting myself on purpose in order to be unpredictable. It makes me even more angry—it's so unlike me to go to Tamaraki that it's what I want to do because no one would think to look for me there, and what's more, some part of my brain thinks it's a wise idea to keep the reasons secret from myself. I'm brainwashed.

Inside, I wipe the snow from my shoulders and I can see the warmth of the place melting the flakes at the same time. I become transfixed, watching them. My cheeks go red. It smells clean and salty—there are bright lights, just as I'd hoped, and many colors and many people spread across the big, open dining room. There's a hum of conversation. I think I hear ancient flutes. A few diners from their meals turn to look at me and I do my best to look like some guy coming in from the snow.

"Can I get you something?" the bartender asks.

"What's the Japanese beer called, again? The famous one?"

"Sapporo?"

"Yes," I say. "That."

"I'll get you one," he says, smiling.

"That would be great of you," I say, "since you're the bartender." But who is it that says such hostile things? Me, nexus of anger.

He doesn't move.

"Big one or small one?" he asks.

"I don't understand what that means."

"We have big bottles and small bottles. There are two sizes."

"Why?"

"Why?"

"Why."

"It's just how they come."

"How big is big?"

"I think they're twenty-two ounces."

"I want one big bottle of Sapporo," I say.

He has remained chipper through this, to his credit. Bartenders—even bartenders at sushi restaurants—tend to handle my need for confrontation better than most. Assholes, I think. It's because they're so used to serving assholes. He nods and turns away.

I look to my right. There's a woman at the bar by herself, looking at me. She looks like she's 40, maybe just done with work, judging by her outfit. Quick dinner alone. She lives a long ways from beautiful and somewhere in the suburbs of ugly.

"You remind me," she says, "exactly," she says, "of someone I know."

"I'm sorry," I say.

I get the feeling she wants to talk to me, no matter what. She is smiling. I'm not good in situations like this, but tonight, I want to talk to people. I truly do. It probably won't work, but I do. When it comes to strangers, I'm like a golem trying to handle puppies. I have incredible strength in my hands and forearms and tend to accidentally crush their internal organs while trying to pet them. Then I walk around crying with their little bodies in my arms, lamenting the classical ironies. Yet now, it feels as though a better, deeper part of myself is urging me forward. Just talk. Just let words go into their heads and let theirs come into yours, Aaron, it's simple, just note it. Not all of me is self-destructive. Part of me is trying to save me. Part of me likes me. If you sit in your house all day imagining all the ways you're not in the right kingdom anymore, maybe, instead of staring at the wall, you should talk to people and go back into the right kingdom? There are such things as gates and underground passageways, aren't there? Have new routes vanished in my absence? What is the secret word? Or is the central gate still open? I have no idea.

"I have no idea," I say.

"In terms of sushi?"

She helps me with the menu and suggests a few things to order, and I order, and we talk about all the problems with the CTA and then also discuss clouds. Her name is Katherine or probably Karen. She's a mother but divorced. She's a lawyer. She asks me what I do and I tell her security guard instead of International Conflict Solutions Consultant or murderer. We move on and talk about various types of fish you can eat. We discuss salmon for eons. She says she likes coming here because she can smoke and no one seems to give her the stink eye. When she says that the bartender

comes by and tells us that all Japanese men like to smoke. Categorically.
He says that sometimes there's a convention in town and the whole place
is full of Japanese men eating pounds and pounds of sushi, drinking sake,
and smoking. They have to be smoking, even as they slide rolls into their
mouths. I look around after he says it. There are maybe a dozen suburban
white people in here and no Japanese people at all. When I look back he
says, "We usually have at least one."

I drink quite a lot. This Katarina person then tells me that her husband
used to be a big boat-guy, a real boat-captain, and that it turned out the boat
was an excuse to cheat on her. He did sincerely love boating, she says, but
it was also an excuse. She makes it a point to note the ambiguity, which, in
a moment of clarity, I find endearing. She tells me that, in a way, she always
knew. She tells me about a dream she had about her husband asking her if
it was okay for the boat to sleep with them in the bed. That was one piece
of evidence. She tells me about another dream where she was water-skiing
behind the boat and it suddenly evacuated its bowels and she water-skied
directly into an enormous, floating boat-turd. I eat so much and become
so drunk and so full of fish that I myself stop being able to either speak
or understand what she's saying. I'm not sure if she even eats—it seems
impossible. She is the kind of person who maybe notices her monopoly
on the conversation but keeps talking anyway—not because she talks too
much, but because she wants to make sure there's always a line from one
person to the other. Underground passageways. Above-ground? Like if she
went mute for a second, both of our brains could and probably would seize
up. I can imagine some other moment with her—more intimate, less manic,
just the two of us, and actually in a different dimension where I'm not
married to Lanie—when I am the one talking and she is the one listening.

About twenty minutes after I've paid she says, "Well," and smiles. "This
has been so nice. Aaron, right?"

I nod. I come close to telling her that I'm prone to seeing skeletons
when I stare at people too long. I hold back. Obviously, though, I feel safe.

She says, "Can we—would you like to go out some time? For dinner?"

She blushes, rolls her eyes at herself. The way she says it—the way she smiles, maybe—I can see that she is a deeply kind, thoughtful person. I don't know how I can tell, exactly, but it's a wonderful vision—she actually is definitively kind. There can be no doubt. Not only that, but I can perceive it. I can see that she is somehow afraid, now, as she looks for the right words, that she will either hurt me or hurt herself by asking a strange man on a date.

I put both hands on the bar. "I think that I should—"

"Yes, no," she says. "Of course."

"It's not that, Karla," I say. "I'm married."

"Oh!" she says, honestly surprised. She squints at my hand. "Where's your ring?"

"It's being cleaned."

She laughs at that, like I'm telling her something secret about marriage, but actually, my ring really is at this moment sitting in a jar of hydrochloric acid out in the garage.

"I had a good time, too," she says. I don't really get it, but we hug.

On the walk home, Wes's Suburban drives right by. I dive into some bushes way too late, but Wes keeps driving. After the truck's gone and has disappeared around the corner, I stand, brush myself off, and give a little salute.

★   ✪   ★

I decide to go to Anger Management the next evening—the address and the time are there on the fridge, in Lanie's writing. Her last communiqué to me. I spend the whole day on the kitchen. The sink is a silent, quiet culprit (and don't forget the bacterial hotbed of the drain), and I scrub for so long that by the time I'm done, I'm looking at an entirely new layer of metal. Then I use silver polish on it, then scrub it again. I realize I can still see scratches and so I go to the hardware store, buy a finer grit of steel wool, and go at the whole thing again, this time with more patience. I try to be calm and not press down so hard. More than once I go out to the living room and stand behind the curtains and watch the street through the crack. Today there's no sign of them. I mark all the times I think about Wes's offer by drawing vertical lines on the bottom of my cleaning schedule. By two o'clock, I've thought about rejoining ICS nine times. Europe. There could be plenty to do in Europe. I could potentially assassinate a real king, which would be like unexpectedly and out-of-nowhere getting the hardest item on your scavenger-hunt list. I imagine the cabin, too, and all the safety there. Not because of weapons. We wouldn't have a moat. I think of it as simple, but containing nice electronic features. Sort of a hybrid place, sort of techno-pastoral, sort of out there in-between everything. Very fine linens and a permanent fresh scent.

I decide to call Lanie. I decide it will be interesting to do it while I'm sitting on the back porch, naked.

"That's how you make kids who don't, like, talk," she says to me, when we get to the issue of me locking Justin in the closet. Justin is Lanie's son from an old boyfriend. I shouldn't say it like that, though; he's my stepson. He has been for some time. He has never been too impressed by me, no matter how hard I've tried. That's fine, the kid can do what he wants, he doesn't have to like me, but it's frustrating, not getting respect. Especially if you're like me.

The closet incident is what put Lanie over the edge. She was out with some friends. Justin and I were home. I told him to do his dishes. He kicked the TV screen and busted it and I snapped on him and locked him up with the coats. I left him in there for two hours, until Lanie came home. This kid is nine.

"You can be monstrous."

"I agree."

"It scares me. It has nothing to do with whether or not I love you."

"I'm not a monster," I say. "I know. I lost it."

"That was something a monster would do."

"I know," I say. I'm shivering. I look down and hope, distractedly, that my penis is not frozen to the chair. I don't think it is. I lift it, just in case. "I have a problem," I continue. "It wasn't the right thing to do. I'm going tonight."

"To Anger Management?"

"Yes."

She's silent for a few seconds, mulling. Finally, she says, "I have to admit, I'm surprised."

"Things are getting..." I look at the frozen, gray birdbath and realize, in a moment of awful deflation, that the "dream" I had last night was not actually a dream. I can see the hole I dug in the snow. I can see the fresh dirt I tore up. It's real. I look at my fingernails and see the dirt in them, too. So. Basically, in this dream, it was night, I was in my Barney pajamas, and I went into the backyard and buried a landmine beside the birdbath.

"Things are getting what?"

"Weird."

"Shouldn't I feel," she says, "this big desire to come back when you're all apologetic and you need me? I mean if I'm going to come back? Shouldn't my heart be welling up right now?"

"I don't know, baby. I have no idea what you're supposed to feel."

"That would be the difference between me leaving as a wakeup call to you and me leaving, like, leaving."

"Maybe, yes."

"It seems like I should just know it's the right thing to do."

"I take it you don't."

"You're dangerous," she says. "What do I do with that? My husband is dangerous?"

"I'm not dangerous," I say.

"I just keep thinking about what you were like when you were fourteen," she says. "Can you even believe it? If you think about that? We used to be so young. We were babies when we first met."

"I know." Surprisingly, it makes me sad, even though everyone used to be so young, and I usually don't go in for thinking like this.

"Go to class," she says. "Just call tomorrow. Tell me if it helps."

"It's not a class. It's a group."

"It's a class. You're learning something."

"Can I come over tomorrow? After? I'll apologize to Justin. I need to do that."

"My brother," she says, "is too pissed. Maybe next week."

"Your brother is always too pissed."

"Just when you're around," she says. "Or when we're playing board games."

"I told him I was sorry about the Monopoly incident."

"I don't think it really got through. Maybe because you were screaming it at him."

By the time we're done talking we've gotten back to something we do, some back and forth that doesn't really have any content to it, just the baseline of two people who know each other well trading the bottom things in their minds. I find it to be very normal. It's often warm. I am fucking blue and shivering by the time I go inside.

I take a hot shower and get dressed.

I find an envelope under the door.

Inside the envelope there's a note.

The note says: "You drive a hard bargain, bro! Great news! Chuck gave thumbs up on 120K! I'll stop by later! Aaron: You want to be on this side of the fence, okay? Trust me!"

On the bottom, a postscript:

"I had Norm pull out that landmine, FYI. Careful, kid!"

The beginning of the meeting isn't so bad. It's pretty much like you'd expect. We're not in a high school gym; we're in a church. There's coffee. There are nine people here. Our leader is a therapist named Dr. Billy. Dr. Billy is about 50. He's got a big biker beard and he's stuffed into a brown suit from 1973. He explains that he's just come from a conference in Canada. He uses his hands to illustrate his abstract points and then, out of nowhere, ten minutes into the meeting, I look up and see that he's eating a massive hot Italian beef sandwich.

He's got a smooth, ultra-controlled voice and he talks about how anger really isn't an emotion like the others, it's more like the body's admonition of confusion. I have a nine-inch serrated blade concealed in a sheath on my right calf.

After the break, a sleepy-looking woman named Jill a few seats to the right of me asks if she can say a few words about her week, and Dr. Billy gives her the floor.

She says, "First, I'd like to welcome Aaron," she nods at me. Everyone nods at me and I nod back. Mumbled hellos. "Aaron, I just want you to know that most of us have been coming here for awhile now. It might look like it's not gonna do anything for you. But stick with it. You look so skeptical right now." She smiles. "Try to let go of that."

"I'm not skeptical," I say. "This is just my face."

"Okay," she said. "But I wanted to say it anyway."

"All right," I say. "Thanks, Jill."

She explains that this week, her boss brought her into the office and criticized her for three typos on an outgoing email to a client. Jill explains that a co-worker added a few lines to the email before it went out, and that the typos were all in the addition. She never got a chance to re-proof it. But her boss wouldn't let her speak before he was finished accosting her. She saw it happening and stayed calm. She let him talk, then she told him, calmly, that she hadn't made the mistake. He pretended that it didn't matter and found a way to blame her anyway. Something about how she was the final editorial eye, so all mistakes were her mistakes.

People nod. People in the group go, "Hmmm."

Jill says, then, that this is usually her trigger—when being reasonable isn't enough to get in the way of somebody's drive toward a different goal. Part of me awakens at this characterization. But she smiles then and says that because of group, she recognized it in the moment. She saw it for what it was and because of that, she didn't do anything. She says she got a little mad, but did nothing.

"I used what I learned," she says proudly.

Everyone claps.

Dr. Billy thanks her and then asks me if I want to say anything.

I say, "My trigger is everything in the universe."

Everyone laughs.

I stare back at them, one by one. I hate it when I make people laugh. It's unintentional. I don't joke. To clear this up, I stare at Dr. Billy for a long time. Yes, like a threat.

"I know we sometimes feel that way," says Dr. Billy, after absorbing my look with his fat face. "Of course. But part of the exercise is to hone it down and get more specific."

"No," I say. "I'm being specific when I say that. Everything that exists, now, makes me angry. All. I don't know any other way to say it. All." I nod the last time I say "all"; I'm getting somewhere.

"Hm," says Dr. Billy. "In what way?"

"Nobody, anywhere, has any real sense what is actually going on." This doesn't seem to get a very good reaction from the crowd—no doubt I'm scowling as I say it, but still. I continue: "I don't either, but at least I know I don't. I'm sorry but you people aren't like me." This is me trying to take the edge off. Being friendly. "You haven't done the shit I've done."

"What do you mean by 'going on'?" Billy asks. He does air quotes. "Could you elaborate on that point?"

I have choices here. I could explain to him, for example, that most people, when they wake up in the morning, they don't think about, say, laws and things like that, but they probably feel that those things are there somewhere, all these agreements people have made with one another, in the background of life. Furthermore they probably feel that they are solid, even though they're invisible. And beyond laws, there are other standard powers we acknowledge as part of your human realm: Love, for example. Kinship. Good. Family. Truth. Meaning. I could explain to him that those things are like warm, bending taffy to me, and how actually, something would be wrong with me if they weren't like warm, bending taffy. There is no underlying structure. We live in chaos. So maybe for other people, something happens and that's their trigger. But for me, just walking around and being alive in chaos is mine.

I say, "I find myself getting particularly agitated at movie theatres."

"Why, do you think?" he asks.

"I don't know," I say. "Most endings are disappointing."

"I think there might be more there," Billy says. "Maybe it's stories themselves. The way they often try to present a definitive truth? Maybe it's narrative you're rejecting."

"Your goobledeegob mumbo-jumbo makes no sense, Dr. Billy," I say.

"I've heard that before, son," Dr. Billy says, smiling kindly. "But is that me? Or is that both us?"

★ ✪ ★

After the meeting, I don't go to see Lanie and Justin. I just walk straight west. I'm looking for a neighborhood that makes me uncomfortable so I can clear my head. Lawndale might be nice. I need to walk around in a place where I might possibly die a violent death.

Things look safe for about a half-hour, but after another mile, I'm further west, on an empty street, and my skin comes alive. It's an industrial area, and I've never been here. There is slush and snow everywhere. The streets are empty and there is a gloom wafting from the dilapidated buildings, windows sadly alight with residents who've most likely been put where they are by somebody else. I keep going, past an empty warehouse, past a lot, past a 7-11. Through the window I see the lone attendant behind a wall of bullet-proof glass, leaning on the counter within his small protective cube, smoking, watching television. I push on. The street again darkens. I come to more houses and an apartment complex. This is excellent ghetto, here. No clichés, but danger in the air. Another block and there's a group of teenagers on the corner. I wouldn't call them life-threatening, but they might do; I walk by them and stare with very buggy eyes.

A kid with a huge kicked Bulls hat sees me, watches me, and says, "The fuck you lookin' at, faggot?" and I say nothing but feel adrenaline, joy, other things. I look away, don't respond. I feel them peel away from their corner, begin to follow me. I smile to myself and don't look back. Then I find myself laughing out loud, but accidentally. It's a foreign, high-pitched giggle and it frightens me. I try to think of a dance I can do, but while walking. I try something with rolling my head back and forth and I continue laughing. I hear someone say, "You escape from the loony bin, dude?" and another say, "Motherfucker must be crazy." They all laugh. Perhaps they're reacting to my twitches and feints? I keep going. They are children, they are no older than sixteen. They're just kids making fun of the strange person and I am here because I am bloodthirsty. The most subterranean of my imaginations is hypothesizing about good kill shots with the blade. A wild and horrendous part of me is straining against its bonds in anticipation of multiple liquidations. In the outside world, the same voice says something else and they all start to laugh harder. I missed it. I feel glad they have me to laugh at. Feeling glad makes me think, too, that I'm not Satan, I'm just all bound up inside. This makes me doubly glad.

I go one block, turn right, walk a block, turn right again, and walk all the way back to my car.

I drive home.

I don't see Wes's Suburban on the street. I park a few blocks away and cut through the backyards and climb the side of the house and break in through my own bathroom window. At first I sleep in the closet, holding an assault rifle, but in the middle of the night, in the middle of the darkness, I wake up, still feeling a little glad, leave the rifle, go to the bedroom, get into my pajamas, and go to bed like a normal person.

The morning is crisp, raw, and cloudless. There's no sign of Wes. I decide not to clean. Instead I will go to see Lanie and ask her to come home and also tell her that if she doesn't, I'll be leaving again, only possibly forever, down into the pit of ambient metaphysical chaos. I take no weapons.

I knew her in junior high. We didn't go out then, but we were friendly. We used to live near one another, and sometimes I'd see her playing basketball with her brother. Sometimes I'd play. She met her first man, Justin's dad, at college, but by the time she was back in town she was on her own again and she just had the kid with her. I saw her once or twice—I'd stayed in town for school—and then one day I went to war. When I came back, she was still there.

One night we ran into one another at a bar, talked, and that was that. She said, "Your hair is so weird," and I said, "Your hair is weird, too," even though it was exactly the same as it had been. Mine was longer. I was doing everything I could to distance myself from where I'd just come from. But these things…there are pushes and pulls. ICS sent a mailer, I filled it out. ICS called, ICS offered, I joined.

I don't want to go to Europe, I know that, but truth be told, the skeleton thing is real. Sometimes it's only lightly in the background, but some days I'll be walking around in Home Depot and every single person will literally appear to be a white grinning skeleton to me. No flesh. Is this a hallucination? Can the absence of something be a hallucination? How is it that my mind, in real-time, renders the background reality where the flesh is supposed to be? I once had a ten-minute conversation about bathroom tiles with a skeleton wearing a bright orange vest. One might say that this is fairly clear evidence of malfunction. But that's not true, either. I recognize metaphor. Hallucination can be thought of as metaphor. Dr. Billy knew. Some guy in some gym eating an Italian beef. He could see the truth. I mean they really actually all do look like fucking skeletons, but I see what my mind is doing to me.

I decide it's a good idea to show up at Lanie's brother's with flowers, and so I drive first to the flower shop on Sheffield. Inside, there's a guy with little Charles Dickens spectacles reading the newspaper. He looks up and nods and I tell him that I need something beautiful.

"Okay," he says. "They are flowers. Let's both relax."

"I don't know if I know how to say this right," I say, "but I want something that has no meaning."

"You'll have to explain."

"I don't want a bunch of flowers that have special meaning."

"Ah."

"They say a red rose is this, a white rose is that."

"White rose means happy love."

"Well fuck that."

"Really?"

"No," I say, "not really. Ignore me if I say things quickly."

"Because happy love is not something you can just—"

"There must be flowers that are just flowers."

"Okay," he says. "I see what you're saying. I understand. Interesting."

"Good." I'm relieved that he understands, exhausted by the attempt at communicating. "Good," I say again.

He comes out from behind the counter, animated by the challenge. Together we go to the cooler against the wall. "Last week I had a local pizza-delivery man in here asking for a flower representing the ability to teleport."

"Just straight-up beautiful," I say. "But also simple."

"I heard you," he says, swatting the air in my direction. He's getting irritated now, which is bad, because I get irritated when I'm with someone who's irritated, and I don't want to be irritated. "Don't keep saying the same thing. It makes you seem like a nutjob." Still looking into his coolers, he places a finger on his lips and deliberates. "We're going to start wild," he says, "and go from there."

I step aside and let him do his thing. A new calm comes over me as I watch him experiment with arrangements, maybe something to do with his matter-of-factness, something to do with believing, as I watch, that there truly is a skill to flower-arrangement, and that this man has a palpable and demonstrable talent that is not related to harm. He chats with me. How nice. As he is gathering the ingredients I stare at the metal handle of one of the coolers and take deep breaths, groping at the possibilities implied by such an idea. I turn and start to watch people passing on the sidewalk outside. A man goes by and I am convinced he's wearing a green helmet. A woman with a little girl, and they are rushing. Old man and dog. Other person. People. They are all like me. I try to think of what they do at home at night, or what skills they utilize at work. I see, I'm pretty sure, Wes's Suburban go by, and about a minute later, just as the flower-man is asking if I like what he's assembled, if I like the bubbly purple nubs, and I, eyes glazed, am staring dumbly into the multitude of pleasing colors, the chime rings, and Wes's pal Norman, the IIS guy with the wool socks, comes into the store and starts looking at ferns.

"It's good," I say, taking the bouquet. I hold onto the bouquet very carefully as we go to the cash register. As he rings me up, I look back at the ferns. Norman is there for a moment, but as I watch him, he presses something on his watch, shimmers, becomes translucent, melts into the foliage, and I can't see him anymore.

"Twenty-five dollars."

I pay. To get to the door, I press my back against the wall opposite the ferns. Once outside, I run to my car. When I start the engine, I look up at the mirror and see that Norman is sitting in the back seat. He has a can of lemon soda.

"You'll have to stay with us," he says. "I know you don't believe me, friend, but everyone goes through this. You're one of the better ones. So we got an expense account."

"Please," I say, very calmly, "exit my vehicle, sir."

"I don't understand why you need the flowers," Norman says. "We brought you flowers."

"I needed more flowers," I say.

Norman opens the door. "What's incredible is that we probably don't have to convince you," he says. "Right?"

"Please, sir," I say. "Exit my vehicle."

I actually studied things. I went to college and read Plato and Aristotle. I wrote a long, decent paper on Anaximander. I'm not saying that that necessarily makes me a Whiner automatically, this liberal arts education of mine, or that it makes me special, but I am saying that once in a while, skeletons and all, weapons attached to discreet parts of my body or not, the taste of blood on my lips or not on my lips, I realize it's wise to remember who you used to be. Or, like Lanie says, recall being fourteen years old. People come from somewhere. Wes, I don't doubt, had a mother who treated him very well, and as I drive, flowers in my free hand like a chalice, feeling wise but also afraid, yes, I imagine him. I imagine that he was on a soccer team once. The vision comes alive. Wes, a boy, dribbles. Wes, a boy, scores a goal and throws both arms into the air.

There's no sign of the Suburban as I turn onto Lanie's brother's block. I am clear and lucid. Fuck them. Wes, Norman, Chuck. The other ten-thousand, too. I am going to take my flowers and repair the damage and make it clear that getting turned around is something that happens over the course of time. Even the act of being turned around implies that it can be reversed. Nothing is stuck. I have to believe that. You are never trapped. Say it to yourself, Aaron, over and over again. Say it as you drive with flowers. Say it and also say Lanie, my baby, come back to me, I love you.

"Lanie's not here," her brother tells me, deep concern on his face, "if that's what you're trying to say, Aaron." He clears his throat. "I don't even look like Lanie."

I'm apparently standing at Lanie's brother's door.

"Are you sleepwalking? Or high?"

"No."

He looks at the flowers, then back at me. "Can I ask you a question?"

"Where is she?"

"Let me ask my question first," he says patiently, nodding to acknowledge what I said. "It'll be quick."

"Please, Greg. I'm trying."

"What goes through someone's mind as he's, I don't know, kicking out the tail lights in his brother-in-law's car over a real-estate dispute in the game of Monopoly? Because I've been wondering for a while. Ever since…" He trails off, looking up toward the sky, lips pursed with extreme irony. "Oh, I'm not sure."

"I apologize," I say. "Again."

"This is the first apology."

"I apologize, then."

"Of course you apologize now. How about back then? Or how about not doing it at all?"

"I'm begging you."

"You didn't answer the question."

I stare at him. It could be, I realize, that this, really, is my trigger. Whenever anyone asks my why. Why are there incidents? Why are you so angry? I can't even conceive of an answer. I can mumble about reality, but that's no answer. All I would like is to be able to produce an answer.

I try one.

"I just want somebody," I say, "to understand what I've done."

Greg is a deep, calm guy. He's a teacher. I'm afraid of him for all of these reasons. He stands there, arms crossed, thinking about it. He's guessing that he'll never be able to understand what I've done, and he's wondering about whether his sister will be able to, and probably doubting it. Of course he's right to worry about the future and wonder what will come of all this. Behind him I see his little daughter run down the hall, screaming happily, dragging a blanket behind her. I catch a glimpse of Justin, too, all the way back in the kitchen. He's at the table, eating cereal. He's not looking our way. Greg's little girl runs around and keeps screaming. Greg doesn't even flinch. Instead he adjusts his glasses and says, "She went back to your house."

"Thank you."

"I urged her to divorce you."

"I understand."

"She still might."

"That's okay. She probably should. I would if I were her."

"So would I," Greg says. "Lucky she's her."

I turn to go.

"Aaron," he says.

I turn back.

"The flowers are pretty."

Wes's Suburban is parked in my driveway when I get home.

When I run into the kitchen, he looks up, bright-eyed, and says, "Hey, man! I already got the flowers, remember? Norman told me what a cornball you were being."

Lanie is there at the kitchen table with them. I am prepared to go berserk if I have to. There are four grenades stashed in the oven and I could get to them in roughly four seconds. The uzi is up behind the pots and pans. I could turn this house into a fucking inferno. I could destroy everything. All of us. If that's what Wes wants, that's what I'll give him.

I wait for a hint.

She does not seem to have been tortured. In fact, she smiles at me, then gives me a little wave from the table.

Norman nods at me, holds up a glass of yellow liquid.

"Your own urine?" I say.

He says, "It turns out you did have lemonade. You didn't look hard enough. It was behind the milk."

"Leave," I say to them. "Get out."

"We were just getting to know—"

"Get out." It would be impossible to describe to you just how much I want to scream it. But I'm not going to. You can't scream your way through these people. You can't be angry. If you are you'll be stuck.

Lanie, thankfully, looks like she doesn't care one way or the other. Later, as she's pulling Wes's flowers from the vase and replacing them with mine, she will tell me that Wes came in and started telling her some rather sensitive things, work-wise. It will make sense to me. That's the last card to play if you're in Wes's position—Chuck at his throat, a world of shit all around him, orders to pull people back into it because no one, really, wants to be doing it at all. Yes, Wes, I can see you. You told the woman I love about the horrible things I have done. She listened and absorbed it. Contrary to your plans and expectations, she did not cease to love me, because you've failed to understand something crucial, at the core of love, which is neither good nor bad but simply your story so far, and I was not made into the nihilist you needed me to be to get me back. Don't you see that since I've been back, since she's been gone, all I've wanted to do is confess? Wes? To lie down in her lap, cry, and tell her about the evil I've personally added to the world? Wes: Do you see how you helped me? Thank you. I cannot help you, but thank you.

"It's time to get out of my house," I say again.

Now I point to the door with the flowers, which are somehow in my hand. Lanie is looking at me. Is she proud? Wes's skeleton looks saddened. Norman's looks old and bulky and worn, like it has carried too much weight for too long, committed too many atrocities, even for a Pro. Yes, Norman, I can see you as well. I hope there's a limit to the havoc one human frame can wreak during a lifetime, for your sake. The skull of Norman has long scratches and one bigger crack down the side. Was he once hit in the head with a hammer? We can only guess.

Lanie's skeleton is small and elegant. I can see her bad posture clearly. I can see the miniature architecture of rib and vertebrae and shoulder. I can see the interlocking of bones in my own wrist and hand as I continue to point at the door. I can see the flowers have no skeleton, and remain flowers. They have chlorophyll. I can see we are motionless in this death-frieze for some time.

Then Wes's skeleton stands up, and Norman's does, too, and I follow them both to the door.

"Apparently you don't want to work for us anymore," Wes says cheerfully. Norman is down on the ground, putting on his shoes again. "You win!"

"Go."

"Twenty years from now, Aaron," he says. "Twenty years from now you'll think of this moment."

I don't respond to that. Then there are skeletons walking through the snow, adorned in winter clothing, lords of doom, those privy to the lifting of the veil, and this is the end of this day. I'm not healed, nor are they vanquished.

I retreat to the kitchen.

Lanie's at the sink, cleaning Norman's lemonade glass. Did she see any of it? The hidden world?

When she turns and sees me in the doorway with the flowers, she says, "Those are great. It's really clean in here." I help her finish in the kitchen and then take her down into the basement to show her what work I've done since she's been gone. I show her the new carpet.

She says, "I'm not necessarily back. I came to have coffee. We should talk it through, Aaron. We need to talk."

I say, "That's fine. That's good."

But now I can see the skin taut on her cheekbone. I can see the two freckles below her temple. I can see her earlobe and the empty holes of her old and angry teenage piercings.

Nothing's there anymore. Her skin still shines youth. I know this person well, I think. I really do know her.

The Son

I feel the knife go in and of all the things you'd think it'd make you feel, I feel sadness. Mind just skips the surprise and skips the pain and goes right to knowing that I've come to the end and more than anything, it's too sad to believe, but you believe it, though, because there's the knife sticking in your side. Crazy. I mean of all the things. There's also relief, like at least I'm allowed to stop pretending, not even sure what exactly, but the real feeling is the feeling of sadness. That's all it is.

I'll back up—the situation is strange. All I'm doing is walking down the street. I'm up north near the triangle but I gotta get down to class. Last night was crazy but I made it a thing now to never miss class because something gets crazy. And I've got my hands in my pockets and I'm listening to some pretty backwards Dr. Octagon I got from this old stoner in my building and out of nowhere now on the sidewalk some dude grabs my shoulder from behind and twists me. Here's what Octagon is saying even though he's not up too loud: "Astronauts get played, tough like the ukulele, as I move in rockets, overriding levels, nothing's aware, same data, same system." But since he's not loud I can hear what Colonel Sanders says at the same time (dude who stabs me looks like Colonel Sanders) right before he pushes his big-ass kitchen knife or whatever right into my side, right under my ribs on the left: "I am loving you and I am sending you off, my brother." Which is hilarious, if you think about the dude in charge of Kentucky Fried Chicken calling me his brother, saying he loves me, and killing me. I stare in his eyes. So it goes in and at first it's not too far from what it's like getting a shot, just real focused on one spot and this weird panic coming up from your body saying some shit like, "Not supposed to be going in like that's going in," but as he really pushed and his blade's all the way in there, into my stomach, him kinda hugging me and I don't think anyone on the sidewalk even knows what's happening, everything pretty much shuts off and that's when I'm sad, like I started. So then time is real off from here forward and I'm living like a month every time he pulls it out and sticks it back in. I think then people start to notice. And it's like another year later by the time I'm on the ground.

My mother. That's who he's really killing. I saw her at my sister's funeral and that was some shit so strange, speaking of strange, it wasn't even sad anymore. I read this book that had Irish women swooning when they found out their dudes had been killed in battle or whatever but I thought that shit was just made up for the story, to be honest. But there's something in women—maybe not just women, okay—but you push a person far enough and give them something that's so sad they gather up this power they have and they blow up, they just blow up. They blow up. It's a big blow up of a person.

My mother didn't just throw herself down on my sister's coffin at that place. No. She started shrieking in this way I'd just never heard. I saw this word, this *Lord of the Flies* word: ululations. That's what I thought when I heard the sound of my mother screaming at my sister's body, when I saw her leaning over, grabbing at her, knocking over flowers and the portrait, just straight-up out of her mind. Ululation. We got animals inside of us, man. We've got all this power.

And so there I am, standing there in my suit, watching my mom do this. It scares me and I can't even move, I can't do nothing. But all the old folks, it was like they weren't even surprised. Not even the old folks, actually—just everyone who wasn't a kid, maybe. But all these people there, it was like it was normal to see someone turn into this screaming beast, and a couple of the old-timers just kind of went up and held her there while she was screaming. They held her up. She didn't fight them, really, but still, she kept struggling, because she was fighting something, it just wasn't there in front of us.

So this is when I realize what I'm seeing.

What I'm seeing is my mother actually making one more last try to change the world.

Put it like this: right then at the moment, while she's ululating, my mother on some level believes, believes completely, that she's gonna say, *Ah hell no* loud enough, to time, and what's happened, and not just that, but that shit's gonna *work*. It's really gonna work. Not even like a story about how the metaphor of it worked, I mean it's gonna *work* work, and Nicole's gonna rise up from that coffin, and she's gonna be alive again. If my mother screams loud enough—so she's thinking—and strange enough—if she empties herself—enough—she's gonna change what has happened.

Does it work?

It doesn't work.

But for a second, it seems like it might.

Back to this. So then I'm at the hospital and I've got no idea what I'm doing and still all it really is is sad. I don't know. I'm lying there and I've got no shirt, someone cut it off. Some doctor's leaning down towards me, talking to me. All I think is: Who was that dude? Colonel Sanders? What did he say? No idea. Why? No idea. Fuck if I want to die, man—I want to **live**—but still it's like my mind, it knows, even though I don't want to admit it.

I'm doing my wailing as well, even though I'm only half-here for it. Funny to find yourself screaming because it makes you think that all along, you're not the one who's been in control of anything, that being alive is someone else is running you and you're just hooked up to a bunch of dummy instruments like a fake steering wheel.

But either way, I'm doing my ululating.

Time's slow. I've got time to say all my goodbyes. Who knows how it comes out. Here I am dying. You're watching it. I do have time to say all my goodbyes, in my way. I mean the right people are here. But you're right here, so I'll say them to you.

The Machine of Understanding Other People

★ ❶ ★
THE DOWNWARD SPIRAL

The situation is not so good on the morning Tom Sanderson receives the telegram. The man who brings it looks to be about ten years younger than him and has an impressive wave of black hair cresting just above bushy, caterpillar eyebrows. He's handsome; he's wearing a blue suit and blue tie and very professionally hands over the cream-white envelope, unsealed, perhaps even perfumed, and Tom, surprisingly awake from the night before, wearing only bathrobe, suit-pants, vomit-stained undershirt, and really big bomber hat, standing ankle-deep in a small sea of his own unread mail, thinks to himself that yes, it makes perfect sense that I am receiving a telegram, considering what an important figure I am in the world. He reaches out and takes it from the stranger with a squint and—accidentally—a burning liquid burp.

There is a moment of tentative eye contact after the burp. Then both men stand in silence as Tom studies the envelope for a long time and the odor of partially-digested Jameson, which is the only thing in Tom's stomach at the moment, expands in an invisible cloud between their faces, mixing with the envelope's musk.

Tom says, "Like a real telegram?"

"Yes."

"But a real one?" Tom says again, looking up at the messenger. "It says STOP." He holds up the envelope, one eyebrow raised, Sherlockian gambit.

"I'm not sure I understand," says the messenger.

"What is that accent you have?" Tom asks the man, changing tone, cocking his head. "Where are you from? What is that? Dutch?"

"My accent is totally standard American, sir," says the messenger, whose name is (unfortunately) Dick Ball and who is now feeling uncomfortable about this delivery.

Tom Sanderson, despite the veneer of aristocratic, disheveled confidence, something he's always had about him and now really only keeps when he's within his apartment, feels self-conscious, too; it's about the stains on his v-neck and having said anything about the accent to this man because it's true, now that he thinks about it, this handsome messenger in the blue suit has no accent at all, actually, just a weird eye-contact thing. So this is awkward. Tom frowns meaningfully and turns his attention back to the envelope. It occurs to him that he could open and read the message as a way of making the messenger go away, but he also realizes he can just sort of drift backwards with a creepy goodbye-smile on his face and nod a little and mumble a thank-you as he closes the door in the guy's face. And this is what he does, and it works: after the latch clicks Tom finds himself again alone in his foyer, just like before, only now he is holding a telegram.

Tom is pretty far down a downward spiral at the moment, which he knows full well, but he also isn't quite sure where the bottom of the spiral is or whether it even has a bottom, which he sometimes finds sort of funny, say early in the evenings, when he's sipping his first whiskey, but later on, into the night, when he sits alone in his too-big apartment, absolutely toasted, usually watching DVR'd reality television but sometimes puttering around in order to waste time and avoid going to bed, where he will probably lie drunk and awake for hours, he catches glimpses of a whole new landscape of life's secret horrors, grotesque sights, really, things that make previous selves seem like naïve children attending only the kindergarten of human desperation; the feeling is pure but only lasts a second or two: it's the human mind trapped by itself in a vacuum, but there's a very small window somehow within this empty and airless prison, he's not unlike Steve

McQueen looking out through his small wired window in the side of his cell in *The Great Escape*, how he has to jump up to do it, and through that window the only visible thing is another forty or fifty years of life's slow and efficient meat-grinder tractor chewing away at some field that is the soul until the grand, totally anticlimactic finale of death, about which no one will really care, which is itself represented in the metaphor by the tractor just totally blowing up.

The drinking got serious a few years back, at around the same time the feeling began, and his wife Sherry left because of the drinking, ostensibly, but she knew he was broken, like he knew he was broken, maybe even all done. He never really tried to tell her about the feeling *specifically*, in part because it was embarrassing to admit how afraid he had become of walking around in the regular world after having been so confident and comfortable in his own skin for decades, an absurd thought, to be agoraphobic or whatever it is he's become, but also because it all seemed so scripted, so predictable. It was the sort of thing he'd read about in college English classes, the most boring ones with the most asinine and pompous rich students on campus...a special kind of contemporary numbness of the spirit, they always said, *ennui*, Zooey Glassinitis, *angst, dread*, **nothing**, *a dearth of Existenz*, and back then he didn't think much of it, as it was so utterly unrelatable, such a privileged condition, like someone had just made it up because there weren't any interesting wars to write about at the time. Now, actually *feeling* that feeling...well, it is apparently a real thing and not a good feeling. Not at all. But is there a bottom to the spiral? Tom used to pride himself on his financial successes, investments and whatnot, which, until lately, had been impressive. Then came Great Depression 2. He was born poor and had made himself rich. That is impressive. Not so much now, as the entire American economy is dead. He's still pretty rich, mind you, but being pretty rich doesn't feel quite like it used to.

Could that help him, though? The old Sanderson savvy? One of Tom's deepest and oldest drives has always been to find ways to make the bad into the good, somehow, that's how he made the money, he's sure of it, and he feels he could maybe turn this whole situation into a positive situation if he acts as a kind of Jacques Cousteau of depression in this case, heading into deeper and colder waters with some kind of little robot friend as he looks for all the weird translucent albino creature-emotions with glowlights on their foreheads and spiky orange teeth, which he guesses would represent different kinds of self-hatred. He is 41 years old; since last month, twice-divorced. That's not that bad. It's not good, but not that bad. For fifteen years he was a corporate lawyer at a massive Chicago firm, never made partner, probably due to his ridiculous social life, and lost his job two weeks ago. That's pretty bad. And finally, sometimes at night he dresses up in his best suits and goes out to dinner alone at fancy restaurants, where he gets a good head-start on drinking and looks at his watch as though he's waiting for someone who's stood him up. So there's that. And it's inexplicable, because it wasn't always this way, Tom has many likable qualities, he has a good smile, he's intelligent, he can sometimes laugh at himself, but he doesn't have a single friend. Not one friend. How did *that* happen? Somewhere along the way, he supposes. In any case, he knows no one who would send him an amazingly weird telegram.

Because it is weird. Here. He removes the thin sheet of yellowish paper from the envelope and reads the message's brief lines:

MR. SANDERSON, YOUR PRESENCE REQUESTED IN
MANCHESTER, LOST ARISTOCRATIC UNCLE HERMAN
DEAD STOP. PLEASE CALL 44-20-6547-2117 STOP.
SUBSTANTIAL INHERITANCE STOP.

Tom stands here in the foyer and reads the curious message through a few times. This is silly. Although it does indeed appear to be an English telephone number. That part looks good. What seems kind of suspicious, though, is the Lost Aristocratic Uncle Herman part, since he has no Uncle Herman at all, but then again the message clearly notes that this Herman is a lost uncle, and so Tom probably wouldn't know about him, aristocratic or not, right? His grandfather on his father's side had been in the war, he'd spent some time in England, maybe there had been a young Red Cross lass plus some martinis plus an unspoken sexy rendezvous in a dark hospital bed that has somehow led to this.

He will solve this now and not think about it again, as tonight, like all nights, he is occupied with drinking. He goes to the phone.

He has to think a minute to remember what he needs to dial to get to England, but when he tries the number on the telegram he gets no answer, and is eventually sent to the voicemail of a blustering lawyer named Grayspool. Tom leaves a message in his most professional, lawyerly voice, cool and casz, which he is glad to find he still has, at least for the time being. He leaves his home number and says he may or may not be available, depending on the time, as there's a chance he could be out at a nice restaurant, alone, drinking a lot and checking his watch.

He calls his mother and asks her if she has any secret aristocratic brothers by the name of Herman and she tells him no, not that she knows of.

"Do you think Dad had any secret brothers named Herman?" he asks. "Or aristocrat brothers? Or the combo?"

"Hm," his mother says, pondering. He can imagine her squinting her one eye and cocking her head out there in Scottsdale. "As far as I know, he didn't. But then again if it says he was a lost—"

"I've already gone through that, Ma."

Afterwards, he decides to take a shower—first one in a week. As he scrubs himself he considers how similar this telegram is to all the email scams that stream into the junk box, then considers how much it all comes off as a stupid hoax, not real, the kind of thing he would have torn up and forgotten about within five minutes back when he used to be his whole self.

Granted, it's a strange one, but in the end no doubt just an elaborate form of junk mail, right? Didn't he just the other day get something in the mail that appeared to have a handwritten extra little hello scribbled on the edge? But upon further inspection it was obviously laser-printed onto the envelope and just a cheap trick to get him to open it up and find the REFINANCE NOW letter inside? He used to deride and shake his head at all the poor fucks out in the universe who got taken in by the rhetorical human noise that comes floating into our lives, through all the channels, in all the mediums, all crafted to *take*—how could you not see those things for what they were? Right away? It's like they screamed bullshit. Couldn't everyone see? But no, they couldn't, and so many people sent away their money to false charities, signed up for magazines they didn't want, lost what was theirs because they so needed and so wanted to be special. *Special.* That was it. When it came down to it, this was the desire that could make virtually anyone believe in anything, wasn't it? To be told that there is no one else in the whole world quite like you. Uniqueness. People want that for whatever reason. Maybe true, maybe not, but it took a certain kind of permission to get there. Jesus. *Jesus.* People are goddamned morons.

But as he dries off, he looks at himself in the mirror, a middle-aged and washed up sod, Tom Sanderson, formerly Tommy, child, and he knows he is exactly the same, there's no getting around, and it makes him sad, staring at himself, but sad in a very simple way, not sad in the newer, complicated ways—sad that he sees how he wants to be special, too, and how he is just the same as everyone.

Sometime around midnight, Tom is extraordinarily intoxicated and eating a *huge* microwaveable corndog when his phone rings and the lawyer, a Mr. Cedric Grayspool, is there at the other end, stumbling and bumbling over his words in what sounds like an upper-crust English basso. "Yes, yes, hello. Mr. Sanderson? Is this a Mr. *Tom* Sanderson? I say, can you turn down that music please, sir? Hello?" Grayspool is presumably referring to the Electric Light

Orchestra Tom's got rocking on his Krell in the living room; Tom mutters an apology as he jogs past the couch and kills the noise. Impressed with himself for not falling down either to or fro, Tom returns to the kitchen and picks up the cordless and says, "Little party going on here."

"Ah."

"We're doing a group glory hole thing."

"Yes, of course," says Grayspool. "I should be the one to apologize, calling you at such a ridiculous hour on a Friday night—*your* Friday, I should say. It's just that this is a matter of the utmost importance, and when I heard your message this morning, I thought I'd give it a go. Did you say a *glory hole?*"

"There's not really a glory hole," says Tom.

"Ah."

"I should apologize for saying that."

"No need."

"What day did you say it was? Grayspool, is it?"

Grayspool repeats that it's a Friday—but it's Tom's Friday.

Tom is pleased to learn that it's Friday, as this will mean college football awaiting him on the TV when he rolls out of bed tomorrow. Then he thinks about it for a second more, looking down at his half-eaten corndog, and he realizes that it's already Saturday for the man on the phone, which blows his mind a little.

"You're in early," Tom says. "On a Saturday. What are you thinking?"

Grayspool guffaws. "No rest for the weary, I suppose."

"No rest for the wicked, either, eh Grayspool?" Tom says, and he bites into the corndog, having no idea what he means by the comment. He just likes the sound of the saying. He also likes the sound of this Grayspool—seems like a nice person, definitely not some charlatan calling him from a basement in Mogadishu. Maybe there's something to this Uncle Herman after all?

On the table, there is a half-empty package of Boursin cheese, its foil folded out for greater access, and beside it, a small knife. Still chewing, continuing what he was doing before the phone rang, Tom begins to slather more of the cheese onto the corndog's remaining fried nub, then a little more onto the top of the wooden stick, so he can lick it off as something of a finish line. In recent days he's discovered that Boursin cheese can make anything—even the best things—better. He decides to tell Grayspool.

"I'd imagine it does," says Grayspool philosophically.

"It does," says Tom.

"If you don't mind, just to leapfrog to the matter at hand," says Grayspool. "Your inheritance. As you called our offices I presume you received the telegram we sent?"

"I did," says Tom. "I gotta tell you, though, Grayspool, this feels a little like a scam to me. I mean I like you and all, so far I mean, you seem like a nice guy, but…Well, for starters, I have no Uncle Herman. But on top of that I'm sort of desolate here, maybe an easy mark? I mean I'm sitting here at my lowest and this feels a little coincidental? Get me? Like, do you *know* about the downward spiral thing that's happening here?"

"I thought the telegram along with the check and the packet of materials regarding your genome would be sufficient proof."

"Packet?" says Tom, stopping himself before going in for the last Boursin lick. "Check? What packet with what check? What's a genome again?" He is moving toward his pile of mail now, still eating the cheese, phone tucked under his chin. "I'm not sure…"

"Don't have it?" Grayspool asks. "Sent October second, received October seventh. From our end it looks as though you signed for it. We have the confirmation, anyhow. Ah, yes. I have your signature up in front of me on the screen. It looks like you signed as Wilford Brimley."

"Might have blacked out after or while I signed, Grayspool," says Tom, not remembering signing for anything as Wilford Brimley. "But I very well could have signed for that package."

"Ah. Excellent."

"Hm," Tom says suspiciously, looking down now at the moose-sized pile of mail—along with a few small boxes—in the hallway beside his front door. He's been a little sloppy with household organizing in the last month or so. He can admit it to himself. Should not have fired the maid. "What's the date today?" he asks, walking over toward the door. As though that will somehow help him.

"It's the eleventh here," says Grayspool. "Tenth for you."

"Hold on."

Tom gets down into it for awhile, digging around like a badger, phone now on the ground. There really is a lot of mail in the world if you never get rid of it.

"Hold it here, Grayspool," Tom tries to yell toward the phone. "Here we go." He's pretty much inside the pile of mail now, and only his bare legs are coming out from the pile. "We have contact."

He extracts himself with a backward elbow-crawl, holding onto the package, and examines it once free, absently reaching for the phone again. Once the receiver's back at his mouth he says, "Yes, this is it. I'm holding England in my hands."

"Only a small part of it, I'd imagine."

"No need to debate it."

"So you've got it, then?"

"Yes, Grayspool," says Tom. "I've got it."

So it turns out, if Tom is to believe in all the genetics stuff, which—they say— is hard to refute, when it comes down to it, science being science, he really does have a secret lost uncle named Herman. Relative, at least. He really does, and this isn't a scam. How exactly he got one and how in particular they're related is still something of a mystery, but the readout from the genetics report (How did they get Tom's DNA, by the way? A man on the street snipping a lock of his hair? Where has he left a skin cell?) shows that he and Herman share a Y chromosome, which means that—well, Tom's not really sure what that means. He tries to remember back to his high school biology class but gives up and eventually goes to the computer. After some time clicking around and reading he finds that the Y gets passed from male to male in a direct line of fidelity, generation to generation, so his father then had this same Y, and his grandfather had this same Y. Herman might be his actual uncle, his father's unknown (probably?) brother, but Tom realizes it might go back another generation, and that Herman could conceivably be his *grandfather's* brother, too. There may be more possibilities, but Tom's brain hurts. It's the middle of the night. Tom feels tired and alone, sitting here at his desk. That sadness is lingering again, but Tom's not sure if it's this new twist or if it's just the same old. There is suddenly a very new and very real diagonal line in his family tree that throws a lot of things up into the air. That said, everything's already up in the air.

There is little additional information in the packet. According to the letter from Grayspool, Tom is required to show his face in Manchester for a meeting with the executors of the will if he is to find out anything about this mysterious "inheritance." The check is to cover the cost of travel. The letter is vague and there are no messages from this Herman himself—it implies only that Herman was familiar with Tom's existence, felt a fondness for the hidden American side of his family due to the "circumstances of its origin" and a love for "Take The 'A' Train," which he enjoyed harmonizing to, and has decided to divide his estate between his two most promising relatives. No mention at all of who the other relative might be, and no mention at all of the extent of the estate.

Tom stands around in his apartment for a while, looking at the different messes in each room, ashamed that he's allowed it to come to this. There's nothing hilarious about this; there's grimness to it, actually. You can smell the reaper in here. Funny what happens when you find yourself letting go—it's more incremental than it might seem, as it takes a good number of weeks to slowly allow the knots of the self to come undone, let the strings all hang loose. What are we but these cords and knots? He will clean this place up. He'll give himself a week to get himself together. And then he'll go and find out about England.

He writes a brief email to Grayspool telling him when he plans to travel, then goes and hits the sack.

Tom doesn't sleep well. It's the kind of sleep where you think you're not asleep, but you look over at the clock once in awhile and you realize you must have been asleep, as though you've been dreaming a very long dream, in real-time, of yourself lying in your own bed, not sleeping. So it doesn't matter if he's awake or not awake—either way, he's stuck thinking through the major moments in the long line of his life, going over, one by one, what he's always thought to be the bigger turning points, trying to figure out which is the most problematic, which altered the trajectory in the most damaging way. Because the long-term downward spiral is incremental as well, isn't it? This is just a locality on the same ongoing corkscrew? It would help to have a sense of what a good trajectory might have been, all things considered. It's a fruitful thought, actually—Tom's surprised to find he's never spent much time thinking about that question, thinking about what the right way and the right line might be. Maybe it's not the turning points at all? Maybe some other category—like the real question isn't which way the line of life goes but rather what color the line has been all along, or what its thickness has been, some other quality that it's very easy to ignore because you're not thinking about it in the right way. For example, he was once in love, but long before Sherry, even before Marianne, and in a very different way. A girl he met in law school named Christine, soft-spoken and sweet, born and raised in Wyoming, kind to the point where it makes Tom almost want to cry, recalling just her general attitude, what she'd be like when you saw her on campus in passing and ended up just walking a few hundred feet together before you both split and went your separate ways. Where did she get that kindness? Did she know how much it mattered? And wherever she was now, could she possibly imagine that Tom, her old boyfriend who she had certainly *not* loved, not like Tom loved her, because he hadn't actually known, and only figured it out years later, upon reflection—and besides, he didn't even know that he did and never said a thing one way or the other—could be lying in his bed, asleep and awake at the same time, recalling the particulars of how her voice used to go up and down when she would smile and discuss a quality in this or that professor she admired or take note of a little nook in one of the libraries that she considered her own personal hideout? She was not an effusive idiot, though—that's probably what Tom had first thought about her, although he can't now remember. She was smart and she was a skeptic but she'd found a way to fold happiness and kindness into that equation as well. What a wonderful girl she'd been.

Or what about the day when he had just turned thirty and the man attacked him on the street? A homeless man. Middle of the day, right on the sidewalk in the Loop, people all around, watching like it was a spectator sport. The man clearly saw something in Tom—the way he walked, the way he dressed, the way his face spelled out his privileged life or his success, spelled out just his *position* in the grand scheme of American life—and came after him when Tom said, with no eye contact, "Nope," in his response to the request for a little spare change. Tom knew and Tom could remember how much disdain had dribbled from each of the letters in the word "Nope," how the slime of it sort of hung off the lower points of the N and a gelatinous, glistening gob of it hung from the bottom of the p like industrial waste. Had he done that on purpose? Not really—it was just there, just in him. On purpose is a really hard thing to pin down. He usually disguised his distaste when the homeless talked to him but on this day he was feeling good and simply chose not to disguise it. It's not like he said, "I think it's your own fault that you're who you are and I'm who I am and I take credit for my success and you should take credit for your failures, and if you were any kind of man you would figure out a way to put the pieces together, get a job, get an education, be a real member of society instead of being what you are, being a suck on the system, being lazy, being a victim, I don't give a fuck about your clinical depression, I'm not sure such things are real at all," but in a way he had said it, just in the *nope*, and the man had come after him. He'd pushed him in the back and Tom had turned and looked at him in shock. The man had come at him again and Tom had punched him in the stomach and he'd collapsed onto the ground, holding his gut. He was frail. He was very old, Tom saw. Way too old to gut-punch. And Tom saw, too, the looks of the people around him and realized he was **the villain**. At least that's what everybody thought.

Still. Weren't such things insignificant? In a life? And was it really that bad? The guy was fine. The guy attacked him—everyone saw. Tom apologized a bit, helped him up. The guy pushed him away. Tom tried to give him a dollar, the guy ignored him. Tom went back to work. Soon forgotten. But it wasn't so bad, was it? That thing? Don't you have to look out for yourself?

★ ❷ ★
ELIZA

Eliza sits alone on a bench just outside the train station's entrance. She's come in at Piccadilly. It's a gloomy day, not quite raining but it may as well be. The air is heavy with moisture and the wind is gusting with enough force to play with the tails on trench coats.

She watches others walk, watches the cabs and cars pull to the curb and pull away. A policeman with a whistle is keeping order, tooting here and there, swinging his arm, strolling up to vehicles and tapping on the glass, small smile on his face at times. It's choreographed—it's a thing that he's worked on. He seems to be enjoying what he's doing.

Eliza's legs are crossed; one booted foot taps absently through the empty air. One hand holding her phone, although she doesn't look down at it. She watches the people. She's irritated that her escort is not here and has half a mind to hail a cab and find the office herself. Just as she'd told them, she didn't need an escort in the first place, but they'd insisted. And why Manchester? They'd insisted. For the trip, she's had to take a day off of work. It's all very irritating.

But. That's not the *overall* feeling. The overall feeling is still excitement.

Not only that, but if Eliza is being honest, it's the kind of excitement she hasn't felt since she was ten years old. She is determined to mask it, as giddiness is inevitably a weakness. But she woke up this morning and it felt like Christmas. She felt like a fool as she noted the racing of her heart as she showered. She's still somewhat in shock, it's only been a week since the lawyer (the lawyer who she *recognized*, although she didn't quite know it until after he'd gone) appeared at her flat, but the new world has been here long enough to have settled into a deeper sense of disorientation. Her life has changed. It's changed dramatically. That all this seems to be completely real and not some hoax, not some game show, not some reality television scheme, is astounding.

Still, she did not dress up for this—dressed *down* a little, even, perhaps as a tacit screw off to the wealth and power that has slithered up to her so sneakily and suddenly, entreating with its sibilant innocence, but she doesn't quite remember doing it on purpose—because of the lingering worry that despite the assurances and despite the very real appearance of the documentation from within Cedric Grayspool's briefcase, there's a lie here somewhere, she's certain of it, and it would be more humiliating to finally learn the truth *and* be dressed up in her most posh clothes. There are cameras everywhere, of course, but are they the BBC and not security? Can you *believe* this woman *believed* what we told her? Amazing!

She glances up at the ceiling of the overhang above her head and wonders about the man or woman stationed before a monitor in some dark room, observing all of this. She feels bad for that person. She tries to say it to him/her as she stares into the lens.

Instead of dressing up, she went simple. Now she's cold. She's wearing her dark green cargo pants and a T-shirt she bought from a street-artist last summer. It's got a human/bunny hybrid painted on the front:

COOL   CUSTOMER

She also has a light coat folded over her bag that she does not feel like putting on and nothing else to speak of. She has no luggage—she doesn't plan to be here for more than a few hours. Then, back to London.

She's a social worker—27 years old. Children's services. Her parents died nine years ago already, just late enough in her life that she was grown and could take care of herself and could get herself into the proper school and get on the track she wanted and make a life, yes, although that did not quite tell the story of what it had been like to learn of their deaths, what it had been like to move forward, mechanically, ever since. That story might be too long to tell. (We'll see.)

Eliza looks down at her phone.

It's another fifteen minutes before the black sedan with tinted windows pulls up to the curb and she sees Cedric Grayspool get out of the front passenger's side door and hurry toward her, head bowed (already) apologetically. He's in a cream great-coat and is wearing the same black bowler he'd had on when he'd appeared at her door last week; in his right hand is the same cane, which he taps in a perfunctory manner whenever his right foot touches the ground. He's gaunt, tall, tends to smile. Eliza, watching him approach, imagines that he is probably some child's beloved grandfather.

He arrives before her, somewhat out of breath, and bows his head again, this time formerly. "Ms. Dagonet," he says. "So sorry. We had a minor delay at the airport."

"It's fine," Eliza says, standing, and Grayspool goes upright and nods. She sees his cool brown eyes; she's reminded of the documentary she watched about a philosopher, how he talked about eyes. They are the only part of us that don't age—matter-wise, not vision-wise. The only parts that renew themselves over time. Our eyes are always young—even if they've stopped working.

"Shall we be off, then?"

"I've remembered where I met you before, Mr. Grayspool," she says.

Grayspool hesitates. "Ah," he says. "That."

"You might have said something at my flat," she said.

"Yes, well," says Grayspool. "I was instructed to make no mention of it."

She'd had the feeling the entire time he'd been in her living room. She'd seen him somewhere, maybe even spoken with him. Couldn't quite place it. As the content of his speech became more and more outrageous, however, she had concentrated less on figuring out how she knew him and more on determining whether or not the man was completely bonkers.

It was only hours later, as Eliza sat alone in the pub on the corner, drinking pilsners and smoking (she was not a smoker—such was her state following Grayspool's message) that it finally, finally came back to her: her advisor. Grayspool was her advisor.

In graduate school, first year, first week. Her advisor for one day.

An administrative email had told her to go to an office for a meeting. So she went. Not exactly on campus, actually, but in a building close enough to make it seem as though it *could* simply have been a small offshoot of the university. In hindsight, there had maybe been a few red flags: say, for example, the advisor's name, a Dr. Hannibal Yellowyarn, handwritten on a piece of stationary and taped to the door of the office. Like so:

"I suppose next you'll be asking me about Pangea," Eliza says.

"We'll see, we'll see," Grayspool says, turning a bit, one hand hovering behind her back in order to compel her toward the car. If she didn't know better, she'd guess he was embarrassed. No touching. Eliza notes it. Grayspool, whoever he really is, is a gentle man. A gentleman. She smirks to herself, realizing (how can it be for the first time, just now?) that this is where the word comes from. She imagines gentlemen, across time, stabbing one another in the chests with rapiers.

"Please," says Grayspool, motioning toward the car. "After you."

As Eliza walks, she half-turns and says, "You should know, I've spoken with a lawyer. He wanted to come along but I told him there was no need." This is not exactly true. It's not true at all, actually—she's spoken to no one. But she assumes it might be wise to at least make mention of it.

"Yes, probably for the best," says Grayspool, hustling along beside her, nodding vigorously. "That's quite all right. No doubt you'll be needing a dozen attorneys once we're all through. A hundred! It's no small sum. Now's not quite the time, though. However. There's something else."

They've reached the car, and Grayspool leans forward. Hand on the door, he says, "There's another passenger inside."

"Who?"

"An American. It's who we were picking up at the airport. He is—" Grayspool's lips make a flat line. "Well, he's somewhat intoxicated. I apologize in advance. For the smell. His behavior." Grayspool looks at the doors of the sedan. "In fact," he says. "Why don't you ride up front? I'll ride in back with him."

"You're putting me into this car with a drunk American?" Eliza says. "How lovely." She turns her head and looks at the tinted window. "Who is he?"

"That's somewhat complicated," says Grayspool, opening the front door for her. "You'll find out everything at the meeting." He raises his eyebrows and nods at the door. "Please," he says.

Before Eliza can move to get in, though, the tinted back window creaks to life and slowly begins its electric descent.

She and Grayspool both watch it fall.

There is a man in the back seat.

He's wearing sunglasses and looking at them.

"Hey," says the man.

"Hello," says Eliza.

"I'm Tom," he says. He strains to reach his arm out the window and holds out his hand. "Tom Sanderson. Unemployed alcoholic."

"Eliza," she says. She takes his hand. "Dagonet."

He removes his sunglasses with his free hand. He has bloodshot blue eyes. He stares at her.

"Pleasure to meet," she says as they shake.

"Likewise," says Tom. His hand keeps pumping. He puts the glasses back on.

She tries to let go, but he keeps shaking.

"Although probably," he adds, raising his eyebrows, "more pleasure for me than you."

So the guy is a huge creep. It flashed through her mind when they shook hands, but the idea didn't take hold until a few minutes into the ride toward Grayspool's office. There's something off with his whole vibe. It's not even that he's American. It goes much deeper. He's loud and strange in the back seat for the trip through Manchester, talking to Grayspool about whatever seems to come into his mind, but it's not that, either, it's not just that he's chatty. Even though he's not talking about himself back there—he's talking about things like British government and a movie called *Ski Patrol* and what he ate for lunch on Thursday and how many drinks he managed to have on the plane before they cut him off and his theories about Boursin cheese, and maybe from a certain point of view it would all be sort of humorous— Eliza can't help but feel a general, powerful narcissistic energy radiating out from his area of the car. She has met some people who talk too much who are not narcissistic in the least. They just talk too much. But this is more of an elaborate, constructed performance. This is some grander and more complex psychological principal at play that brings two words to mind: personality disorder.

She tries to tune him out and looks out the window at the old buildings of the massive industrial city. She's only been here twice in her life and never fancied it much.

Manchester.

The driver beside her is silent but for the occasional muttered comment to another car. He is Pakistani, surprisingly young, and has a thin mustache he reaches up to stroke whenever the car comes to a stop.

When there's a break in the Americans' ramblings: "And how was the train, Ms. Dagonet?" Grayspool.

"Fine, fine," she says. "Call me Eliza."

"Yes, Grayspool," says Tom. "Call her Eliza, will you?"

"Of course," Grayspool says. In the rearview, Eliza sees the faintest of smiles on Grayspool's lips as he settles further into his seat, both hands on the top of his cane. There is something particularly English about it—a minor amusement at the American's unnecessarily emphatic insistence on informality. Perhaps she agrees with Grayspool a bit on this matter. At the same time, she can't help but be reminded of the same patronizing nods and smiles she receives whenever she tells people—particularly English men— that she's a social worker. Perfect, they are thinking. How perfect for the young lass.

"Where have you come from, Mr. Sanderson?" Eliza asks, turning her (mirrored) eyes to him. She's beginning to wish that she'd chosen to sit in the back of the car, despite Grayspool's insistence. She and the American are far more allied than any other pairing—after all, they are the only two who are completely confused.

"Chicago," he says. "Chicago, America."

"And I take it you are the 'other' relative our Lost Uncle Herman so adored?"

"Oh," he says. "Oh, yeah. I see. So you're the other one."

"We're both the other one."

"Right," says Tom, squinting out the window.

"All will be revealed very soon," says Grayspool. "No need to—"

"Can I ask you a question, Eliza?"

"You may."

"Was your first reaction to all this," he says, "that it was complete bullshit?"

Eliza twists in her seat, looks back at the American. He's looking back at her without a hint of a smile—she guesses that somewhere, beneath the clownish exterior, there's a serious side to him. She likes finding this in people.

"It was," she says. She's embarrassed, though, remembering how quick she was to believe Grayspool's words. Almost immediately.

"And is that still how you're feeling?"

She thinks for a moment. "Well," she says. "I suppose I've come to see."

"Do you know what he left you?"

She turns forward.

"No," she lies.

Tom shuts up and they ride the rest of the way in relative silence; the only penetrating sound is the traffic and the muttering of the driver. It seems to Eliza the stereotypical gothic gloom of the North has made itself manifest for the visit.

Eventually, they pull up alongside an unremarkable stone building. Grayspool ushers them out of the car and into a lobby, and then the three cram into a very small lift. Grayspool inadvertently forces her rather close to Tom, and she can (for the first time) smell the alcohol on his breath. She thinks to ask him about his jet-lag but decides she would rather not engage him. She's never actually known an American. Funny. Just like she's never actually seen, say, a polar bear. But this specimen of American lives up nicely to her expectations. Blond-haired, blue-eyed, cavalier, obnoxious, drunk. Skeptical, mediocre, twenty pounds overweight. Self-centered, conservative. Not as funny as he thinks.

"Is this elevator supposed to have this much weight in it?" Tom asks, as if on cue. "It moves like there's some guy in the basement pulling us up with a rope and a pulley."

"Only one more floor," says Grayspool cheerily, and soon the lift rumbles to a halt and Grayspool pulls open the accordion door.

As far as Eliza can tell, they are at a boutique law firm. She notes the plaque behind the receptionist's desk: Grayspool, Groberman, Leafing and Stewart. They pass quickly, though, and soon Grayspool has shepherded them into a larger conference room. Already seated at the table are three suited men, all of them over 60, and Grayspool leads both her and Tom to chairs and introduces them to the partners.

Stewart has a pipe—the room is smoky.

Groberman tilts his head at them, almost like a challenge.

Leafing appears to look quite like Wilford Brimley.

There is also a short, bearded man standing in the corner. He is wearing a potato sack. He smiles and nods at Eliza.

"Is that the man who's going to rape us?" Tom asks, looking at him dubiously.

The potato-sack man frowns.

"Ho! Ho ho!" laughs Grayspool. "How indecent. And I do say, Herman did like that about you, Mr. Sanderson."

"What's that?"

"Your indecent jokes."

Tom says nothing.

Then Tom says, "What? Was he watching me?"

"Now," continues Grayspool. "Let's get down to real business."

"Okay," says Tom. "Let's." He looks over at the bearded man one more time. Eliza looks, too. She has no idea what to think.

"Welcome, welcome," says Leafing. "We trust you both had excellent travels. A very exciting day for us all, I must say."

Stewart, with his pipe in his mouth, nods deeply and makes an "Mmmnmnm" sound.

Grayspool clears his throat. "As you both know, you each share a relative. A heretofore unknown relative. And that's why you're here. Although I would hasten to add that the two of you are not blood relatives yourself..." As Grayspool begins what feels to Eliza like the formal, possibly rehearsed part of the presentation, the receptionist rolls into the room pushing a cart. Eliza is impressed to see an actual slide projector atop the cart, not a digital projector. It's very quaint.

The receptionist pulls the screen at the front of the room and cuts the lights on her way out.

Once the machine has warmed up, Grayspool kicks in the first slide in

the carousel. Stewart's smoke twirls lazily in the cone of light coming from
the projector. This is what the image shows:

Matilda Sanderson - William Sanderson — — — Beatrice Lyons - Hub Dagonet
|
Herman Lyons
|
Dagonet
Christopher Sanderson - Emily Sanderson
Justine Lyons - Foreign
|
|
Thomas Sanderson
Eliza Dagonet

"As you can both clearly see," says Grayspool, "your shared relative, Mr.
Herman Lyons, was the son of William Sanderson—Tom's grandfather—
and Beatrice Lyons—Eliza's grandmother. According to our employer, the
two had a brief affair in 1945 and never spoke again. William Sanderson
never knew of the pregnancy. In fact, he never knew the name of the woman
he'd impregnated."

"Grandpa," Tom says. "You dog."

Eliza has already seen this tree. (Already seen, too, that they've chosen
to represent her mother as "foreigner.") She's still shocked to see it—or
rather, to understand it. Until Grayspool's visit last week, she'd never heard
the name Beatrice Lyons. Not many people had. For the brief time she'd
known her grandparents on her father's side, they were Hub and Kate
Dagonet. They both died before her tenth birthday.

But it seems as though Tom is now experiencing the same vaguely
uncomfortable feeling she'd felt last week—learning of the infidelity of a
grandparent. Not exactly high on the list of ways the mind can be blown,
but on the other hand, enough to catch your attention.

"Now," says Leafing. "Herman Lyons was an **eccentric**. You also may be
surprised to learn that he was our only client."

"Get out," says Tom, smiling.

"Quite true," Grayspool says. "And his fortune, which came to him via
his mother, was quite large and quite old."

Grayspool, after a nice dramatic pause, changes the slide. It shows this:

After an uncomfortable moment, Tom says, "Who put this slideshow together?"

Grayspool has gotten quite good at ignoring Tom. He doesn't answer. Instead, he launches into the full explanation—finally, new information to Eliza's ears. And she again finds herself in the strange state of both believing and not believing.

Here's the situation:

The two had their affair. Circumstances unclear. The history that really matters, however, is the history of Ms. Beatrice Lyons, a scientist whose name is entirely unknown to us today due to the secrecy of her research between the wars and during the war, but also due to the particularly private nature of the Lyons family itself, which, for around 700 years, had been doing its best to convince the residents of northwestern England that it did not exist at all. Beatrice herself, who trained in physics at Oxford under the name Alexander Periwinkle, was said to be a mathematical genius of the highest order. Trained alongside Bertrand Russell, taught Wittgenstein differential equations, played squash with G.K. Chesterton. Originally, as she had no real ambition beyond some gardening and taking in the occasional article on quantum physics, Beatrice had planned to complete her training and retire to the family estate not far from Cockermouth, but—(at this point in the speech, Grayspool is interrupted for a moment as Tom snorts while drinking his tea, then asks if there really is such a place, and if it is really called Cockermouth, and he is told yes, it is real, and he shakes his head and says, "England," then Grayspool asks if he can continue, and Tom says, "Sorry, sorry. Go ahead. Juvenile.")—in the late-thirties, on a tip from Paul Dirac, the British government approached her and asked if she might be willing to use her gifts in the service of the crown?

And by "use her gifts," they meant something quite specific. They meant devise a weapon.

Beatrice asked what kind.

They said it was up to her.

Sort of a free reign, imagination's workshop kind of thing.

Turing, they said, was making calculating machines.

Beatrice spent a good week considering the proposition. Weaponry, of course, was not exactly the seed of her passion in the sciences, but then again, she was not the type to take hard-line stances about such things, especially when their German neighbors across the channel appeared to be so intent on killing as many people as they could manage. Her family, she knew, had flopped sides many times throughout the Middle Ages; they had shifted allegiances from Henrys to Richards so often there was a special chart in one of the castle's basements, just to keep track. War was a reality of the world and it seemed to her that from a certain point of view, it was her duty to use her talents in this way. But she had never cared for how her colleagues thought or how the thick-skulled government officials thought whenever such subjects came up. A better missile would help us, would it not? Something a might bit bigger than a V2? A V3, say? Alan—poor Alan— of course had conceived of the problem differently, conceived of it in terms of communication, of breaking codes. Alan was a lovely man.

After a week, she told the Ministry of Defense her idea for a useful weapon.

"It has to do with poetry," she said.

"You're mad," said her contact.

"So is Hitler," she said. "So is Stalin. So is Chamberlain, so is Churchill, so is Von Braun, so is Roosevelt, so is Einstein."

The agent leaned back into his leather chair, eyeing the document. "You actually believe this will work?" he asked. "It's not a lark? You're not trying to make a point, are you? Please don't try to make a point, Beatrice."

"It will work," she assured him. "I've already begun my distillations. You can see the results."

The man raised an eyebrow, read for a moment. "What good will it do us?" he asked. "Even if it does work?"

"Quite a lot, I'd imagine," she said. "Considering what a war is. What's a war, Mr. Haperwhale?"

The man said nothing, simply touched his mustache, slowly lit a cigarette.

Much to her surprise, the government agreed to fund further research in the Lake District. On one condition. It came from on-high.

"Please don't tell anybody about this," Churchill wrote in the letter. "It could end up rather embarrassing. But good luck!"

★ ✪ ★

At this point in the history, the lawyers and Eliza all realize Tom is facedown on the conference table.

After some very loud throat-clearing from Stewart, Tom bolts upright.

"Sorry, sorry everyone," he says, rubbing his eyes. "I can't believe how boring this is. Sorry."

Some uncomfortable silence.

"What?" says Tom. "Really? All that exposition?" He looks to Eliza for help. "That's not how to tell a story."

"I found it fascinating," she says.

"Perhaps this is the right time to move to the second part of the presentation?" Grayspool says. "You'll learn the rest in the by and by. And I have to say, this part is quite exciting." Looking at Tom: "I believe you'll find it far more dramatic, Tom."

"Do we find out what we get?" Tom says.

"Precisely," says Grayspool, and as he does, he motions toward the bearded man in the corner, who has stood quietly all along. "Now. Mr. Cankerton. I believe we're ready for your presentation." Grayspool glances back at Eliza and Tom. "Mr. Cankerton is an actor hired by your Great Uncle Herman to play himself at these very proceedings."

"I'm sorry?" says Eliza, looking at the man. He's come to the front of the room and is now adjusting his potato sack.

"I'll be playing the eccentric, previously unknown, aristocratic Uncle Herman," says the man, Cankerton. "A late entrant as a character, nevertheless crucial. Heretofore shrouded in mystery. I'm perfectly qualified. I've done *Pirates of Penzance*."

"Listen, Grayspool," says Tom, swiveling toward the man. "This all seems both unorthodox and unnecessary. Why don't we just cut to the chase? I don't think we need any role-playing."

"Ha!" cries Cankerton, throwing his arms up into the air, and Eliza notes by the glint in the man's eye that he seems to have dropped into the role of Uncle Herman.

He begins to cackle and pace around the room.

She glances at Tom, who glances back.

"I assume you're Herman now," Tom says to the man.

"That's right!" cries Cankerton/Herman, eyes wild, arms still up in the air. He even gets up onto his tiptoes for a second and extends the dance in a more ludicrous manner. "I am your Great Uncle Herman Lyons," he booms, "and I am an eccentric man who lives in a cave from time to time! Some miles from my family's estate! Hellooooo, my long lost relatives!"

He's totally shrieking now. He's standing on one leg.

"Take it down a bit, would you, Cankerton?" says Grayspool. "Herman wasn't quite this eccentric."

Cankerton/Herman looks annoyed. He puts his foot down and brings his arms down, crosses them, says, "Do you want me to play the G-D role or not?"

"Stick to the script, please."

Cankerton makes a big show of sighing, takes a deep breath, closes his eyes, opens them, and begins stroking his beard, which is obviously fake.

"You two are my only living relatives. I've known this for some time and have been watching you both. I am an eccentric, unpredictable man of great power and wealth and I am very, very crafty. I am now dead, obviously, but I live again via this replacement body and the power of acting."

Cankerton/Herman rides a few beats of this. Eliza wonders if this is the zenith of his career.

"After some deliberation," he continues, "I've decided to leave my two greatest treasures to **the two of you**. What do you think of that?" He points at Tom, then Eliza. He also eyes them both mysteriously, then starts stroking his beard.

"Are we allowed to interact with him?" Tom asks Grayspool.

"Not really," says Grayspool. "He's not supposed to be asking questions. I think that one was rhetorical, anyway."

"I could improv answers?" Cankerton suggests.

"Please don't," says Grayspool. "Please just get on with the speech. As it was written."

Cankerton goes through his recalibration routine and once again is in character. Eliza is seriously considering getting up and leaving.

Then Cankerton/Herman gets down to business.

"Eliza," he says, turning to her. "You get the money."

"Please say I get the cave," says Tom.

"Eliza also gets the cave," says Cankerton/Herman. "And the castles."

Tom is frowning.

"Well, fuck," he says.

"Watch your language, my boy."

"What the fuck do I get?"

Cankerton/Herman stares down Tom.

"You get perhaps my greatest treasure, great nephew," he says. He steps forward, touches Tom on the head. Softly, then, and now almost whispering: "You get my mother's invention. You get The Machine of Understanding Other People."

★ ✪ ★

It's later that night and they are still in Manchester. They've put her and Tom Sanderson up in The Palace, a rather fancy-looking hotel with its own clock tower. Why are they both still here? They're both still here because there is, unfortunately, one last condition.

In order for her to receive the money and get started, the two of them must retrieve this Machine of Understanding Other People.

Together.

It's in the Lake District.

Buried.

In the cave.

They have a map.

Tom Sanderson is currently downstairs in the bar, drinking himself into oblivion. Eliza politely declined his half-hearted invitation to join him and opted instead for a bath, some wine, and some thinking. Grayspool, having noted that she arrived with only the clothes on her back, has had a package of outdoor-wear sent to her room along with a backpack, raingear, rations, and a shovel.

"You think of everything, Mr. Grayspool," she said to herself, looking at the items, when she first came in.

Now she is soaking.

Tomorrow, they'll be given a ride to the head of the trail that leads to the cave. It's a good day's hike, and they'll have to spend a night in Herman's cave. They'll be picked up the next afternoon in the same spot they'll have been dropped off.

Perfectly simple.

Eliza, having abandoned her sense of realism last week, has integrated this final condition of the bargain into her state of mind quite casually. Secret wealthy relative? Why not? A machine that helps people to understand others? Why not? A hike through the hills with a drunken boor? Why not? She sinks back further into the tub. Fine. She is to inherit an unfathomable amount of money. Fine. She will do what she has to do.

Cankerton/Herman provided a number of additional details about what he called The Machine of Understanding Other People. Eliza had done her best to pay attention; Tom, upon learning he was set to inherit no money at all, seemed to drift further and further away as the meeting dragged on. According to Cankerton/Herman, the machine was the end result of her grandmother Beatrice's research. The "weapon." Turing had used his computers to crack the Enigma and that had in turn helped defeat the German forces. Very functional, very utilitarian. Beatrice, on the other hand, had focused her considerable gifts on something quite different: devising a piece of technology that distilled the power of romantic poetry into a usable, portable device.

A helmet, actually.

A big helmet that helps you understand other people.

Eliza smiles, impressed with how ridiculous it is. But she knows nothing of science. Who knows? Even more amusing is the American's despondent reaction to what he'd been bequeathed. It's oddly perfect for him, this machine. Even if he doesn't know it.

Narcissists, she thinks, just before pressing her feet against the tub's wall. Her head goes under; she blows some bubbles through her nose.

Narcissists can never tell.

★ ✪ ★

"Just over nine kilometers," Grayspool is saying. He is dressed again in his cream great-coat and black bowler, and he stands at the head of the trail, looking into the forest. Eliza sees a slight distaste in his expression, as though he could do without the natural world, given the opportunity to delete it.

It's still early, just past 8 a.m., and the weather has cleared—the sun is out and the air is crisp. It's not exactly warm, but it's a nice day for a long hike. At least to her eye. She suspects her companion might disagree.

Tom stands beside her, swaddled in his new outdoor gear, which includes a green jumper whose color is surprisingly similar to the color of his face. On the drive to the head of the trail, they were forced to twice pull over to allow him to vomit. The second spot overlooked a rolling pasture dotted with sheep. When Tom came back to the car, he said, "Pretty."

"Have you ever been made to walk this trail, Mr. Grayspool?" asks Eliza. There's something about the look in his eyes. Knowing what she now knows about his "eccentric" employer, it seems entirely possible.

"Yes, yes," he says. "Many times. It's quite beautiful, especially if it's not the middle of the night. It won't be difficult. And I imagine you'll find the cave quite comfortable as your lodgings. It's been recently cleaned."

"Did he die inside?" she asks. "In the cave?"

"No," Grayspool says. "The lake."

"Amazing horseshit," Tom says. He's still clearly disappointed about the distribution of the inheritance. But Eliza also guesses that as her capacity for abiding the strangeness of their situation has increased, his is going down.

"How quickly we adapt to unexpected good fortune, Mr. Sanderson," Eliza says, "and how hard it is to adapt to misfortune. You'd think we weren't being given something for nothing."

"Says the one who got the money," Tom says, looking at the trail.

"I'm quite fascinated by this machine of yours," she says. She is.

"Wanna swap?"

"No," Eliza says. "I don't."

"How much money is it, exactly?" Tom asks. "I missed that during our theatrical event."

"You two best be off," says Grayspool. "We'll be here to meet you tomorrow evening, upon your return. Good luck." He turns, then shakes Tom's hand. "Try to stay hydrated," he says.

"Thanks."

"And try to take good care of our visitor," he says to Eliza, turning to her and shaking her hand. Confederates in Englishness. "The machine is quite valuable," he says, glancing at Tom. "And I assure you, it works. I've used it myself."

"Oh really?" Tom says. "And who did you use it to understand?"

"Your uncle, of course," Grayspool says. "How else do you think I could be compelled to work for such an absurd man?"

"I dunno, Grayspool," says Tom. "Maybe you're just greedy."

Grayspool smiles warmly at them, and in another moment, he and the car have gone.

"Well," Tom says, looking at the trail.

They set out into the low hills at the northwest corner of the park. They aren't far, Eliza knows, from Maryport, where she once went with her grandfather, just a year before he died. The ferry to the Isle of Man goes from Liverpool, and she knows that city well, too. Surprising, but she's never spent any time in the Lake District, close as she used to be in the summers. There was enough on the island.

The landscape here is a rough combination of rocky highland and forest. The trail ascends into the more densely forested hills, and there are no markings to speak of.

They hike in silence for the first twenty minutes. Eliza, knowing she is the stronger hiker and also not hungover, has put Tom in front so she will not outpace him. She's also not too keen on having him stare at her ass the entire way. She can't help but think he would.

Funny, too, that she hasn't been here before, as Coleridge has always been her favorite. She can't entirely remember what she first loved about him, nor can she remember why she found there to be something terribly boring about Wordsworth. In a way, they were part and parcel, but nevertheless she always thought of Coleridge as the real human, Wordsworth as the parody of himself. Perhaps the beard? Was it "Kubla Khan?" The story of somebody interrupting him, how furious he had been? No, no, not that, something else. Could it be so superficial as the simple beauty of his name? Cole-ridge. Gorgeous. Eliza thinks her fascination—her original fascination, at least— could easily have come from it. What more is required to capture a child's imagination than the sound of a single, beautiful word?

Tom is barfing again.

Lost in her thoughts on Coleridge, she did not notice his slow drift to the side of the trail and now nearly runs into his backside as he leans toward the weeds and (loudly) empties the contents of his stomach. At this point, it's mainly water.

"Oh, dear," Eliza says, stopping herself just in time. "Not feeling any better, then?" She resists the urge to reach forward and touch his back as she might do if one of the kids at the after-school program were in similar straits. This is, after all, a grown man, and he's done this to himself.

"No," he says, after another spell.

"The hiking will help eventually," she says. "You'll sweat it out."

Tom nods. He's taken a seat, now, right in the middle of the trail. Eliza stays on her feet. Tom wipes his mouth with a handkerchief.

"What possibly possessed you to drink so much?" she asks.

"Good question," he says. "I wouldn't mind the answer to that question."

"It won't be so bad," Eliza says, looking up the trail. "Only a few hours, really. Then you'll have your machine, and you can take it home and sell it on eBay."

Tom smiles. "Right," he says. "One dollar."

"Maybe not," says Eliza. She does not want to look at Tom because she is guessing at his line of thinking, and she does not like where it's headed. She always has had this talent—no idea where it came from or why she's so good at it, but she can guess what's in the heads of other people, sometimes frighteningly well. She almost always wins at rock-paper-scissors. It's not quite that she can read the faces of her opponents. Usually, it's more of a guess at the other point of view. If I were Sheila, goes the thinking...if I were Sheila, I would prefer to follow rock with rock.

Her guess about Tom Sanderson's thinking: he is right now, as he wipes his mouth, calculating how best to extort money from her.

He does know, after all, that a condition of her receiving her inheritance is that they retrieve this machine together. No retrieval, no money for Eliza. The manner in which she is supposed to spend it will be lost on him entirely. He'll only note the easy logic.

It's sadly predictable, and it fits perfectly into her conception of humankind, actually. See a means of capitalization, calculate the manner and means to exploit it, and fly into action. A simple formula for being. Not hers, but most.

"This is insane," Tom says. He's sipping his water.

"Yes," she says. "Very."

Here it comes, she thinks.

He looks at her.

"And yet strangely," he says, slowly getting to his feet, "I kinda want to find out what happens."

They continue into the hills for another two hours, talking here and there. Tom asks her what she does for a living and even though she can't see his face when she answers, she suspects it displays the wry smile that comes alongside the patronizing pity most people experience when they consider a lifelong career in social work.

Then Tom says the most obvious thing he could say.

"So you're a do-gooder, eh?"

"No," Eliza says. "Just child services."

Tom says nothing. Perhaps he hears the hostility in her voice. For whatever reason, he decides to shut up, which leaves Eliza alone with her thoughts and ongoing images of the American moving along at a slow pace, drifting left and right on the trail. She can hear him panting.

She does not dislike him quite as much as she initially had, although she has no intention of warming up to him anytime along this brief journey. To her, Tom is a vaguely interesting addition to a cataclysmic shake-up of her life, a blink of the eye amidst a paradigm shift.

They break for lunch on a ridge that overlooks a vast lake. Finally, they seem to have finished climbing, and the trail now seems to flatten out and take them toward the base of much rockier hills—one might be tempted to call them mountains, although Eliza has seen enough pictures of the Rocky Mountains to know she would sound foolish if she called them that in front of Tom.

Tom no longer looks hungover. He looks exhausted, but not hungover. He sits atop a chair-sized rock, eating one of the energy bars Grayspool so thoughtfully packed. He's also dug out a small GPS device from the pack, and is now tapping it as he chews.

"Hmph," he says. "We're halfway there." He glances east, out toward the rocky hills in the distance. "It's probably right in there."

"Will we be there before dark, then?" she asks, looking out where he points. It's beautiful. Green hills, still the blue sky above, roving and arching lines of trees and forest. To the south, they can see a small lake, a disc of cobalt.

"I guess so."

Eliza looks back at him.

"I have to say, Tom. You're being an awfully good sport about all of this."

He smiles. "Why do you say that?" he asks. "Because I'm out here hiking in the first place?"

"I suppose."

"Yeah, well," he says. "I didn't have a whole lot going on back home. No kids. I got divorced six months ago. Lost my job." He shrugs. "At the moment Grayspool called me, I was ready to believe just about everything. This is perfect for me."

"Funny, that," she says. "It's the same for me."

"What do you think," Tom asks, "about all this talk of Herman watching us? Over the years, I mean. Did you ever notice anything?"

"Nothing I would have recognized at the time."

"What does that mean?"

"Grayspool," she says. "I've known him for years."

Tom looks, cocks his head. "You're kidding."

"I didn't know I knew him," she says. "He showed up at my school when I was 24. He posed as one of my advisors and gave me…I guess you would say he gave me an assignment. I thought it was a part of the program. And so I did it. It took me an entire year. The first draft, at least."

"What was the assignment?"

"He told me I was to design an institution whose sole purpose was to prevent the destruction of the world."

"Huh?"

"Given no financial constraints, what would such an institution look like?"

Tom is smiling, his eyebrows up.

"That's kinda neat," he says.

"I thought it was annoying," she says. "But I did it—I thought I had to do it. And I arrived at the offices a year later with this...enormous document, hundreds of pages, and told them I was there to hand in my project. They asked me which project, and I told them. They looked at me like I was mad."

Tom laughs. "From what, though?" he asks.

"Come again?"

"Prevent the destruction of the world from what? What's gonna destroy us? A band of aliens?"

"Yes, well," says Eliza. "Grayspool never directly responded to that question, even though I asked the same thing at the meeting. He said I need only glance at the previous century to find plenty of candidates."

"I suppose that's true."

"War, technology. Pollution, destruction of the environment. Starvation, overpopulation. Unpredictable catastrophe. There are already plenty of choices. We don't need aliens. Although there is a Department of Extraterrestrial Diplomacy."

"Say what?"

"In case they come," Eliza says. "We do need to have some people who know how to **talk** to them, don't we?"

"I guess so?"

"We do."

"So wait, hold on," says Tom. "What exactly did you come up with? What's the institution you made?"

"Well," she says, "it's rather complex."

"Okay. I'd imagine, sure. How so?"

"There are quite a lot," she says, "of departments."

"Departments?"

"You know," she says. "Branches. To address the different issues. It's essentially a university. But a free university."

"Ah."

"We study—well, we study unusual branches of knowledges."

"Knowledges?"

"Yes," she says. "Knowledges."

"I didn't know the word was plural."

"No," she says. "You wouldn't know. If you don't know."

"I see."

"Do you remember the feeling," Eliza asks, "when you were back in school, when you were just a child? And you had a project to do. Or you gave it to yourself?"

"I remember a whole lot of coloring."

"Not what I mean."

"What, then?"

"It was really one of my first ideas, actually," Eliza says. "You know. Here I am with my papers out, writing up this or that idea, thinking about it all. And what I found was that it's really quite enjoyable to be working on a project. Something that's your own project, I mean. It doesn't matter if it makes any sense or not. You have your own rules, all of that. You must have done something like it. Didn't you?"

"I guess I made a castle once," Tom says. "Out of snow. And made myself the king."

"More like that, yes," Eliza says. "But I thought what I might do is spread schools all around. In every city. Schools that had no real name, no real purpose. No goal, no credential of any value. And all you would do, at these skills, is work on projects. Like your castle."

"For children, you mean? Daycare."

"No, Tom. For adults."

"That's incredibly stupid."

"It's really quite silly. You're right."

"I mean I'd like to be enthusiastic with you," he says. "I'd like to embrace how cute the world is. But come on. Don't you think you'd just be better off—I don't know. Better off trying to find every mine that's still in the world and disabling it? Wouldn't that make a lot more sense?"

"It would seem to, yes," she says.

"But you ignored that impulse."

"To be practical? Yes. I did."

"You ignored any sense of realism."

"I did. It seemed important. Look at the adult world."

"You mean our world?"

"Yes."

"I find that to be deeply cynical," he says. "And I'm supposed to be the cynical one."

"You think I'm cynical?"

"Only inasmuch as a willful refusal to look the world in the eye, for what it is, is cynical."

"It's quite a lot to assume that we can do that in the first place, isn't it? Where is the world's eye? For me to look into it? I would if you could tell me."

"You know," he says. "Two-thirds up its face."

"Right."

"And what's this thing called?"

"What? The institution?"

"Whatever this whole project of yours," Tom says, "is called."

"My free university? Designed to save the world from various threats?"

"Yes."

"It's called Pangea."

As they hike onward—Eliza now in front, keeping a reasonable pace for Tom, who, she noticed at lunch, has begun to drink again—she does her best to outline the project for him and describe her whimsical institution, ignoring the frequent intrusions of skepticism that erupt, again and again, from his mouth. Because it is whimsical. Very. Is that not the point. It's not as though she can't see that, even though Tom tries to imply that she cannot. But she was 24 years old when she began to design it, focused on spending her life doing something to make the world slightly better instead of slightly worse, and thus unencumbered by anything resembling real experience in the world or a real understanding of human suffering beyond the struggles and experiences of her own young life. Was there not a certain value to deductions springing from this initial perspective? She thinks so. To how youth looked out at the world? Money, in the exercise, was not a constraint. Nor was practicality. In truth—and she remembers now, as she describes it to Tom, how she had become obsessed with the project, how exciting she found it to simply imagine on such a mass scale, to do a project, if for no other reason than to see where it might lead. Pangea (or Pangea University, as she sometimes thinks of it) is by far the most absurd thing she had ever done.[1] Which had made it all the stranger when she realized the mercurial "Dr. Yellowyarn" had been taking a piss all along.

Funny thing was, she hadn't ever really stopped working on the project, even after she realized it was a hoax. She set it aside, of course, but now and then she would have a new idea for a new department or a new wing—a new initiative so bizarre that it would never exist, not really, but perhaps so outrageous it might nevertheless produce something

---

1. Some departments and programs at Pangea U: The Department of Meaningless Projects; Anti-Gravity Fucking; Murder Studies; Sweetness; Earthquake Prediction, Prevention, and Manipulation; Finally Ending Bull-Fighting, Which is Awful; The Department of Large-Scale Global Revolution (and Fomenting *Coup d'etat*); Ponerology; Fishies; The Department of Anti-Science; Cetacean Role-Play; Carbonated Beverage Studies; Bomb-Sniffing for People; The Department of Postmodern Submersion; Trash Heaps; Voyeurism Studies; Creating Propaganda; Eddy Van Der Paardt; Escaping Propaganda; Ghouls; The History of Dirt; Methane; BP Destroyed a Huge Part of the Gulf and They Will Just Change Their Name; Methane Bubbles; The Department of People Flying; Getting Back Mastodons— Now; Understanding Joy; Giving Gifts; Gifts; Gift Giving.

unexpectedly good? Pangea had always been her secret, her private joke on the world. Wouldn't it be interesting if this existed, or if this were true? It didn't matter what was possible. I don't care if it cannot. And the pleasure she took in whimsy only grew as she got older; for each year she watched children slowly disappear into the bureaucratic cogs of the British government and for each moment she looked at a young person in the eyes and thought to herself: you are damaged beyond repair; we are not able to fix you; your lifetime will be a lifetime of suffering—most likely you will cause it for others, too. Or for all the times she missed her mother and father and wished with all her heart she were not essentially alone in the world, trying to steer her way through it with no help whatsoever. For all these things, whimsy. For all these things, Pangea. It truly did help to just imagine.

Tom, she is learning, is a very logical person, despite the obnoxious veneer of stupidity. And so eventually, when she feels they must be getting near their final destination, he asks the next logical question, and she is not surprised.

"Wait a minute," he says, and she looks back and sees that he has stopped walking.

She stops, too, and looks at him.

"Jesus," he says. "Wait. How much money did Herman actually leave you?"

Eliza says, "Four billion, three hundred and seventy-two million pounds."

Tom continues to stare.

"I'm going to make it," she says. "You're right. I'm going to use the money and make Pangea real."

They arrive at Uncle Herman's secret cave an hour later.

It's a pretty strange cave.

For starters, it has a door.

"Not unlike hobbits," Eliza says.

"I've always hated those little fuckers."

"Oh."

"So," Tom says. "Do we knock?"

They're standing in a small clearing outside of the cave's entrance. Small, simple signs with red arrows led them off the main path and down a small trail. The door is a deep oak brown and looks as though it belongs on a house. There is also a mailbox, a lamp, and a welcome mat. And a doorbell.

"Oh," Tom says.

He steps forward, rings the bell.

"Easy," he says.

"I have a feeling nobody's home."

"You never know," Tom says, frowning at the door. But there is no sign of anyone, no noises to speak of. "Would you really be surprised if Grayspool opened the door? Wearing, like, a kimono and a wig and a dildo?"

"Probably."

"You know what I'm saying."

Eliza looks at the door a moment longer, shrugs, and reaches for the knob. When she finds she has not been electrocuted, she twists.

Not locked. She pushes. The door swings open.

In the way that it's completely unexpected, the situation inside of Herman's cave dwelling is somewhat predictable to Eliza. A wave of musty air washes over them and track-lighting along the rock ceiling as bolted to the sides of stalactites clicks itself on, light by light, until little darkness remains within the vast cavern. Eliza hears Tom blow out through his rounded lips in a half-whistle as he absorbs the scenery. Things here are decorated rather nicely.

"This sort of reminds me," Tom says, "uh…" He stops, finger on his lip. "What is this?" he says.

Eliza doesn't know. Two chiseled rock steps lead down into the main space, where two long couches form an L-shape atop a bright orange shag carpet. In front of the couches is a low glass coffee table with a fanned display of magazines across its surface. In the back corner of the cavern is a kitchenette, and on the other side, elevated a few feet on a rocky plateau and accessible by more carved steps, a large, plush, king-sized bed. Near them, just to the left of the entrance—and with plenty of space around it—is a yellow ping-pong table.

"A pretty tastefully done bachelor pad?"

They take a few steps into the cavern.

"I can't say I'm really into the yellow on the table there."

Somewhere deep in the cavern, a ventilation system comes to life.

Tom looks up. There's a vent above them.

"And here's where we die," he says. "Here comes the green gas."

But Eliza only feels cold air sweeping down onto the top of her head.

"Fuck me," Tom says. "A/C."

For a few minutes, the two of them explore. They set their packs down near the door and fan out. Eliza finds some very nice built-in (rock) cabinetry along the western wall. Tom, who has gone to the kitchenette, alerts her of the very nice rock refrigerator.

"I gotta say," calls Tom, his voice echoing slightly. "I'm liking Uncle Herman more and more. He has those…um…he has those poetry magnet things here on the fridge? Even though it's made out of rock. Weird."

Eliza, who has drifted over near the ping-pong table, is now looking down at a conspicuously soft, sandy part of the floor near the corner. It's also conspicuous because it has a giant red X running across it.

"Maybe there's some kind of code or puzzle we can solve with these poetry magnets," Tom is saying. "We put them into the right order, spell out the right poem, and then a secret door opens and leads us into another chamber…And in that chamber, we find what we're looking for. There's gotta be a riddle…there's a riddle and you and I are going to solve it. Right now."

"Tom?" she says.

No answer.

She looks up from the red X and sees that he's leaning over a boulder.

"What are you doing?"

"Sorry," Tom says. "Found the bar. Do you want a martini, or...?"

"Tom," she says, this time sternly, as though she's talking to a teenager.

He looks up.

"Come here."

He does. When he sees the X, he says, "No riddle, I guess."

He goes to his pack, up near the open door, and returns with his small spade. He approaches the X, drops to his knees, and begins to dig.

Eliza steps back and watches him work. Both are silent—the only sound is the soft sand parting way as the spade easily cuts downward. And then: the sharp clank of metal on metal.

Soon, Tom has unearthed the top of a sturdy-looking chest. He begins to dig around the sides. Eliza drops to her knees now, too, and instead of going to retrieve her own shovel, she uses her hands to push away the remaining mounds of cool, wet sand.

After a few more minutes of digging, enough sand has been moved.

Tom reaches forward, unlatches the chest's heavy metal clips.

There's an engraving. Just these lines:

> WITH LIPS UNBRIGHTENED, WREATHLESS BROW, I STROLL:
>
> AND WOULD YOU LEARN THE SPELLS THAT DROWSE MY SOUL?
>
> WORK WITHOUT HOPE DRAWS NECTAR IN A SIEVE,
>
> AND HOPE WITHOUT AN OBJECT CANNOT LIVE.

"Well," Tom says. "Don't fucking understand that."

Eliza, looking down, says, "I think it's Coleridge."

"How nice," Tom says.

He lifts the lid.

And right there is The Machine of Understanding Other People:

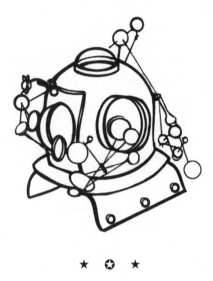

★ ✪ ★

It's night. Hours later. Eliza is on the couch, paging through a copy of *Domino*, vaguely aware of Tom at work in the kitchenette, cooking dinner. The cave has filled with the smell of garlic. It is perhaps the eighth or ninth excuse he has invented to avoid acknowledging the situation, and the thing they've just dug up.

A part of Eliza can't help but understand Tom's hesitation at tangling with his inheritance. The look of it alone is somewhat intimidating. Seen from the top, Eliza immediately thought of *20,000 Leagues Under the Sea*, the old-timey helmets divers used to wear. Bubble-like, a little gladiatorial, steel, glass window at the front the size of an obscenely large salad bowl, hole at the top, perhaps for an air-tube. Or something.

But there's more. Dappled across the curved top and sides of the helmet, there are oddly shaped, apparently articulated antennae and sensors of some kind. They are different three-dimensional shapes—mainly spheres—held in place by thin stalks of steel. And on other stalks at the front, thinner stalks hold delicate-looking lenses, each with its own jointed arm, as though they can be twisted and stacked in different orders and orientations, yielding different optical results.

It is a helmet.

It is a large, greenish, absurd, ungainly helmet.

It does not seem safe.

"Did you say you wanted salad?" Tom asks, still in the kitchenette.

"I didn't say."

"That means you **get** salad."

Eliza again looks over at the hole near the ping-pong table. They have not yet touched the device. After a few moments of looking down at it, Tom said, "Let's just leave that right there for a while." Eliza did reach out gingerly to touch it. She wanted to feel what it might feel like, feel the tiny lenses. Before she could, though, Tom grabbed her wrist and said, "Don't."

"Why?"

"Because," he said, "it's so dumb."

It's his inheritance, she supposes. If he doesn't want to take it out, he doesn't have to take it out.

"We have arugula!" Tom sings, coming down toward the couches, two small (rock) bowls in his hands. "Herman likes to keep his pad stocked, apparently. Even being dead and all." He sets the salad down in front of her. "Pepper?" he asks.

"Tom."

He's standing near, holding the rock pepper shaker, smiling.

"?"

"I think," she says, "you should try it."

"The pepper? I already did. It's good."

"No."

"What?" Tom says. "That thing?" He straightens up and looks over toward the hole. "Why?"

"Well," she says. "Perhaps you might find out if it...does anything. Aren't you curious?"

Tom sets the pepper shaker down on the table and goes over to his own salad. He finds a cherry tomato on the top, pops it into his mouth, chews.

"Here's the thing," he says, but then says nothing else.

"Are you afraid of it?"

"Yes," Tom says immediately.

"Why?"

"Does it not look like something a French king might put onto the head of some sad little French prince for, like, a decade? Or does it not, actually, I don't know, look like something that might, say, implode my skull when I put it on? Have you seen those fucking *Saw* movies? You know?"

"I think you'd have to admit," she says, "that everything we've been up to lately is an act of faith. You came here, didn't you? You're sitting in your Great Uncle Herman's cave home, aren't you?"

"Sure," Tom says. "This is just the first time I've been asked to wear a helmet. Call it a new level of faith, then. Say there are rings of faith. Levels. I don't want to jump another one."

"Do you know what I think?"

"That you getting the money is a much, much, much better inheritance?"

"I think you're afraid."

"I just admitted that," he says. "Yes. Not hiding it. You're right."

"Not like that," she says. "I think you're afraid it might actually *work*."

"That thing," he says, pointing with his fork, "doesn't do shit. I promise you."

"No?"

"No."

Maybe it's the accumulated pressure of this last week, the slow and steady dissolution of her belief in all that's normal, consistent, and predictable about the world. The sun will always rise the next day, cause-and-effect, Hume and all of that. But of course that's not quite true, is it? Not necessarily, at least? As she looks at the hole, Eliza feels it come over her, just as the musty air of this place had come over them only hours before: our sense of what's real, our sense of what's true, our sense of what's possible, our sense of the world, our sense of being here, on Earth, now, and living this life, which we have not asked for, having this body, having this heart...

it's all an act of faith, anyway. It's a miracle of the highest order that we are not presented, day after day, with miracles. Or that we're all here in the first place. It's all the same. And she is therefore certain that the helmet will work. She knows it—she has felt it for the whole day, during the whole oddly beautiful walk with this inexplicable man. It's as though because they are here, within this particular story, the helmet will have to work.

"I'll try it, then." She stands. "If you don't mind."

"I'd rather you didn't," Tom says. "What will I do with your body?"

"Too bad, Tom."

With that, Eliza crosses the room and goes to the hole, thinking of her grandmother, Beatrice, wondering at the specifics of the logic behind such things. She passes the ping-pong table; Tom has stayed put.

"Okay," she says, looking down at the helmet.

Tom is standing. "Really?"

"Yup."

She squats, reaches down. If she is to be the type of person who will head up an organization designed to save the dying world—for real—it's not as though she can be afraid of such things. The metal is cool and feels cleaner than she expected it to feel. For some reason, she expected there to be something slimy about it. But the greenish hue is apparently a quality of the metal itself.

When she pulls upward, gripping the helmet, she nearly rolls backward, ass-over-tea-kettle. It feels light enough to be made of plastic.

"It's so light!" she says.

Standing up straight, holding it at her waist, she looks at Tom, who's pointing.

"There's something dangling from it."

She looks down. Tom's right. A simple stick, the size of a conductor's wand, is indeed dangling from the helmet, attached by a cord no thicker than a speaker-wire.

Eliza tucks the helmet under her right arm and holds the lower rim tightly. Using her left hand, she dips and plucks the wand from the air.

"What do you suppose this is?" she says, looking at it.

"You're asking me?'

She squints at the inscrutable little stick.

"If that thing kills you, I'm taking the money," Tom says. "And I am not using it to save the world. I'm using it on yachts."

"Just watch me, please," she says. "Make sure I'm all right."

"Really," he says, and she can see that he's not joking. "You don't need to put it on. I get your point."

"What's my point?"

"I don't know," he says. "Something...fruity and liberal."

"I'm putting it on."

And she puts it on.

At first: just darkness, a hint of her own claustrophobia as her mind realizes she's lost her peripheral vision. Then she can hear the high-pitched whine of small motors. She sees a glint of movement above her brow.

"What's happening?" she asks.

Her voice is lost and tinny, as though she's speaking from the bottom of a well. Tom has come over and is standing right in front of her. Her voice bounces off the glass bubble and washes back over her, but she sees that he can hear her.

"The things," he says, pointing above your head. His voice is small and distant to her ears, even though he's right there. "The little gizmos are all kinda...kinda moving around. It's like your head's in the middle of a...a watch." He flicks his eyes down to her eyes. "Is anything happening? Do you feel anything?"

"No."

She remembers, then, what she's holding in her left hand. She tilts her head to look down at the little stick, then looks back at Tom.

"Maybe this?"

She points the thing at Tom's face.

Her brain explodes.

Well. Such is the initial feeling, such is how it seems to Eliza as the leading edge of Tom's consciousness rolls into her own, as though his is a wave and hers is a wave and they have merged and amplified one another in the process. She first feels the muted inebriation Tom must right now be feeling, even though you wouldn't quite know it, looking at him. And although drunkenness isn't one of her regular states, at least it makes sense. What comes next does not make much sense.

It's his mood. It's his mood right now, she can feel it, and it's not one she's ever quite known. There's an arrogance and a fear together. Below that, a sadness, a kind of desperation, hidden. Not the sadness of what it's like to lose one's parents, her only real barometer of extreme emotion. Eliza glimpses—no, feels—that Tom's mother and father are alive and well. One is in Arizona. One in the Florida Keys. It's not that. It's a sadness much closer to disappointment in oneself. It takes multiple decades of failure. It's a foreign feeling and terrifying to Eliza; she feels, too, how the booze mutes it.

New layers, now, as though she's peeling back onionskins. She is deeper again. She has roved to a place of being where she can see herself as she is in Tom's mind. She feels tremendous lust—in an instant, one hundred images of her own body pass through her mind, a nonlinear catalogue of her lips, her eyes, her breasts, and (she was right, she knew it, even though she hasn't sensed Tom hitting on her at all) her ass during the second half of the hike. Further back, down into other corridors, are things Tom has imagined about her, she is sure. It is her but it's not what she's done. All in this short time! She does not go further down those corridors. She doesn't want to see.

Because there's far more to see, anyway. She tumbles down a shoot and finds herself swept up in Tom's sense of beautiful things. First she sees the landscape of the day's hike, just as she saw it, but time no longer being a straight line, at least not from the inside of someone, she knows that Tom used to love math and used to be good at it. Now it's simply a tool he uses to calculate tips, but there, back in his school days, in high school: Tom is at work on some quiz, and the meaning of the problem snaps into sharp relief on the paper, and along with it, a deeper and abstract sense for the concept haunting the subtext of the problem. This place is peaceful. If she stayed here longer she might see how Tom is amazed that math even works, that numbers map properly atop our universe, how that seems to be a miracle, and it's like her thoughts on miracles from right before she put the helmet on her head. They're the same in that way.

Near beauty is a place where Tom keeps his knowledge of love. It may as well be a strip mine in his brain, not the heart at all. She sees two wives. A first wife, a second wife. He sees the second wife—Sherry—and feels the weight and power of fifteen years together. There's a vastness to it. She has never come close to something like this; she has only ever attended the kindergarten of romantic love, she has only ever had two or three real boyfriends. Here is a destitute man who has felt more than she has felt. He is not shallow—and in fact, the whole concept, now, here, is ludicrous, because there is no such thing as shallowness if you consider the unbearable, unfathomable depth of any one single—

She's on the ground.

Flash.

She's lying on the ground, hyperventilating.

Tom is yelling

"—holding up? Eliza! *Goddammit*, you're looking at me but I can't—tell me if you're *awake*. Can you *hear* this?"

"No," she says.

Tom looks relieved when he hears her voice. "Are you looking at me?" He waves his hand in front of her eyes. "Are you in there?"

"No," she says again. But she is. She's on the ground, looking up at him. She takes a deep breath through her nose, then sees the helmet behind Tom and to the right. "Yes," she says. "I mean yes. What happened?"

She sits up.

"I tore it off you," he says. "You looked like you were having a seizure in there."

She looks at the helmet, then looks into Tom's eyes.

"I know," she says. "Thank you."

★ ✪ ★

After this experience, Eliza has learned a number of things about The Machine of Understanding Other People. Beyond the obvious—it works—she's discovered that: 1) to probe a mind makes you very thirsty, and 2) to probe a mind makes the thought of talking—any kind of talking, at any length, at any volume, regarding any subject—completely unbearable. For the thirst, she simply drinks water for the rest of the night, what feels like gallons and gallons. Still, she can't quite quench it.

Before they go to bed, the problem with talking is a little trickier, especially because Tom immediately takes to quizzing her about the helmet. It's not as though she doesn't want to talk, to tell Tom about it, to explain to him the strange details of what it felt like to be her being him. It's only that the thought of communicating—finding the ideas and building the words atop them and uttering the sounds—and watching his reaction and listening to his responses and thinking about them and developing responses in return—feels impossible. It's as though she would have to consciously perform each step, one by one, instead of her mind simply doing it for her, as it usually does.

She has an empathy hangover.

"Is there a reason," Tom says, about an hour later, "you're not talking?"

She shakes her head no.

"You're just resting."

She nods.

He looks dubiously at the helmet, then goes to make another drink.

She's staring at the helmet, too, going over in her head what she saw in Tom's head, when he comes back to the couches and sets a drink down on the table for her, too.

"Seems appropriate," he says.

She agrees. She takes the glass and drinks. It's scotch on the rocks, and it helps.

"I guess I'll just be up in the bedroom area," he says, pointing. "Or, um.

Why don't you, actually? Why don't you take the bed? You look tired, I'm beat...We can talk about that—well, that thing—" he nods at the helmet—"in the morning."

They will never talk about it.

She doesn't dream.

She doesn't sleep well, either, despite the intense thread-count of Uncle Herman's sheets. More than anything, she feels sad. Sad for Tom. Sad for larger things.

She drifts off, then wakes. Drifts and wakes.

Once she wakes and the cave is pitch-black. She hears a scraping sound, then nothing.

She falls asleep again.

And Eliza will wonder, in the coming weeks and months, if she should perhaps have tried harder, either that night or the next morning, to explain to Tom what she saw when she pointed the stick at him. Could he even see himself? Perhaps not. Perhaps now no one on Earth knew him better, not even himself. Because she felt much better when she woke early the next morning, she felt much more able to communicate, she might have made a stronger effort. And would that have mattered? I see—I *see* you, Tom, she might have said. People need that. She rolled to the side and saw Tom asleep on the couch, remembered about the helmet. But say he woke up and they talked. What more could she have told him, if he pressed for details? That she knew how terrible it was to be him? That she had felt what it was to be his particular kind of frightened narcissist, and that she had never in her life imagined one might be so trapped within one mind? To be Tom was to be very different, no doubt: he was a man, of course, although Eliza was not so sure the deep differences between the two of them fundamentally came down to gender. To be Tom was to be a kind of sourness. To be so steeped in the verified disappointments of the world was to believe something *not* disappointing was almost not possible, not imaginable, and *that*, she knew—although she could not quite put words to it, not yet—went strongly against what it was to be Eliza.

But then again, wasn't it to be experienced? Here was a man who had seen more, done more, felt more, and lived more? She was young. She was sheltered—she'd done it to herself. She had few friends, she had little beyond work and books. So maybe there was something to Tom's pessimism that needed to be cherished, too? Could such negativity be cherished? Wasn't there a place for the deep skepticism of a cynic? For the realpolitik of the man who had seen things, seen real pain, was unable to deny its existence just for the sake of whimsy? Pangea was foolish in the light of most minds. But his way—it certainly was not wisdom. She hoped. More like: to be Tom was to be smugly satisfied with hopelessness. As though the only true, adult, reasonable point of view was to be hopeless? And that was not acceptable. No matter her age, no matter what she had or had not seen.

That morning, he does not press for details. The day, from the start, feels somber, as though they've walked all this way to attend to a funeral.

Tom has the helmet strapped to his backpack when she emerges from the rock shower. He's in the kitchenette, making coffee. His back is to her, and as she looks at the helmet, it occurs to her that it may be strange, to be naked but for a towel, so close to a man she doesn't really know. And yet she knows him. But he can't know how well she knows him.

She stands, dripping, watching him. He's scrubbing the counters. She feels as though he could be her older brother.

"Almost ready, then?" she asks.

He spins. "Howdy," he says, smiling a little. "I'll go outside while you get dressed. There's coffee, yeah." He nods at it. "Oh, also: it's a wee bit rainy out there. Wear your jacket."

"I'm sorry I didn't talk to you," she says. "It's hard to describe."

"Hey, no worries," he says. "I know. I mean I don't, but it's okay."

"It works," she says. "It really does."

"And so that means you saw me?"

"More like…I *was* you. Briefly."

"Uh-huh," he says, nodding. She can tell that he's embarrassed. He turns back to the coffee. It makes her sad again.

So she'll wonder about Tom—she really will wonder. She'll wonder why they said virtually nothing to one another the next day, the whole hike back to the pickup. If anything, should not this wealth of understanding have opened doors between them? Maybe it was too extreme.

She'll wonder what it is to really know another person. She will wonder why her grandmother seemed to think that this particular invention would be the thing to stop the war. What could you learn about a Nazi that would make the Nazi make more sense? See that he has children, or that he's felt pain, too? The string of decisions required to find oneself a member of the party? It seems a worthless thing to do, considering the amount of evil involved. Why understand evil? As she works she will sometimes imagine it, though: Dunkirk, but all the young soldiers creeping through that exodus with helmets on their heads, pointing sticks up at the sky as German pilots dropped their bombs. Pointing them at one another, pointing them at themselves. What could that do? Either way, destruction. In fact, it will seem to her a worse way to die, to bear witness to the cold and mathematical indifference of a man who's just pushed the button. Whimsy did not trump destruction.

But why didn't they say more to each other at the end? That's what she'll wonder, and it will seem as though the answer to the question is the same answer to the question of why, in the weeks to come, she will not seriously consider sitting down to write him, to tell him about her progress, to call him, to invite him to join. It could not have been because Grayspool was there, sitting at the wheel of the car, rain coming down, the three of them waiting for Tom to get out, to take his luggage, to get back on the plane, to go home to Chicago as though they'd never met.

"Well," Tom says, right then.

She can hardly look at him.

"We do all hope you can make some use of that device," Grayspool says. "Herman had it in his head you were the right man for the job."

"That makes no sense," Tom says.

He smiles, turns to Eliza. "Goodbye," he says.

She manages a smile, turns, hugs him, kisses him softly on the cheek. "Good luck, Tom," she says. "You'll do well."

"Geez, what's the big deal?" he says, looking at her. "I'm not about to be executed here." When she doesn't smile in return, and instead just nods, he says, "It was nice to get to know you. Good luck with all that Pangea stuff." And he's gone.

She'll wonder, now and then, even as the weeks go on, even as she slowly begins to page though all her notes on Pangea, as she sets her mind to the task before her. As the lawyers come, as the paperwork begins. As the press catches wind of the massive financial transactions, then catches wind of what she intends to do. As the government begins to come around, to ask their questions, too. As she finds herself with less and less time, with more and more problems, all of them caused by the money. As she slowly learns that there are dangers to this, that it's not simply whim. That to make an institution like Pangea will instantly create enemies. Thousands of enemies, infuriated at the very thought, let alone the details of her departments as they begin to trickle out. Infuriated at the thought of what is whimsical, strange, unlikely, or magic gaining any foothold anywhere. Whether or not any of it is true. As she slowly sees, too, that she can't control it.

Not at all.

Sometimes, when she gets a moment, she'll wonder about Tom.

★ ❸ ★
THE MACHINE OF
UNDERSTANDING OTHER PEOPLE

Tom lives in a part of Chicago sometimes called The Viagra Triangle. It's real. They call it this because there are—apparently—a lot of men like Tom snurfing around: divorced middle-aged professionals, prowlers reliving their (failed) bachelordom, only this time they've got money. Tom was vaguely aware of the neighborhood's reputation when he signed the lease after the divorce, and for a few months he rode a wave of illusory optimism about his new freedom, even got into the groove at a couple nearby martini bars and tried his hand at talking up some **ladies**. It had been a long time, but still, he talked his way into a couple of disappointing humps.

One date was good. She was a blond attorney with a gravelly voice and her name was Katherine. She was a few years older than him, divorced as well, and they'd gotten along okay. Their date was at a place called Joe's Stone Crab and Big Steak Shack.

They drank too much; Tom even noticed, as they ate and chatted, that she seemed to pull booze down into her body at a rate far greater than your typical person and a lot closer to his own rate. Kindred spirit. She told him about her daughter, who wanted to be an attorney as well, despite Katherine's constant warnings.

"Sometimes you're talking to them," she said, "and they're just hearing the exact opposite of what you're saying. You know?"

"That sounds about right," Tom said. He had no idea.

"You said you don't have kids, didn't you?"

"Never had a kid," Tom said. "We thought about it. Time just went by. Never seemed quite right."

Katherine smirked a quirky smirk, sipped her drink.

"My first wife was more interested," Tom said.

"First wife?" Katherine said, eyes lighting up a bit, mock-scandalized. "You didn't tell me you were married twice. Bad!" She chuckled; Tom liked her. He could tell she didn't care one way or the other. He could tell, too, that she had a nice, easygoing sense of humor.

"Long time ago," Tom said. "And it was so short, I don't think it counts."

"I bet they were working you to death at that firm."

"Yes," Tom said. "They were. But that wasn't the issue."

"What was?"

"Well," he said. "She died. Actually."

"Who? Your wife?"

Tom nodded.

"Oh my God," Katherine said. "I'm so sorry, Jesus. I'm prying." She looked at her empty plate. "I'm drunk."

"No, no," Tom said. "It's okay. It was a long time ago."

It was also a lie. Well—it was something of a lie. Marianne was dead. She just didn't die while they were together, and in fact, Tom hadn't heard from her in at least five years when he heard the news. She'd drowned. Some kind of boating accident with her second husband. Washed up on the shore of Lake Superior. But Marianne had left him much in the same way Sherry had left him. The only difference was how much younger the two of them had been. Both times, all his fault. Totally. No denying it. Tuned out, uncommunicative, distant, vain, detached, unhealthy, completely obsessed with money.

"It was terrible at the time," Tom said. Why was he doing this? He did not know. Still, though, he kept going: "But I moved on," he added, and yes, Jesus, he was trying to look thoughtfully sad.

Two things came of this lie. Tom never knew how direct or indirect the cause-and-effect really was, but the basics were pretty obvious.

That night, he slept with this Katherine.

Later—like the next day—is when the downward spiral began.

Maybe this would only be an unpleasant memory of Tom at his ethical worst—after all, every person has his or her bottom, his or her peak—if you look at your life, you can see your worst moment, too, and you probably recovered from it. I hope you remember it. But there was more. Only a day after his return from England, Katherine called and asked if he wanted to get dinner.

"We had fun, right?" she said on the phone. "Why didn't we ever try it again?"

Because you remind me, Tom thought, of the worst in me.

"I'm not sure," Tom said.

"Well," she said. "Let's get sushi. Fuck it."

Tom, still a little jet-lagged, almost said no. He didn't need to be back in that psychic place, especially now that he had this goddamned helmet to deal with, especially now that he'd spent those…days with Eliza. He wasn't feeling so hot, not hot at all, but Tom was impressed to notice how this was not the same feeling as the feeling of the downward spiral, the feeling before he'd gone to England. This was something new, and it was comfortable in a different way.

He waffled; she prodded him a bit about his waffling.

Then she said, "Come *aaawwhwhn*, Tommy," in an accent so thick with Chicago he found himself smiling.

They got real drunk.

Tom, even now, can't remember everything about that night. He remembers drinking big beers straight from the bottle and shoveling fish into his mouth, he remembers laughing hysterically at her serial killer jokes. (Because there was, the police were saying, a serial killer in and around Chicago. He was a stabber, and Katherine had some good material about what it might be like to get knifed by a psychopath.)

He just barely remembers the two of them, arm-in-arm, stumbling their way along the sidewalk, Tom pretending to practice some kind of karate.

He just barely remembers giggling as he told her about a "business trip" to England he'd been on.

And did she fall down as they entered his apartment? Onto the pile of mail? Did she also then pretend to swim in it?

Maybe.

From the sex, he remembers the weird smirk back on her face, only this time, he swears he saw it on her face while he was right in the middle of coming, as though she were somehow victorious, she'd gotten another one, and had been expecting victory all along. She smoked a cigarette in his bed, then, without getting up. She said she only ever liked to do it lying on her back.

He passed out, she passed out.

A few hours later, just before dawn, he woke up, still a little drunk, and could not fall back asleep. All the sugar in whiskey, someone once told him. Something about metabolism.

He went to the kitchen, drank a glass of water.

In the living room, he stood and stared at his luggage, still unpacked. The steamer trunk, given to him by Grayspool.

Then Tom stood at the foot of his bed, naked, helmet on. Stick pointing. Katherine, asleep, flowing into him.

What he felt was the unbearable, alien sadness of this woman's history—or maybe her perception of her own history. He could not be sure. He remembered, through her, how it had felt to be on their first date a few months ago, back at Joe's Stone Crab and Giant Steak Shack, he felt the odd optimism she had about Tom. He saw his own lie. He saw her sympathy for him when he said it. The old engines of emotion used against her. He saw how she liked him. Behind it, a kind of rippling desperation that had gained strength in the last ten years.

Behind that, he saw at least a hundred disappointing, mediocre men, each with an attendant stain of optimism, too.

He saw—really disturbing—how perfectly he fit into that list.

Tom, right now, stands in the terminal, looking down at the same steamer trunk, worried there will be a problem with security. When he first came home, the helmet slipped through unnoticed, but you never know; he's not sure whether the terrorism alert has gone up in the last two months.

It's December. **Now.** *Here.*

He does not want to have to explain to some idiot rent-a-cop what he's doing with an enormous metal helmet, or why he's taking it with him to London. Or why, for that matter, he appears to be so upset.

Tom is going back. It's December 18, 2010, a week before Christmas, and he's going back to find out about Eliza.

Eliza's gotten herself into some trouble.

Some very bad trouble.

He knows she's not dead; beyond that, he's not too sure.

Yes, so that was back in mid-October, that time he'd humped Katherine, slept with her for the second time, actually, but also the first time he'd used the helmet. And really, it wasn't quite so bad and desolate as that—he did have a mind-blowing orgasm—and you didn't always happen to point the thing toward deep depression. Tom saw better things as the weeks went by and he started to use the helmet on a regular basis, looking around at people here and there.

He realized early on that despite the strangeness of experiencing another person and despite the wicked empathy hangover, it was a good feeling, too. It drew you in. It freed you. It opened you up, this knowing people. It stabilized you. It was something good to understand another person, if not for a couple of minutes. He'd never really thought about it before. How there was something inherently good in that. And considering how few inherently good things Tom perceived in the world, he took note.

For example: once, Tom was up on the roof—he figured out pretty quickly that the range of the helmet was easily a few hundred yards, he could point the stick at people down on the sidewalk and get quick, fleeting jolts, far safer, far less intense—and he found a girl who'd fallen in love.

So nice when you see that.

She was a graduate student, the sciences. At that moment, on that day, in that moment, to be her was to be as light as a cloud.

Tom liked it. He recalled that feeling. She turned the corner and was gone.

He leaned back, let the stick fall, tried to linger in that good place as it faded, before the hangover would come.

She'd had a terrible time in high school, but things were better now—he closed his eyes, breathed, tried to remember.

There it was, that story from a few years back. But you already know it. He saw her running.

★ ✪ ★

Now, though, here, as in the present, *in December on the plane*, Tom can't get comfortable, and he knows that there's no chance he'll be able to sleep. He'd take Ambien if he had any, but he doesn't. He supposes it's a situation in which it's okay to have a drink or two, even though he's been trying to limit his intake of alcohol of late. When the attendant comes by with the drink cart, he gets a small bottle of Jim Beam and a can of soda, then leaves both on his tray-table, unopened, and looks down at the clouds.

The flight is full; Tom's sitting somewhere near the midpoint of the 747, and he lucked out with a window seat and an empty in front of him, even though there was no time to make special requests, nothing like that. He bought the ticket late last night, on the internet, for about ten times what it would normally cost, but what else could he do? He hadn't been able to get in touch with Grayspool after the initial call, could find no real contact information for Pangea University. It was either too young, too obscure, or they were trying to hide it.

There's a child sitting next to him, a young boy who, based on the size of his headphones, has little interest in interacting with anybody on this flight. His eyes are closed, but the amount of noise seeping out from the giant orbs on each side of the kid's head suggests that it would be a miracle if he were actually asleep. The woman sitting beside the boy does not seem to be his mother, nor has she been behaving as though she knows the boy at all. She's reading the newspaper.

When she flips the pages, Tom catches a glimpse of Eliza's face. It's the *London Times*; Eliza is on the front page.

"Excuse me?" Tom says to the woman. "Could I take that from you? When you're through?"

She smiles at him. "You want the front pages?" she asks, then starts removing folded sections for herself. Tom is surprised to hear that she has a southern accent—probably because of the paper, or the flight itself, he was expecting someone English. She's middle-aged, with curly blond hair, a little stocky. She's wearing a festive red sweater and Tom again is reminded that the holidays are upon them.

He thinks back to the tree in his apartment. He is stunned—stunned— that he went out and got a tree for himself. And decorated it. For himself. When he was with Sherry, he had constantly complained about the rituals of Christmas, always sought to point out this or that banality of the tradition, as though everyone hadn't heard all of the banalities before. As though it weren't completely boring to be the realist, the one to bring the whole illusion down.

This year, unlike previous years—he doesn't know if it's because he's alone because the helmet has changed him, because yes, at this point he's pretty sure that the helmet has changed him—is the first year he's realized that people celebrate Christmas knowing full well it's bullshit.

They like it—it makes them feel good.

He never quite noticed that before.

The woman hands over the front section, and Tom does his best to not disturb the kid between them, even though the kid's noise is disturbing him. But he's not distracted. He looks at the photograph of Eliza on the front page, feels again the same pang of sadness that he felt last night, when Grayspool called:

Ms. Eliza Dagonet, founder of Pangea, the controversial non-profit organisation whose London offices were bombed on Sunday. Ms. Dagonet remains in critical condition.

★ ✪ ★

Tom only really got swinging with the helmet on Halloween. Even though it had worked on Katherine and even though it worked from the roof, it's not as though the thing didn't still scare the bejeezus out of him. And besides, why do it at all? Why run around investigating the minds of other people? There was no goal, no endpoint. There were no more conditions from Herman, there was no next step to the whole process. There was just him and the helmet. Alone in Chicago. Sherry was still gone, he was still fired. He was still stuck being himself, Tom Sanderson, middle-aged sod. There were a thousand reasons to get rid of the thing. Just throw it in the trash.

He didn't do it.

One time he went to a coffee shop.

But people, it turned out, tended to react poorly to a man wearing something large and complicated over his face, and so Tom tried to be discreet, on the roof, and waited for Halloween to come. What better night to walk about the neighborhoods of Chicago? Free and open?

He had found what appeared to be an ON/OFF switch on the side of the behemoth, which allowed him to spend a few evening hours pacing the streets and smiling at people he passed without blasting his mind with the secret news of their own minds. It wasn't quite that he was afraid to do it, even though Eliza had been right that night, he had been deeply disturbed by the very concept...

It was just that sometimes...sometimes, it was too much.

He went to a different neighborhood, way up on the far north side, trying to escape the typical rigmarole of his own neighborhood, where it was far less likely to see children and their parents out on the street.

He wanted to find something different, something new.

Where he ended up, in Edgewater, had neighborhoods, houses, and yards. He parked his BMW and began to walk. He strolled up and down Glenwood Avenue.

Tom saw many things that night. First at dusk, and then, after darkness.

★ ✪ ★

Even though it kills him to do it, Tom decides to take a cab from Heathrow. The train to Paddington is cheaper and faster, but he's still lugging around the helmet, and he's too exhausted to fight the crowds. Besides, now's not a time to be cheap.

When he tells the cabbie where he's headed, the deep-voiced man cranes his neck a bit and says, "Where the building just got bombed, then?"

"Yes."

"Why you going there?" asks the man, pulling away from the pickup site. "You one of those terrorism tourists?"

"Are you joking?"

"Course not," says the man. "There's a whole group out there that goes from site to site. Whenever there's an explosion, there they are, snappin' their photos. It's a whole thing—they've got a website and everything. Kind of a club."

"That's sick," Tom says. "Is that a thing?"

"They're called *journalists*," cries the cabby, and he then begins to cackle.

Tom, in no mood to talk, looks out the window at the outskirts of London.

"Terrible, that, though," says the cabby, once he's recovered from his own joke. "All that with Pangea. Just when we were getting used to this batty little tart, someone goes and blows the poor girl up."

"Is there any new news?" Tom asks. "About who did it?"

"Yes, yes. They're saying that they might've found someone. One bloke."

"Who is he?"

"Don't know. Just rumors. They don't think al-Qaeda or any of them, though."

Tom only got the news last night, from Grayspool. Gone was the lawyer's typical cheer, replaced by a rattled, quiet distraction. Eliza had been wasting no time making Pangea's missions and goals public, and they seemed to be even more audacious than she'd intimated on their hike. Status Quo Studies? Perhaps it wasn't a surprise that some people in England—some people everywhere—took exception to the idea that the status quo had been the thing to doom the Earth, or that some unknown woman in London was starting to throw quite a lot of money around to say it.

"I can't quite get a sense," Tom says. "Do people—regular people, I mean—do people like her here? In America, the news all says she's crazy."

"Ah, yes. I expect they do. I mean it's all a little strange, isn't it? All her talk of revolutions and learning how to parlay with aliens? But right off the bat she goes and drops two hundred million quid into the ocean like she did and you have to admit, something might be a little off with her head."

Tom remembers reading about the story. The first major action of Pangea, a week after he'd left her there in the car. Eliza, via Pangea, had dumped, in various coinage and currency, within enormous treasure chests, a rather large sum of money into the oceans of the world, weighted down and sunk to the ocean's floors. No real explanation. And of course there was an uproar when the video of it began coming out on the internet, all of the cargo palettes stamped with the Pangea name and logo. Tom even remembers a chest or two launched into space. Everyone was up in arms. Conservatives: rabid. Leftists: confounded. From all sides, the words poured in: superficial, facile, meaningless, wasteful, immoral, ungodly, dangerous, immature, and deeply irresponsible.

It all got quite a bit of coverage.

And Pangea's first official press release? As a means of explanation? Two words:

 PANGEA University

Well. Obviously.

"So everyone thinks she's crazy."

"Absolutely bonkers, yes, but I can't say that's necessarily such a bad thing. And besides, she says she has her plans to give all those billions away to the people, eventually. But have you heard about the hot air balloons? And the banana cream pies?"

Tom tunes out as the cabby chatters on, cycling through a few more of Pangea's new initiatives. It is possible, he thinks, that Eliza is certifiably insane. *Was* insane all along. Perhaps it's not even true that she was caught off guard by Uncle Herman? Or that she knew, her entire life, what was coming, and Tom was the only one in the dark? At this point he'd believe anything. He can think of nothing, from their short time together, that might prove any of this, and besides, he'd been preoccupied with his own concerns in those days. His initial appraisal of Eliza was succinct and happened very fast: He'd noticed that she was beautiful; he'd noticed that there was something to her, some substance that he liked, but that she was young, she was predictable, she was a liberal idealist, and in that sense, an idiot. By the end of their time together, perhaps he had shifted his thoughts. Somewhat. But in either case, he'd never had much reason to think she was nuts.

It takes them 45 minutes to get to the Pangea offices. Tom can see, through the cab's window, the damage on one side of the building, and he has trouble imagining how anyone could have survived such a blast in the first place. He pays the cabby, who thanks him, then steps out of the cab. The cabby deals with the steamer trunk. It's raining; Tom's wearing his trench coat. There are a few cameras around and a noticeable police presence, but the story is no longer BRAND NEW, and there are regular people about, too, going about their business, ignoring it all.

"All right then, sir," says the cabby. "Have a fine visit."

"Thank you," Tom says, still looking up at the hole in the building. After a moment, the cab pulls away.

"Rather disturbing, isn't it?"

He turns. Grayspool, holding an umbrella, yellow flower in his lapel.

"No more jokes about glory holes, are there, Tom?"

"No," he says. "Not at all."

"It seems your great uncle's experiment is a failure."

"Oh, I don't know why you say that," Tom says, looking back up at the hole.

"Thank you for coming."

"Hey," Tom says. "You need the helmet, I bring the helmet."

Grayspool's driver has appeared, and Tom sees Grayspool give a nod. The man—the same Pakistani from Manchester—is lifting the steamer, apparently intent on loading it into the car. Tom can't say that he cares. He's done with it. Seeing the kid get stabbed was too much. There are some experiences he doesn't want to understand.

"Yes, that," Grayspool says. "It may be useful, but I doubt it."

"Then why am I here?"

Tom looks at him, suddenly angry. Not because he's in England. Because of what's happened. Because of everything.

"She's asking to see you," Grayspool says.

"Is she going to die?"

"Yes," Grayspool says carefully. "But she's stable. For the moment."

"Why would she want to see me?"

"I'll explain in the car," Grayspool says, motioning with his arm. "We have to get to Lancashire. There are only so many ferries."

★ ✪ ★

After Halloween, he began experimenting with the many lenses on the helmet, and had quickly discovered a previously unknown detail about its operations. Move the different lenses around, line them up in different ways, and you could increase the helmet's power. You could turn it up.

He had a rather intense experience, in mid-November, pointing the wand at a businessman downtown.

He did it from across the street, leaning against a hot dog stand. The man was not well, it turned out. And with the power turned up higher, Tom was pulled in deeper, and had far more trouble extracting himself, or even lowering the wand. The smell of hot dogs got mixed up. It was as though he were being electrocuted; he couldn't move, and could only feel the guy. Maybe not just that. He got the distinct impression that the experience had not necessarily been a one-way affair, either, that maybe the guy could feel him. Rather than reading the man's mind, he felt, for a moment, that he was in it, thinking along with him, participating, maybe even introducing his own ideas to the small storm of consciousness. How else would the man have gotten the word "pangea" into his head? Magic? No—more likely, from Tom.

That one took a whole day for Tom to get over.

But of course he went back.

He kept going back.

Day after day, person after person.

Winter came, then, and he went back once, and that's when he saw the murder.

So fast, and in such a cloud of confusion—people moving and running and screaming—that he had no time to warn the kid, even though he saw it coming, knew what was about to happen. What would he have done? Yelled down, "Behind you!" at the top of his lungs? Tom was up on his roof, Thanksgiving alone had depressed him, he had started to drink again, and this was better, to go up here and watch, almost like channel-surfing on the tube, but a deeper link to the heart. Letting the wand drift from mind-to-mind. Here was a frustrated mother, there was a lonesome father. It felt good to see it. Not because it felt good to see the pain of others and compare himself to them, to rank his lot alongside theirs. Harder to see; more that other people were real. Other consciousnesses—they existed.

About an hour into this session, beer in left hand, Tom focused on a man—a white-haired man, hands in his pockets—and instantly felt something different, something far darker and far more divorced from reality than anything he'd ever felt before. To be this man—this normal-seeming man—was to live permanently immersed in a psychic scream of pain.

This man was dangerous.

And just like that, it happened.

The man may as well have been pulling change from his pocket to give to the homeless vet nearby. Instead, he withdrew a knife, and just like that, he stabbed someone.

A young man.

No sound.

A boy, really.

Tom saw it all. He saw the cops, he saw the chase. He had the perfect vantage point.

After that, he quit the helmet altogether.

★   ✪   ★

The ferry to the Isle of Man takes two hours, and Tom spends most of it on deck, in the mist, looking north across the dark and frigid waters of the Irish Sea. It smells like fish. Seagulls have been following the boat. Tom, grim, feels empty.

On the drive, they'd heard more news about the man—the bomber—captured in Bulgaria. Two items, actually. First: he was dead. He killed himself with a cyanide tooth.

Second, he was thought to be a private contractor. An American mercenary.

"Mmm," Grayspool had growled thoughtfully, frowning at the radio. "Surprising. Of course that means very little. There are so damned many of them. We'll never know who hired him, I doubt."

Tom can't say he cares too much about the details or the intrigue surrounding the assassin, a nameless tool of the larger forces. If not this bomber, another bomber, no doubt. Eliza, and Pangea, could not be abided, not with the power of those finances. More important than how it happened: Tom, right now, is increasingly terrified about actually seeing Eliza. To see her, yes—he knows her face is horribly burned, Grayspool told him as much, but it's not that. He is terrified to talk to her. What could she possibly say? And what might he say back?

Grayspool eventually finds him out on the deck.

"Have you ever been?" he asks.

"Where?" Tom asks. "The island? No."

They can see it, now, but it's still far off.

"They used to think it was Avalon."

"You don't say."

"Either way, the island's god was called Manannan."

"Fantastic."

"Among other powers—most of the magics, you know—he had a great cloak of mist which he'd draw around the island to protect it from invaders. Irish, English, Scots, Norse, Welsh. Anyone out looking for trouble."

Tom, for a second, pictures an enormous figure made of dark clouds—or made of a collective imagination—hovering above the island, drawing this misty cloak into a cylinder, a shield.

There's something beautiful about it, he supposes. Something that's just right. And how alone we all are, how locked in that same way within our own camouflages, and how much difference it might make if we had better knowledge of those cloaks as well. All of us.

"Protection from invaders," Tom says.

"Indeed."

Tom thinks long and hard about that massive figure, about that cloak. It's a few minutes later when he finally speaks again.

"How could he not have guessed what would happen to her?" Tom says quietly.

"What?"

But there is anger at the root of this—he feels it growing. He doesn't care that it's not Grayspool's fault. Grayspool will have to receive it. "You can't just give someone a fortune like that and expect it to be all fun and games," he says, his voice rising. "I mean what is this? A joke? A big game for Herman? Go and do good in the world? You can't encourage someone to spend money on the craziest batshit shit they can think up, Grayspool, and then just stand back and watch great things happen in the world. Do you think it's easy? Do you really think it's easy?"

"Tom—"

"No, listen. That's not how it works. That's sophomoric. It's not

FIGURE 24.7k8: MANANNAN CLOAKS THE ISLAND IN MIST

goddamned practical. But beyond that, it's dangerous. It killed her. And we're talking about whimsy."

"Yes," Grayspool says, after a moment of calm and silence comes between the two men. "You're probably right. And I suppose eccentricity is not much of a defense. Now."

There's something in his voice—Tom hears it, but it's far away, veiled as well, like some old personal god of Grayspool's invention has let loose its shawl, too, to keep an old thing hidden.

Tom shakes his head. "You know something odd, Grayspool?"

"What's that?"

"After I stopped wearing the helmet around—after I saw this kid get killed—things went back to normal for a few days. Got myself together. Started thinking about finding a job somewhere. I started thinking okay, yeah, maybe it was all right to have this thing. Maybe I learned something, maybe it was good Herman gave it to me. Why the fuck he did, I don't know. But maybe it was okay."

"That's nice, Tom. I know he believed in you."

"Then I was watching TV," Tom says, "and that kid's mom was getting interviewed. She was crying, talking about the day, talking about what the kid was like, how God had a plan for everyone. And I sat there looking at her, just listening to her talk. And I felt it anyway."

"Felt what?"

"Just for a second," Tom says, "but I felt what it would be like—well, no—what it might be like, to be her. To find out that your kid just got killed. By some crazy fuck." Tom looks at him. "And this without the helmet."

Tom looks back at the island, which seems to be growing. What would be the point of that? To teach someone that lesson?

He looks back at Grayspool.

"Don't you find that interesting?"

★ ❹ ★
PROGRESS & CATASTROPHE:
THE ISLE OF MAN

Eliza's family's country house is very normal. There are no magical or fantastical aspects to it at all—just a really nice view of the sea. A private road leads up to the house itself, back and forth, back and forth, switchback and gravel up through the bluffs, and at the end of the road, the Georgian home stands quiet and still, looking westward toward Ireland. Eliza's parents were successful people, no doubt; her father was an English investment banker with Pendragon & Wilperstein, and he made millions as a young man—he was far more successful (and focused) than the likes of a Tom Sanderson. He'd met his wife, a Pakistani woman named Nita, in Hong Kong, of all places. And it was Nita, after a trip to the Isle of Man, who insisted on a country home. Nothing too excessive, but something private, and something that looked out over the water.

Over the years, summer after summer, Nita never understood why she loved the island so much, but the feeling had overtaken her on the ferry that day and had stayed with her for the whole visit. Even afterwards. She was pregnant with Eliza, then, and only just married. She loved her husband, she did, but she was afraid, too, of her prospects in another country, of what she might become, over time. It's not that she wasn't fond of London. She loved London. This, though, the Isle of Man, was different—she felt here the remainder of something painfully, blissfully, tranquilly old. She wanted to be near it whenever she could.

Eliza, in all honesty, has some money of her own, even though she's always kept this very quiet, and has always been privately disgusted with her family's affluence. Even had she inherited nothing from Herman, she could have lived, at her whim, a life of retirement and luxury. She knew, too, that this played a role in her decision to be a social worker, she could not pretend that her desire to work with the less fortunate had not grown, partly, from guilt of her good fortunes. No one at school ever knew. Certainly, no one at work knew, either. She concealed it well. She affected an accent, made sure her attitude on certain topics was just so. She'd begun to do all this even before her parents died.

The house is three stories. There are many cars in the drive and there are many people here. Most are gathered in the drawing room on the first floor, quietly discussing what they might do next. They are all members of Pangea, in some way shape or form; they are bureaucrats, lawyers, artists, teachers, and weirdos. All people Eliza began to gather toward Pangea, or people who came to her once they realized what she aimed to do. They are, basically, the strangest people in the world. They are here to use their strange to save it. They are an army of odd.

Eliza is in a third-floor bedroom, alone but for a doctor and a nurse, and at the moment, she isn't conscious. Her face is wrapped tight in bandages; her hair is gone, burned away. What's left of her lips are wrapped, too, but in a softer matrix of bandages, which the doctor has just now changed.

Before, when she was conscious, she made the plans to come here.

The doctor doesn't want her here, nor does she like the task with which she's been charged, as it runs counter to the central tenant of her profession. Eliza is not going to live. Eliza knows this. Eliza came here, to her old country house, to die.

There are to be no more surgeries, only the lightest of treatments. Only fresh bandages, moisturizer, drugs to ease the pain. Eliza made it very clear to the doctor: only keep me alive for a day or two. Enough time to make plans for the money. If possible, to talk to Tom once more.

Tom is in the car that even now is rolling slowly up the private road, so maybe she'll get to.

Eliza, of course, were she conscious, would remember almost nothing from the explosion. She would have no idea how the bomb first came into the offices. It seems the security budget was penciled in a little low, even for the early stages of their project, but how was she to have guessed? She had known there would perhaps be a few rough patches, but never had she guessed at the vitriol that lurked behind disbelief, behind shock—never had she imagined there could be such swift and focused hatred for the absurd.

Never had she guessed at the systemic abhorrence, quick to pounce, snake-like, when someone as unusual as her came to power, unconstrained by the usual paths of power-grabbing. Grayspool—God bless Grayspool—had had an inclination all along. Grayspool had warned her, had tried to protect her, but she had none of it. Even when he'd said, quite accurately, that the amount of money she controlled was enough to kill her a thousand times over, reasons be damned. The fact that she'd started out by dumping 5% of it into the ocean had not helped.

"Pardon me, Eliza," Grayspool had said, upon first reading the memo. (She was proud of it: the first on Pangea letterhead.) "Why would you like to do this? Humor a confounded old man."

"To create jobs, of course," she said.

"Humor him more."

"The treasure hunters," Eliza said. "They'll need labor, won't they? Deckhands, cooks, support crews? They'll need new boats, they'll need to buy all new scuba gear. Perhaps someone will even commission a submarine? Imagine the spike in labor then. Are you aware of the unemployment rates around the world today?"

"And why not just hire people?"

"To do what? No. People want to be looking for treasure, Cedric."

"I see."

"You don't," she said. "But eventually."

Now. Here is Eliza: a clump of mummified white cotton on a bed. Someone blew her up.

She's unconscious. But she's not dead yet.

Tom is sort of uncomfortable when a good thirty people stop chatting and stop what they're doing and all look up at him in the doorway of the house. He's helping the driver with the steamer trunk, and at first, he doesn't realize that he's the center of attention.

When he finally looks up, though, and looks around the room, he says, awkwardly bent forward, "Oh. Sorry. Hi everyone."

Grayspool says, "Everyone, here's Tom. Tom, everyone."

"Hi. Everyone."

Embarrassing. You wouldn't think it at a time like this, but it's embarrassing. Tom gives a meek wave. Some servants hurry up and take over with the steamer—they quickly disappear up the stairs, hauling it and the rest of Tom's things.

Tom straightens up and looks at them. He does not know who these people are. They seem to know who he is. He remembers the day, long ago, when he stood in front of his mirror and mused on the idea of being special. Here it is, happening. Not quite what he had in mind.

The room is very smoky.

"No need to gawk, everyone," Grayspool says, escorting Tom across the room. "It's Tom, not Jesus. I assure you, he is both real and human."

Tom notices someone near the bar is dressed as a platypus.

"Who exactly are these people, Grayspool?" Tom asks.

"The beginnings of our staff," he says, leading Tom to the foot of the stairs. "They've all come on their own accord. Freaks, really. Aren't they? Eliza said it was all right."

"Is that Jonathan Rhys Davies?" asks Tom, looking over his shoulder.

Grayspool compels him up the stairs, nodding absently. "Probably," he says. "He's been with us since the first week."

Tom slows and turns forward and looks warily at the staircase, knowing what's at the top.

"She really wants to see me?" he says.

"Yes."

"She's got Rhys Davies down here and she wants to talk to me? Have you seen him in *Indiana Jones*? Or as **Gimley**?"

"Tom," says Grayspool. "Please. She's dying."

Tom sighs, looks at Grayspool.

"It's not a joke. It's real."

Tom knows. He just doesn't want to see her in this state. He doesn't think he can take it.

★ ✪ ★

Eliza told Grayspool that she needed him to bring Tom to England during her only real coherent moment of consciousness. That was yesterday, not terribly long after the explosion, and since then, she's only faded in and out. She's not talked. Looking at her, Grayspool hopes that she somehow senses that she's back here at the house, back in her old room. She has not woken up in hours.

He and Tom stand silently at the foot of her bed.

Grayspool is a master of concealing his emotions, always has been, but if he were not, he would certainly turn to Tom and tell him, through tears, how terribly hard he's finding this, how it's difficult to see her like this. True, it's his job to look after her, but this cuts far deeper than a mere job. For Grayspool, the line between his work and his life has always been somewhat blurry, but he has known the girl, and been her silent ward, for years. He was the one to arrange a suitable foster home when her parents died; he was the one to shape the trust. He was the one to steer her toward the school, to set her on the path of her particular project. He saw her grow up, just as he'd seen his own children grow. She might as well be one of them.

The doctor is irritated to have more visitors. It's an impossible task as it is, just keeping her alive, not trying to aggressively keep her alive. And in these conditions! The last thing the doctor needs is two men lurking here like vultures, waiting for the poor girl to open her eyes. What do they expect? To kiss her on the lips and wake her? She doesn't even have lips anymore. She has absorbed the blast of a bomb.

The nurse just wishes she were back in Liverpool.

"Is her face…" Tom says, but he doesn't complete the thought.

"It's quite bad," says Grayspool. "Yes."

"Were you with her?"

"Not at the blast, no," Grayspool says. "But I found her."

Tom tries to imagine what it might be like for Grayspool to have heard the blast, come running. To have come into the smoky room, felt the wind blowing through the opening. And there she was on the floor.

"She had hoped to be able to speak with you," says Grayspool. "But as she's not awake, and there's little time, I'll have to speak in her place. I know her wishes."

"Just as long," Tom says, "as you don't role-play anything."

"Eliza has requested that you take over management of her institution."

Tom stares.

"Me?"

"She's asked that you run it, yes. She said she thought you'd do a fine job."

"Me?" Tom asks again. "Pangea? I'd be awful."

"That's not what she thought."

"I told her I'd buy yachts," Tom says, looking back at her. "Big yachts. She has to remember that."

"I believe she does."

"I'm the one who thinks the whole thing is childish," Tom says. "I think she should have just created a hedge fund. Or something. Something better than what she did."

"Yes, well. She thought you might use the helmet on her. Before she dies, that is. Just to get a sense of what she thinks, how she's been approaching the job. Thoughts on Pangea. That way you might remember, you know… remember her as something of a guide. She can be your Virgil, Tom."

"That's some dark shit, Grayspool," Tom says.

"Perhaps, yes. But practical. Isn't that what you're interested in? Practicality?"

"Do you not understand what I'm saying here, though? I can't run Pangea. I don't give a fuck about anything, let alone a huge, silly—I mean maybe myself, maybe I give a small fuck about myself. But that's it. The end of the world? Are you kidding me?"

"All I can tell you is that she seemed to know you quite well," Grayspool insists. "And that you'd be perfect for the job."

Tom thinks back to that night, how he watched her point the wand at him. The looks on her face, through the helmet's glass. He could see. He hadn't understood, then, had no idea what it might have been like for her to see him. Now that he knows how the helmet works, he can only shudder at the thought of what she saw in his heart. He has never quite had the nerve to point the thing at himself.

"I'm sorry," Tom says, "but I can't. No."

"You can," Grayspool insists. "At the very least, you can—"

"I'm not doing it," Tom says. "I'm sorry. And I'm not pointing that thing at her. I'm done with it, we should all just be done with it and let her die in peace. It's already over."

To brush shoulders with death in that way, in passing, is like riding an elevator, for one floor, with the Grim Reaper. At your back, you feel his cold. Even her, even here—he can't do it again. He can't.

"She was being idealistic," Tom says. "She was being romantic and goo-goo eyed about people. About me. It's stupid, Grayspool. And besides, you know as well as I do that Pangea is a waste of that fortune. That people have a right to be furious at how she plans to spend it."

Now it's Grayspool's turn to stand silent. Tom knows there's something sensible in him, deep down.

"He was crazy, wasn't he?" Tom says. "Herman. He was mad as a hatter."

Still, silence.

Tom looks once more at Eliza.

"And he did this. To her."

With that, Tom says that he's going to bed. He finds his room—it's on the second floor. He looks up at the ceiling. When a servant goes by, Tom catches his attention. He tells the man to bring Scotch.

What you have to understand is that Beatrice Lyons, seventy years in the past, never believed that the helmet would actually work. She never had the faintest clue as to how she'd made it work, either. Besides a few very complicated, somewhat arbitrary mathematical analyses, all she'd really done was distill, distill, distill. The Machine—once operational—scared the living daylights out of her, and she only once wore it herself. She trained the wand on a bat, actually, which ended up being a very uncomfortable experience.

Tom, no longer quite the champion drinker he was a few short months ago, drinks himself to the edge of oblivion in a very short amount of time. Sitting in a plush chair, legs up on an ottoman, fire crackling beside him, he wonders, blurrily, if he loves Eliza. Not romantically, not really in that way—but still, there's some connection, something more like family. Could it happen in just a few days? Two days? A trip to a cave? Or could you meet someone, and not even know it, but then remember—maybe years later—remember back and reconstruct the time and realize all the feelings that you'd missed, originally? It's stupid—he knows how stupid it is. Something that a child might think. But he wonders. He does wonder.

He passes out.

The house falls into silence as the night moves on.

The many gathered downstairs find nooks and couches and chairs while the few staff on hand do their best to clean around them.

Cedric Grayspool, restless, struggling to maintain a suitable demeanor, walks the paths outside, wondering if perhaps Tom might not be right after all.

And Eliza still doesn't wake up. She's lost in something below a dream and different than sleep.

Pain of that degree will follow someone anywhere—it will only turn back at the gates of the underworld.

Eliza is dying.

The island is still.

Manannan isn't here.

There are not many houses nearby, and most people live east, in Douglas. Douglas sleeps.

Hours go.

The sun, then, coming up over the sea.

Tom, surprisingly, is awake to see it.

He's outside. Metabolizing again? He's not sure. But as dawn comes and the orange light begins to creep along the rocks and grass outside the house, Tom is there, sitting on a bench, freezing, watching the arrival of the light.

Tom's reconsidering.

Tom thinks:

We're it.

And we're at best a maybe.

What he couldn't have conceived of months ago—hours ago—seems strangely obvious to him now, sitting here, watching the sunrise. He thinks of the press release: well, obviously. It makes little difference what he thinks of Pangea, or even what he thinks of Herman, of the helmet. There's something far clearer and far simpler afoot.

Life.

It took some hours for it to settle over him, but he knew, even then, arguing with Grayspool. Probably why he argued in the first place. Something more in harmony with mornings than with nights. How is it that he's sober? He isn't sure.

It's Christmas Eve.

It's Christmas Eve, 2010.

Tom goes into the house, finds the kitchen, and asks the servant for a chisel and a hammer.

Upstairs, kneeling in front of the helmet, Tom pauses, concerned that the noise might wake everyone. If it does, someone—Grayspool, probably—might try to stop him. He closes his door, leans a chair up against the knob.

He starts by tearing off all the attachments, all the wiry arms and orbs and lenses. They come free with distinct, satisfying snaps, and as he plucks them off, Tom realizes that a part of him has grown to hate this helmet.

Hate it.

He goes after the main contraption with the chisel, wedging it down into a welded seam and pounding with the hammer. At first, the pounding does little more than create noise, but Tom continues, hammering with more and more fury. Because what right had she had, so long ago, to make such a thing at all? Really? As though it would have stopped the war, a war of real death, of real pain? Thousands of years of death and dismemberment, man at the hand of man—as though such a thing could stop inertia like that. It is what we are. As though it would have closed down concentration camps, reunited families, made bombs fly back upward, sucked the flames back into ordinance? Fuck that. It was a disgrace to those who'd died. And what right had Herman had? To spy on them, to orchestrate their lives, to toy with them as though they were marionettes. Fuck that. People, Tom knows, are not marionettes.

Show some courage, he thinks. Show yourself, Herman.

There is another loud crackle.

Tom starts hammering with more passion. The seam has split. There is knocking on the door—he can hear it alongside his pounding. The top of the helmet has cracked open.

After a few more strikes, Tom takes hold of the two split pieces of metal and begins to pull with all his strength. There is louder pounding at the door—Tom hears Grayspool's voice. He's concerned. Tom's almost there. Just a little more and...

Crrraaaaaccckkkkle.

There. Finally.

Another seam gives, this time at the side.

The helmet cracks open like an egg.

Tom, hands aching, leans back onto his knees, surveying what's before him. The innards of the machine are twisting tubes and wires. There are a few small lights glowing softly. More lenses, too, dirtier, stacked horizontally. The wires and tubes all wind around a central space, a kind of heart at the helmet's center.

And resting there, the centerpiece of everything, is a single glass vial with a cork.

Within the vial, a transparent liquid.

The tiniest of tubes runs through the cork, siphoning liquid out into the network of conduits.

Tom takes hold of the vial and lifts it out of the machine.

Carefully, he pulls free the tiny straw. The vial is disconnected, and he holds it up to the light.

A moment later, Grayspool's knocking is interrupted by Tom flinging open the door.

"Hey," Tom says.

Their eyes meet, and Grayspool, for a moment, looks over Tom's shoulder. Tom glances back; they both take in the deconstructed helmet.

"What have you done?" Grayspool says. He sees the vial in Tom's hand. "What is that?"

"Work without hope," Tom says, "draws nectar in a sieve."

Grayspool, frowning, swivels and begins to follow Tom toward the stairs. "Tom, I don't understand. What are you—"

"Coleridge," Tom says. "One of your guys."

As he sets foot on the first step, Tom pops the cork from the top of the vial. "I can't really run Pangea, Grayspool," he says. "I'm not the right person. I mean come on. Look at me."

Tom starts to climb again. Grayspool hustles up behind him. "I'd prefer if you'd just slow down and tell me—"

"Let's be honest—I mean really honest. The drinking alone would probably bring down the whole thing a lot faster than any assassin, than any fucking...mercenary. I'd like to think I could stop, but I honestly just don't know. Sometimes I think it's impossible. Once you go far enough along."

Reaching the top of the stairs, Tom turns, looks back at Grayspool. It's not happiness, not quite, whatever it is that he's feeling. But he does feel the peace that comes with resolve, with certainty.

"She's dying," Grayspool says. He's reached the top of the stairs; the two stand side-by-side, feet from Eliza's door. "There aren't any other options."

"No," Tom says. "She's not dying."

He holds out his hand. "Goodbye, Grayspool. I liked you right away."

Grayspool, out of breath and eminently flustered, warily takes the hand. They shake.

"Where are you—"

Tom turns, takes a breath, opens the door to Eliza's room. The morning sunlight angles across from the window, lighting both Eliza's still body and all the machines beside her bed. She looks peaceful. Her linens all look clean.

Tom puts the vial to his lips, closes his eyes
and drinks.

He has time—a second or two—to make his way to the bed before he begins to feel it. At first gust a glimmer of Grayspool and his annoyingly English reserve standing there behind him, arm on the doorframe. Soon, though, Grayspool's mind is washed away by Eliza, who is lost, adrift atop a sea of drugs and pain, which he must first sink down through before he gets to something more real. Tom got pretty good, back in Chicago, at dealing with other people and their minds. He has to admit. They're all mazes, but there are common turns, common architectures. Dealing with both Grayspool and Eliza at the same time feels doable. At first.

But Tom drank the whole vial, all of it. A thousand times the strength of the wand and the helmet, when all is working properly. Because that's what the helmet is, isn't it? You can see that. Not a focusing agent but an object to retard the strength of everybody else's thoughts and heart. The liquid inside—it's too powerful. The helmet around it is for control. It won't be just Eliza and Grayspool, Tom knows. Eyes closed, he rests his hand on Eliza's bandaged forehead. And

there, it starts, he begins to feel the pain. How many are there on the first floor? 30? He feels them all, one by one, but at the same time, all at once. The rush is overwhelming; the rush is slow. It's as though he's a man on a beach, looking out, and a tidal wave had risen up and struck him, leaving him there on the beach in no hurry, dripping but not washed away. Still, though, in that crowd, in the congestion of all those minds, Tom tries to stay focused on Eliza. He begins to gather up her pain.

As he does this, the radius is all the while expanding, sweeping out across the island, and Tom now senses the moods and minds and histories of hundreds, then thousands—this when the radius reaches

Douglas, when the weight of an entire city's people crushes him, and he can barely breathe amidst each distinct life, of so much pain, of so much consciousness. There's more pain than joy out there, Tom sees, but is that a surprise? He tries to stay focused on the one. Even as England and Ireland and Scotland and Wales hit him, geometrically larger waves, he stays standing on his shore, rooted. He feels as though he'll be ripped apart, or crushed, or both at once, and he

concentrates on her, on the bomb, on each burnt nerve ending, each ruined cell of skin, each neuron in her mind that relined and overloaded when the explosives ignited. He pulls her pain into himself. He'll feel it instead. He can take it from her. She's better than him, better in almost every conceivable way. He feels the pain of the burns spreading out across his face as they recede from hers, feels his skin dissolving away. He even feels the individual, still-smoldering fires hidden across the charred skin of her shoulders. He feels her mind becoming aware of him, too, beginning to feel relief the more he takes away. He feels her coming out of her hiding place. He couldn't have imagined the pain. Something in him is screaming. He might be screaming. Still, the radius is expanding. All across Europe, now? Maybe over the ocean, and Tom goes further down, still. He continues drawing out all the poison he can locate in her body. He puts it into himself. Sure, he'll take the bioaccumulation, too: the mercury, the lead, the pesticides, the polychlorinated biphenyls, the cadmium, the Teflon, the brominated flame retardants, whatever—he'll take them. Fuck it. There are too many— and they're in everyone, too. Will it even matter that he takes them from her? Perhaps the world has already ended. Hasn't it, if this is inside of us? We're all dead already, right? He finds shrapnel in his stomach and he puts it in his own. He takes every iota of pain he can find until he's nothing more than a pyre kneeling beside her, overcome with so much agony that he finally—after how long?—feels himself slipping. He tries to hold on. He doesn't know where the radius is anymore. Maybe it's gone all around. But he can't see now, his eyes aren't really working. Eliza. Eliza is sitting up. She has a hand on his cheek, he thinks, and Tom feels tremendous relief. He's not sure if it's his or hers, as he can no longer tell the difference. He feels, briefly, her surprise and her confusion, trying to understand what he's done. He feels her shock when she looks at him. She sees how all her wounds have transferred onto his own face.

He collapses.

"Tom," she says, is saying, her face hovering over his. But is he in her? He sees himself now. She looks down into his eyes, concerned. He sees himself through them. He does not look good. But Tom can't talk—he's down at the bottom of a well, looking up, "Tom," she says, is saying. Softly, though. Not panicked. No need to say a thing. Go on, my friend. Go further down.

Tom goes further down.

"Tom."

She's better. The bandages are off. He can see that she's better.

"Tom."

She'll be better, Tom knows. Better for the world than he would have been. In lots of different ways. Tom has no ideas anymore, not really. Tom's never had a whole lot to give. Tom learned how to **take** well, sure, but he knows he's not the type to have new ideas, to generate something that makes the world better. People like Eliza can do that. You have to care a lot and not care at the same time. It never felt quite right, did it? Alive in his own skin? That may have been the problem all along, but of course you can't see that about yourself, you can't see the deepest of the flaws, what started so long ago that it is now transparent to your eyes. Never quite right. He could point to some good moments. But never quite right.

"Tom?"

Now she's just a voice.

She'll do well. She'll scare billions, which will be a nice shake of the shoulders. Maybe that will be all she does. Shake shoulders. Knock on Earth's forehead. That's good. Wake up! Eliza will say.

Tom has drifted down. Going down is okay.

He's so far down the well that he can't even feel the pain anymore, neither the pain nor the other people.

There are so many other people.

So much pain.

But there's a small chance, too.

Knowing this, relieved and a little sad, Tom lets go.

Acknowledgments

This book is an attempt at answering a handful of worrisome questions. Like a lot of people, I began to wonder about these (admittedly abstract) questions in my twenties and could never shake their hold. And not to be annoyingly mysterious, but I hope there's no need to restate the questions themselves here; if they're not somehow in the book already, there's a problem, and it's my fault completely.

However, due to my furtive ways in and around academia and the slow, piecemeal development of this book, many of the kind people I want to thank have no idea who I am. No matter. I'm thanking them anyway.

To various philosophy, cognitive science, and sociology professors scattered across the country: I was the one sitting in the back, probably not qualified to be in your class, listening with keen interest and occasionally asking non sequitur questions about poetry. Thanks to David Lindberg, Hannah Ginsberg, Richard Boyd, David Grusky, Ronald Kline, Shimon Edelman, Aaron Lambert, and many others.

Thank you, too, to the wonderful, talented, and oft underappreciated science-fiction and fantasy writers who painted my formative reading years with so much unusual and perfect color: Margaret Weis, Tracy Hickman, Paul B. Thompson, Tonya C. Cook, Douglas Niles, Timothy Zahn, Kurt Vonnegut, Douglas Adams, Doug Naylor, Rob Grant, Ursula K. Le Guin, R.A. Salvatore, and Troy Denning. Troy, *The Amber Enchantress* got me three detentions from my eighth-grade Spanish teacher. I was reading it under my desk.

And finally, thank you so much to all the people I actually do know who helped with this book along the way. First and foremost on that list is my wife Alexis, who actually abides my presence—amazing. Tremendous thanks as well to Zach Dodson and Jonathan Messinger, legitimately insane co-founders of featherproof books, no explanation required. And more thanks to many others, too: Gina Frangello, Emily Tedrowe, Thea Goodman, Maggie Vandermeer, Dika Lam, Betsy Crane, Roy Kesey, Jami Attenberg, Mike Fowler, Brettne Bloom, Oliver Haslegrave, Reagan Arthur, Ben Warner, Steve Somerville, Lee Somerville, Sara Prohaska, Cecilia Phillips, Mark Rader, Rob Funderburk, J. Robert Lennon, Alex Kostiw, Audrey Niffenegger, Sam Axelrod, Allison Burque, and okay, dude at the CVS, guy walking down the street with the white poofy hair, Melvin Jones Bukiet, dickface at the kayak rental kiosk in Ithaca, tatted-up girl at the coffee shop. Whether you meant to or not or even knew I was there, you all helped in some way. Books are funny like that.

About the Author

PATRICK SOMERVILLE's first book of stories, *Trouble*, was named 2006's Best Book by a Chicago Author by *Time Out Chicago*, and his novel, *The Cradle*, was a finalist for The Center for Fiction First Novel Prize. He has taught creative writing and English at Cornell, Northwestern University, Auburn State Correctional Facility, and The Graham School in Chicago. He lives with his wife in Chicago.

featherproof
BOOKS

featherproof books is an indie publisher dedicated to doing whatever we want. We live in Chicago and publish idiosyncratic novels and downloadable mini-books, as well as 333-word stories for the iPhone. Visit featherproof.com, OK?

WE PUBLISH **STUFF**

www.*featherproof*.com

Daddy's by Lindsay Hunter

Lindsay Hunter tells the stories no one else will in ways no one else can. In her down and dirty debut, she draws vivid portraits of bad people in worse places. A woman struggles to survive her boyfriend's terror preparations. A wife finds the key to her sex life lies in her dog's electric collar. Two teenagers violently tip the scales of their friendship. A rising star of the new fast fiction, Hunter bares all before you can blink in her bold, beautiful stories. In this collection of slim southern gothics, she offers an exploration not of the human heart but of the spine; mixing sex, violence and love into a harrowing, head-spinning read.

($14.95, 978-0-9825808-0-6, eBook: 978-0-9825808-8-2)

The Awful Possibilities by Christian TeBordo

A girl among kidney thieves masters the art of forgetting. A motivational speaker skins his best friend to impress his wife. A man outlines the rules and regulations for sadistic child-rearing. A teen in Brooklyn, Iowa, deals with the fallout of his brother's rise to hip hop fame. You've heard these people whispering in hallways, mumbling in diners, shouting in the apartment next door. In brilliantly strange set pieces that explode the boundaries of short fiction, Christian TeBordo locates the awe in the awful possibilities we could never have imagined.

($14.95, 978-0-9771992-9-7, eBook: 978-0-9825808-7-5)

Scorch Atlas by Blake Butler

A novel of 14 interlocking stories set in ruined
American locales where birds speak gibberish, the sky
rains gravel, and millions starve, disappear or grow
coats of mold. In 'The Disappeared,' a father is arrested
for missing free throws, leaving his son to search alone
for his lost mother. In 'The Ruined Child,' a boy
swells to fill his parents' ransacked attic. Rendered in a
variety of narrative forms, from a psychedelic fable to
a skewed insurance claim questionnaire, Blake Butler's
full-length fiction debut paints a gorgeously grotesque
version of America, bringing to mind both Kelly Link
and William Gass, yet turned with Butler's own eye for
the apocalyptic and bizarre.

($14.95, 978-0-9771992-8-0)

AM/PM by Amelia Gray

If anything's going to save the characters in Amelia
Gray's debut from their troubled romances, their social
improprieties, or their hands turning into claws, it's
a John Mayer concert tee. In *AM/PM*, Gray's flash-
fiction collection, impish humor is on full display. Tour
through the lives of 23 characters across 120 stories
full of lizard tails, Schrödinger boxes and volcano love.
Follow June, who wakes up one morning covered in
seeds; Leonard, who falls in love with a chaise lounge;
and Andrew, who talks to his house in times of crisis.
An intermittent love story as seen through a darkly
comic lens, Gray mixes poetry and prose, humor and
hubris to create a truly original piece of fiction.

($12.95, 978-0-9771992-7-3)

boring boring boring boring boring boring boring by Zach Plague

When the mysterious gray book that drives their twisted relationship goes missing, Ollister and Adelaide lose their post-modern marbles. He plots revenge against art patriarch The Platypus, while she obsesses over their anti-love affair. Meanwhile, the art school set experiments with bad drugs, bad sex, and bad ideas. But none of these desperate young minds has counted on the intrusion of a punk named Punk and his potent sex drug. This wild slew of characters get caught up in the gravitational pull of The Platypus' giant art ball, where a confused art terrorism cell threatens a ludicrous and hilarious implosion. Zach Plague has written and designed a hybrid typo/graphic novel which skewers the art world, and those boring enough to fall into its traps.

($14.95, 978-0-9771992-5-9)

This Will Go Down on Your Permanent Record by Susannah Felts, $9.95, 978-0-9771992-4-2

Hiding Out by Jonathan Messinger, $13.95, 978-0-9771992-3-5

Sons of the Rapture by Todd Dills, $12.95, 978-0-9771992-1-1

The Enchanters vs. Sprawlburg Springs by Brian Costello, $12.95, 978-0-9771992-0-4

*FREE Mini-Books by over 50 exciting writers, downloadable from *featherproof.*com

www.*featherproof.*com

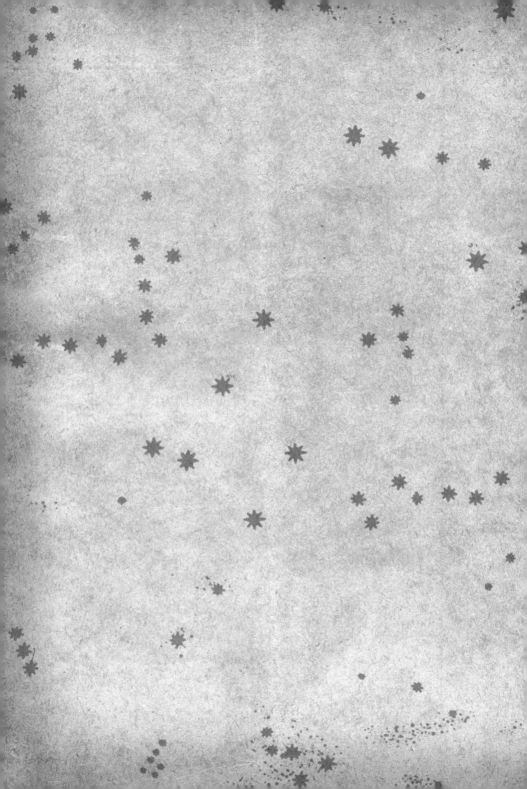